Edward Augustus Freeman

Historical and Architectural Sketches

chiefly Italian

Edward Augustus Freeman

Historical and Architectural Sketches
chiefly Italian

ISBN/EAN: 9783337096465

Printed in Europe, USA, Canada, Australia, Japan

Cover: Foto ©Andreas Hilbeck / pixelio.de

More available books at **www.hansebooks.com**

HISTORICAL AND ARCHITECTURAL

SKETCHES:

CHIEFLY ITALIAN.

BY

EDWARD A. FREEMAN, D.C.L., LL.D.,

LATE FELLOW OF TRINITY COLLEGE, OXFORD,
CORRESPONDING MEMBER OF THE IMPERIAL ACADEMY OF SCIENCES OF SAINT PETERSBURG.

WITH TWENTY-TWO ILLUSTRATIONS FROM DRAWINGS BY THE AUTHOR.

London:

MACMILLAN AND CO.

1876.

LONDON:
PRINTED BY WILLIAM CLOWES AND SONS,
STAMFORD STREET AND CHARING CROSS.

PREFACE.

THE following pieces, with two exceptions, are re-printed from the *Saturday Review*. That · headed "Trier" appeared in the *Pall Mall Gazette*, and that headed "Vercelli" is now printed for the first time. My best thanks are due to the Editors of the two papers concerned for the leave kindly given me to reprint the articles.

Some of the papers were written at or near the places spoken of, with little or no help from books. Others were written after my return home, with the same means of reference as any other of my writings. I do not doubt that the reader will easily mark the difference between the two classes. All the papers of both classes have been carefully revised, and corrected and improved where there was need; but I did not think it right to recast the first class of articles, or to take away from them the character of first impressions, even when I might by this means have made them more complete.

The illustrations, made by photography from my

own pen-and-ink drawings, arc an experiment. I fear
that the result of the process has been to exaggerate
the necessary defects of the rough sketches, and at the
same time to take off something from their life and
force. But in any case they will serve to give a
general idea of the outlines of the buildings represented.

I think it right to mention that, just at the time
when several of the literary journals had announced that
I had this little book in hand, large extracts from the
articles in the *Saturday Review* appeared in a book by
Mr. Augustus Hare, called 'Cities of Central and
Northern Italy.' This was done without any leave
either from me or from the Editor of the *Saturday
Review*, and, by a further breach of the rules of literary
etiquette, Mr. Hare thought proper to add my name to
pieces which were still anonymous. To conduct of this
kind it is hardly needful to give a name. I, like every
other scholar, am always glad to find myself quoted
in moderation by any brother-scholar. It is another
thing to be made wholesale spoil of for the profit of a
blundering compilation, whose workman cannot even
copy accurately what he—in the sense of the wise—
"conveys" from others. Mr. Hare is very fond of
sneering at what he thinks it decent to call the "Sardinian government." It would seem that he has learned
his notions of the rights of property in those parts of

the Italian kingdom where the authority of the "Sardinian government" is least fully established. They certainly savour of Calabria and Sicily, rather than of Lombardy and Piedmont.

The present collection is wholly Italian, except that to the account of Ravenna I thought it well to join three other pieces, which, as describing Imperial dwelling-places elsewhere, had a close connexion historically, though not geographically. Of two of these cities, Ravenna and Trier, I have spoken more at length in articles in the *British Quarterly Review;* but, as those articles rather belong to a series of a different character, that seemed no reason for suppressing the papers which gave my impressions on the spot. I hope that I may some day be able to continue the present attempt by other collections, from our own island, from France and other parts of Gaul, from Germany, and, above all, from Dalmatia.

Le Mans, June 1st, **1876.**

CONTENTS.

LIST OF ILLUSTRATIONS.

THE VENETIAN MARCH.

B

ALL roads lead to Rome; and, among all the roads that lead thither, each has some special merit or attraction of its own to plead. To one who is about to enter Italy for the first time, it is hard to pick one out to recommend as distinctly superior to all others. But there is much to be said on many grounds in favour of entering Italy by the Brenner pass. It is a road to be specially recommended to the architectural traveller. By this road he will not enter Italy suddenly; he will find, long before he reaches the frontier, forms which will prepare him for what is coming, forms which will show him how deep was the artistic influence of Rome on the land whose Kings claimed to be her Emperors. That influence spreads indeed over all Germany, as in truth it spreads over all Western Europe. But he who is making his way into Italy through the Teutonic kingdom will perhaps begin more distinctly to feel its influence if he tarries in the former capital of the ecclesiastical princes of Würzburg, the city whose Bishops bore the proud title of Dukes of the elder Francia.

The tall towers of the cathedral church, much in the church of St. Kilian, and not a little in the general architecture of Würzburg, will make him feel that there, in the heart of Germany, he has come within the direct influence of the art of Italy both in earlier and later times.

From Würzburg then let him make his start. He will pass along the pleasant banks of the Main ; he will mark the small fortified towns like Heidingsfeld and Ochsenfurt, towns of the smallest size, yet girt about with walls and towers, reminding us of days when no man dared to risk himself beyond the protection of a town wall except those who were strong enough to make their neighbourhood unsafe for others. He will mark here and there, even in a passing glimpse, tall, slender, towers, akin to those of Würzburg, again bespeaking the influence of Italy in Northern lands. He may perhaps pass lightly through the artistic capital of Bavaria. If eager either for Italian skies or for Italian bell-towers, he may think it enough to visit the huge Friars' church of brick, of a type so different either from Rostock on the one hand or from Verona on the other. But there he will not fail to do his homage at the tomb of the Bavarian Cæsar who fills so large a place in our own history, Lewis, the ally of England, the enemy of Avignon and of France. Innsbrück, with its girdle of mountains, with its richer

Imperial store, will be more likely to detain him. He will there perhaps see some signs of nearness to the Southern land in the street arcades ; and, whatever his errand, he will hardly turn away without a sight of the wondrous tomb of Maximilian. He will look round at the royal and princely group which surrounds the stately resting-place of the penniless Emperor-elect; he will look with curiosity on the full features of Charles of Burgundy; and he will perhaps venture on a smile when he sees among the company a personage so oddly described as "Arthur, King of England." But two forms on the northern side of the tomb will specially attract the eye of the student of Imperial history. King Albert the Second appears with the sacred robe over his armour. But Frederick the Third, on whose person aught of warlike attire may have been thought incongruous, appears in all the splendour of that ecclesiastical garb which reminded men that the successor of Augustus was, within his own province, no less God's Vicar on earth than the successor of Peter.

Innsbrück seen, the wonder-working powers of modern engineering skill will carry the traveller over the great barrier which so long cut off the peninsular lands of Southern Europe from the great central mass. He goes, if between rugged mountains, yet among green and pleasant valleys, dotted with villages and churches

nestling on the mountain-side, each of whose towers
may pass for a stage in the great process by which the
art of Italy made its way beyond the Alps.   He
hurries by Brixen, and remembers that in old times
that city was deemed the frontier of Italy and Bavaria;
he hurries by Bozen or Bolzano, and feels from the
double name that he is still on debateable ground.   At
last the true border is passed.   He has now made his
way from the episcopal principality on the Main to
another princely bishoprick, placed on the very border
of the two chief Imperial kingdoms, a city one event
in whose history makes its name familiar to every ear,
but which otherwise would be perhaps less known than
the seat of the ecclesiastical Dukes of the Franks.
Trent, a name borne by two English rivers and at
least one English parish, is also the English name of
the city which is famous as the seat of what lately
was the latest self-styled Œcumenical Council.   Tri-
dentum, Trento, Trient, Trent, lies on one of the high
roads of Europe, and its position has ever made it a
border city.   Its present political *status* is one of the
anomalies of the map of Europe.   Lying south of
the Alps, Italian in speech and bearing in all things
the aspect of an Italian city, Trent still remains one
of the many outlying provinces which so strangely
gather round the royal diadem of Hungary and the
archiducal coronet of Austria.   It is hard, at first

sight, to see on what ground of reason or policy Trent and Aquileia should be denied that union with the one national body which has been already won for Venice and Verona. Yet the paradox is not new. Some influence or other has certainly from early times drawn Trent politically northwards. Though of old times counted as part of the Lombard kingdom, it has been for centuries counted part of that of Germany, and its history under its ecclesiastical princes has been that of a German rather than of an Italian town. In purely Italian history it bears little part, save when it fell under the power of Eccelino in the thirteenth century. Trent had little share in the wars and revolutions of the neighbouring common-wealths of Lombardy. It had more to do with its northern neighbours, vassals, and advocates, the Counts of Tyrol. Yet its architecture, as well as its language, is decidedly Italian; to a traveller entering Italy by the Brenner pass it will be his first Italian city. For an Italian city he will certainly deem it. What-ever ancient or modern arrangements may have decreed as to its political position, he feels that Trent and the land in which it stands are truly part of Italy.

The position of Trent almost forces a comparison with the position of Innsbrück. But in this matter no one can hesitate as to giving the higher place to the

undoubted German city. Both lie among mountains;
but there is this difference, that Innsbrück lies in the
strictest sense among the mountains; it is girded by
them on every side, while Trent simply has mountains
on each side of it. That is to say, Innsbrück lies at
the point of meeting of several valleys, while Trent
merely lies in the valley between two mountain ranges.
Hence, noble as the site of Trent is, it is not like Innsbrück, where it is hardly possible to look up from any
point of the town without seeing each end of the street
guarded by Alps. The result is that, while the views
round about Trent are nearly equal to those round
about Innsbrück, the streets of the town itself do not
present such striking and startling contrasts as meet us
at every step in Innsbrück. The loss of the noble
stream of the Inn is also no small disadvantage on the
part of Trent. In architecture, on the other hand, the
advantage is no less indisputably on the side of Trent.
Innsbrück offers but little beyond some fine street
arcades and projecting windows. The churches are
worthless; as Innsbrück never was a Bishop's see,
there is no *dom*, and the principal church, that
which contains the tomb of Maximilian, is chiefly
remarkable for the perverse ingenuity with which all
traces of mediæval effect have been got rid of from a
church evidently of original mediæval design. Trent,
on the other hand, has a noble *duomo* of the second

class, and the other churches, though otherwise of no value, have towers which again help to carry on the line of connexion between the arts of Italy and those of the North.

To an eye as yet unaccustomed to Italian forms the first sight of the cathedral church of Trent is very striking. The traveller will most likely first approach it from the north, where the nave and north transept occupy the southern side of the great square of the city. Everything at once tells him that he is in Italy. The central cupola, the open galleries running along nave and transept, are features which have their representatives in Germany. But here they seem clothed with a new character and a new meaning; and the few and small windows, the porch above all, with its columns resting on the backs of lions, are distinctly and characteristically Italian. The student may remark the windows of the aisle, where the double splay characteristic of German Romanesque is relieved by a profusion of external shafts and arches, in marked contrast to the usage of England and Normandy. He may mark this as a happy means of adorning a feature which, when treated as it commonly is in Germany, always has a certain look of rudeness and bareness. In the wheel window of the transept he will also mark a form of a familiar feature which will show that he has wandered far away from either Lincoln or Amiens. From this

point of view the east end is lost. It is embedded in
a mass of buildings of which the most prominent feature
is a tower, as tall and almost as slender as an Irish
round tower, but with two rows of the characteristic
coupled windows with mid-wall shafts. Here too he
will mark for the first time the peculiar battlement
which, from its frequent use at Verona, has got the
name of *Scala*, while on another machicolated tower
which forms part of the group he will see a developed
shape of the stepped battlement of Ireland. He will
not be inclined to tarry long over the west front, with
its incongruous tower; but, unless he at once enters
the building, he will most likely make his way to the
north-east, by far the finest point for a general view
of the church and its adjoining buildings. The group
is a noble one. The central octagon, with its domical
covering, rises above the choir and south transept, the
latter finished with an attached apse, and with an
eastern porch, with the pillar-bearing lions and with
one of the pillars itself twisted like the mystic pair at
Würzburg. The tall aisleless choir, with its gallery,
its tall shafted windows, its stately apse unencumbered
by surrounding chapels, may perhaps again suggest
the memory of Würzburg, not indeed in its *dom*,
but in its lesser minster. But in St. Kilian's we see
a distinctly classical tinge; while at Trent all is
late and richly developed, but still perfectly pure,

EAST END OF CATHEDRAL, PALACE, ETC., TRENT.

To face page 10.

NAVE OF CATHEDRAL, TRENT.

To face page 11.

Romanesque. And this rich Romanesque of the church itself contrasts in a marked way with the adjoining buildings, once the episcopal palace, where we see windows of the ruder German type and an apse of clearly earlier date than that of the church. The machicolated tower also comes in well from the same point. In fact, few more striking groups can be found anywhere.

We turn to the inside, and we find something for which the outside has hardly prepared us. The gloom of the church, the low clerestory with its very small windows, is thoroughly Italian; the absence of the triforium is also Italian, and sometimes German; but the piers, except in their prodigious height, are those of an English or Norman church. We have here neither the square piers of Mainz and Zürich nor the basilican columns of Murano and Torcello, nor yet the alternation of the two in St. Zeno at Verona and St. Burchard at Würzburg. The section of the piers and their attached shafts, their capitals, their whole appearance, are all thoroughly Norman, save only that they and the arches which they bear are carried up to a height which is rare in Romanesque of any kind, and whose proportion is really more like that of the latest English Gothic. But the likeness does not go beyond the proportion. The tall pillars of a church in eastern or western England bear a clerestory which sometimes becomes a very wall of glass ; those of Trent carry an upper range which is small indeed, and pierced, as the sky of Italy demands, with the smallest of windows.

It is hardly conceivable that this nave, formed of six arches such as we have just described, can come from the same hand as the enriched Romanesque of the outside of the choir. On turning to the local history the matter becomes perfectly plain. Udalric, the second Bishop of that name, was consecrated in 1022; he received the grant of the temporal principality from the Emperor Conrad the Second in 1027, and died in 1055. He rebuilt the church, or at least its eastern part; for his crypt survived till 1740, when it was destroyed to make room for the present high altar. Of the church of the first Prince-Bishop there is no reason to think that any trace remains. Work of his is more likely to be found in the adjoining buildings than in the church itself. But there seems no absolute necessity to attribute anything to an earlier date than the episcopate of Bishop Altmann, who held the see from 1124 to 1149, and who is recorded to have performed a ceremony of consecration. The arcades of the nave are doubtless his work. But the building received its present character from Bishop Frederick, who reigned from 1207 to 1218, and who, about 1212, rebuilt the choir, enriched the church outside and in with marbles and sculptures, and made some changes in the adjoining palace, which may most likely be traced in the upper range of triple windows. His work gives us a distinct specimen of pure and unmixed Romanesque, of a naturally developed round-arched style, admitting of much elegance and refinement, living on into the thirteenth century. The style had thrown off all rudeness, but it had not begun to imitate any features inconsistent with itself. There is no sign of any falling back on merely classical forms, no sign of any striving after those forms of the Northern Gothic whose true spirit Italy could never realize. Already at Trent we have seen enough to tell us that the Romanesque of Italy is a good, pure, national style, which it was pity indeed to exchange for the cold and dead imitations of foreign forms which presently set in.

Two other churches, of no other importance in themselves, claim attention on account of their towers. *Santa Maria Maggiore*, as being in some sort the scene of the Council, ought to be the most historic monument in Trent. But the church has been rebuilt since those days, and there is certainly nothing about it to attract on its own account. But attached to it is a campanile of pure and noble Italian work, with two ranges of windows with coupled shafts. St. Anne's church has a gabled tower crowned by a spire, which has therefore more of a German look, and it is worth notice that it has a stage with mid-wall shafts over a stage with pointed windows. The steeple of St. Mary's shows plainly that we are truly in Italy; but that of St. Anne steps in to show that, though we are in Italy, the land is still only an Italian march.

ROMANESQUE ARCHITECTURE IN VENETIA.

A VAST deal has been written from various points of view on the ancient architecture of Italy, yet one very important aspect of the subject has, to say the least, never been thoroughly worked out. We mean its relation to the early architecture of Germany, and still more to that of England. The more German and Italian buildings the antiquary examines, the more carefully he compares them with the little which is left in England of the eleventh century and of earlier date, the more fully does he become convinced of the essential unity of the early Romanesque style in all three countries. The buildings in England of the class commonly called "Anglo-Saxon," some of them earlier than the Norman Conquest, some of them a little later, are so few and so rude that we may be easily tempted to pass them by as not being examples of any definite style of any kind. But any one who bears them in his mind as he studies the German and Italian buildings of the eleventh and twelfth centuries will easily recognize them as simply smaller and ruder specimens of the same class. The fact is this: in England a distinctly new style was introduced in the eleventh century, the Norman style, the *novum compositionis genus* in which Eadward the Confessor rebuilt the church o Westminster. In that great building age, from the middle of the eleventh century onwards, all the great churches of England were rebuilt in the new style; the older forms survived only in a few obscure buildings here and there. In Germany and Italy the same age was equally fruitful in buildings; but there no new style was introduced; the existing native style was simply improved and developed. The great German and Italian churches of the twelfth century exhibit features which in England we see only in the rudest structures of the eleventh or of a still earlier time.

The likeness between our early towers and the Italian campaniles has often been remarked; in fact, it is more than likeness; the two things are absolutely the same. It is of course less striking in the grander and richer Italian towers; but take some of the smaller and ruder. There are towers both in Verona and in Venice which no one would feel to be out of place in company with Coleswegen's towers at Lincoln. In fact, with such examples as the church of the Apostles and the little church by the great Scala tombs at Verona, it can hardly be said that the English

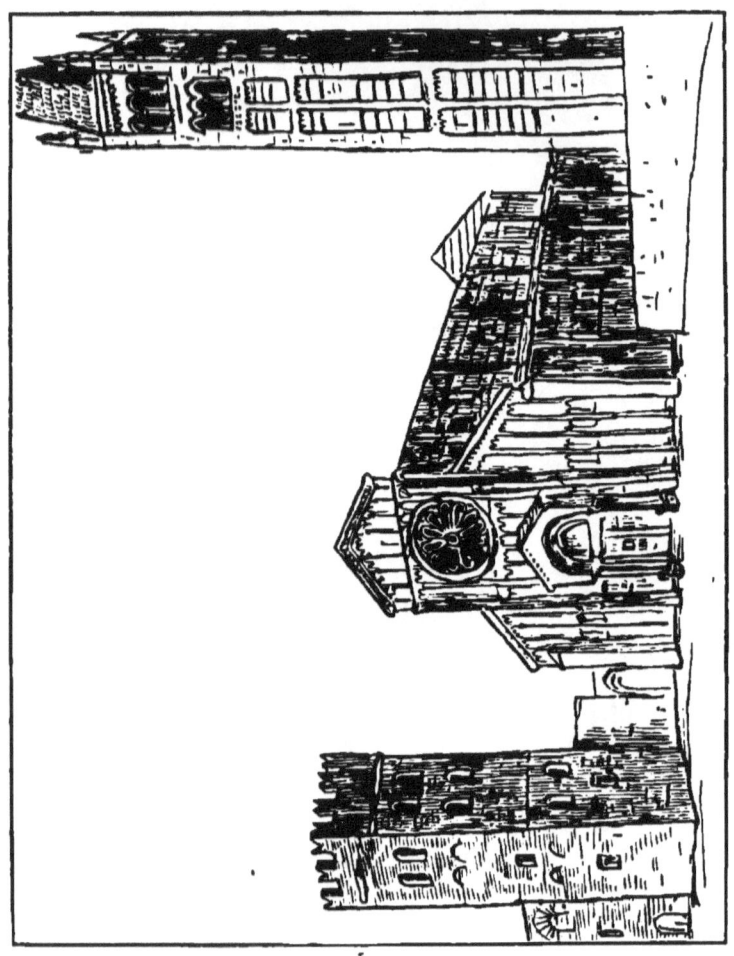

ST. ZENO, VERONA.

To face page 11.

examples are ruder than the Italian.   Yet these towers
differ in nothing but their rudeness from the mighty
campaniles of Murano and Torcello, and from the
noblest of its class on this side of the Hadriatic, the
tower of St. Zeno at Verona.   The tall, slender, unbuttressed, tower, with its mid-wall shafts in the belfry
stage, with its ornaments, if it has any, confined to flat
pilasters and arcades, is the tower common to all Western
Europe up to the eleventh century.   We find it in our
own island; we find it over all Germany from Schaff-
hausen to Bremen; we find it in the valleys of the
Pyrenees and in the heart of the Burgundian Alps.   But
Italy is its birthplace, and it is in Italy alone that we
can study its origin and meaning.   What at once distinguishes the Italian campaniles and the towers which
follow their model is their height and the absence of
buttresses.   This last feature indeed they share with
Romanesque buildings of all kinds; our own Norman
in its purity has no true buttresses; it never gets
beyond flat pilasters.   But in the towers of later date
the buttresses become features of such special importance that an unbuttressed tower strikes us more than
any other unbuttressed portion of a building.   The
height again is a characteristic of bell-towers as bell-
towers; the low massive Norman tower always shows
to most advantage as a central lantern; it is the de-
scendant, not of the campanile, but of the cupola.   The

flat pilasters and arcades which are the common ornaments of Romanesque buildings assume a special prominence in the case of these tall towers, whose apparent
height and squareness they seem to increase by dividing
them by a series of vertical strips. These strips in a
ruder form were long ago noticed as a characteristic of
the so-called "Anglo-Saxon" style in England; but
they are characteristic of it only as being one variety
of this common Primitive style. The Italian and the
English towers differ, not as members of two different
classes, but only as highly finished examples of one
class differ from ruder examples of the same.

The same truth comes out also, if we look a little
more into detail. The *long-and-short* work at the
angles of the English towers, the great slabs of stone
used in the construction of early doorways in England,
and still more in Ireland—all are, as we soon learn at
Verona, imitations of Roman masonry. So again, such
capitals, if we can so call them, as we see in the tower-
arch of St. Benet's at Cambridge are clearly copied
from work like that in the archway of the Palace called
Theodoric's at Ravenna. The mid-wall shafts of the
windows are well nigh universal in the Italian towers,
and a little further study of the details of the Italian
Romanesque easily explains their history. Next to
the introduction of the arch itself, the greatest invention in the whole history of architecture was the

improvement by which the architect of Diocletian's palace at Spálato ventured to make an arch spring at once from the capitals of a pair of columns. But this great invention was not at once universally received.   In the twelfth-century basilicas of Murano and Torcello the pattern of Spálato is followed in all its fulness, but in St. Zeno at Verona, and even in St. Burchard at Würzburg, there is something over the capitals more than can be fairly called an abacus, something which is distinctly a memory of the entablature.   Long before this, in the basilicas of Ravenna, a large stone, a kind of enormous double abacus, was interposed between the arch and the capital, and, at St. Vital, as often in Byzantine work, this grows into a distinct double capital.   In this way it became usual for a shaft to support something with a projection greater than that of a genuine capital.   In Italy we find this form used in various positions; use it in a coupled window, and we may at once get the midwall shaft.   These windows, set in groups of two, three, or four, with mid-wall shafts between each and no shafts in the jambs, effectually distinguish towers of this type from those of the Norman type, where the windows, if they are at all finished, have shafts in the jambs, and where the central shafts are set, not in the middle of the wall, but much nearer its outer surface.   A triforium again has much in common with a tower window, and in the cathedral at Modena we find a distinct example of the mid-wall shaft in the triforium. The form most commonly taken by the stone resting on the shaft, both in such finished examples as St. Zeno and in such rude windows as those of St. Stephen's in the same city, is essentially the same as that of the great Byzantine capitals in St. Vital at Ravenna and St. Mark's at Venice. And a form nearly the same is found in a singular object in the great basilica of St. Apollinaris in Classe, at a date as late, it would seem, as the fourteenth century. This is the support of a stone book, which takes the shape of a more graceful variety of those balusters which range from Jarrow to Tewkesbury, and which is finished with a stone of this kind alike for its capital and for its base. Hardly a detail of our Primitive Romanesque can be pointed out which does not appear in a more finished shape in Germany, and still more in Italy.

If we go on with the towers, as the strongest case, we shall see that the type which in England lasted only till the eleventh century, and in Scotland and Germany only till the twelfth, in Italy never went out of use at all. A glance at the towers of Verona and Venice soon confirms us in the belief which may perhaps have suggested itself to us at Trent, that the type which died out so early in the North can in Italy hardly be said ever to have died out. There are a crowd of towers in

Verona only, towers of much later date, towers of the fourteenth or fifteenth century, contemporary with our later Gothic buildings, the general effect of which does not differ from that of St. Zeno. They still keep the mid-wall shafts, the pilasters and arcades, all that gives the type its peculiar character. The noble campanile of St. Euphemia almost rivals St. Zeno, and there are also very fine towers at St. Firmus, and at the otherwise worthless church attached to the workhouse, the dedication of which we think is the Holy Trinity. There are other towers of nearly the same general effect in which the characteristic details are lost, and are replaced by the forms either of the pseudo-Gothic of Italy or of the revived classical. The outline is kept, and the same general form is given even to the windows. To go beyond our immediate district, the great square of Bologna is surrounded by a group of towers—the town-tower, that of the cathedral, and that of St. Petronius—which have forsaken the true Romanesque detail, but which have by no means lost the true Romanesque feeling. And more remarkable still is the tower of the church of St. Peter in the Castle at Venice, which was the patriarchal church till the see was removed to St. Mark's. Let us tell our own experience with regard to it. We saw it first from the water, in the direction of Murano and Torcello. At a distance it had thoroughly the air of a third ancient campanile,

the compeer of those of the two island basilicas. It was
only on coming near enough to study the details that
we saw that it was really a work of the revived classical
style of the sixteenth century. So thoroughly had the
architect caught the spirit of a type of which he despised
the detail; so slight is the boundary which, in the
native land of both, divides the style which continued
Roman forms by unbroken tradition from that which fell
back upon them by conscious imitation.

Passing from the towers to Romanesque work of
other kinds, the great Venetian cities seem on the
whole less rich in buildings of that class than some
other parts of Italy. Venice, we must never forget,
is for our purposes no part of Italy, no part of the
dominions of the Western Emperor. It is a fragment
of the Empire of the East, which gradually became independent of the East, but never admitted the supremacy of the West. ‘Ημεῖς δοῦλοι θέλομεν εἶναι τοῦ
‘Ρωμαίων Βασιλεως are the words put into the mouth of
the islanders by the Imperial historian; and they ceased to
be subjects of the Eastern Cæsar only in becoming Lords
of One Fourth and One Eighth of his Empire. Both
as subjects and as lords they were equally disciples. The
ducal chapel of Venice repeats the patriarchal church of
Constantinople, as it is itself so strangely repeated in the
far distant abbey of Périgueux. On St. Mark's it is need-
less to enlarge. All the world knows the one building

in which constructive and decorative art meet on absolutely equal terms, where the domes and arches stand
in as much need of the mosaics as the mosaics do of the
domes and arches. The apse of St. Mark's kindled by
the western sun into one blaze of gold fairly rivals the
storied windows of Rheims in all the glory of the same
happy moment. How much of the unrivalled effect of
St. Mark's is due to its gorgeous mosaics is best felt by
comparing it with such a church as that of St. Antony
at Padua, where the domes—of no contemptible design,
at least within—cry aloud for the same kind of relief to
their bareness and whiteness. But St. Mark's may be
studied from a humbler point of view as an inexhaustible
store of capitals, plundered and imitated from all kinds
of sources, classical, Byzantine, and Romanesque. And
many of them again teach us the lesson into what
gorgeous forms it is easy to carve the rude stone which
rests on the mid-wall shafts of Jarrow and Earl's Barton.

But, if the great glory of Venice is not Romanesque
but Byzantine, the spot which is the real cradle, the
real centre of the life, of the great commonwealth, has
somewhat more in common with western forms. The
little chapel on Rialto, the first ecclesiastical home of
the new-born city, is of much the same type as that
grand series of twelfth century palaces dotted up and
down among the ranges of buildings of later work
which fringe the Grand Canal. It is a strange feeling

to see in a short sail more Romanesque domestic work
than we have seen in our whole lives before. At Lincoln, at Bury, at Christchurch, at Dol, at Le Mans, we
have eagerly traced out a few doorways and windows,
with an uncomfortable feeling that perhaps all were,
as some certainly were, the work of the Hebrews
within our gates. But here are lines of windows and
arcades which equal in their way the nave of Bayeux
or the hall of Oakham. Perhaps it was not wholly
inappropriate that the noblest of the series became
in after days the possession of the Turkey merchants.
Here and there, in the stilted arches and the general
air of the whole, we almost seem to see some touch of
a Saracenic hand.

The two outlying insular basilicas of Murano and
Torcello will interest the inquirer at any stage; they
will amaze him till he has seen Ravenna. Basilicas
they undoubtedly are, though they do not show the
basilican type in such purity of the genuine thing itself
as Ravenna, or even as the churches at Lucca, which
are perhaps contemporary with themselves. The east
ends, with the many apses at Torcello, with the large
open gallery at Murano, depart from the stern simplicity of the Ravennese and even of the Lucchese
buildings. After all, the basilica at Torcello is less
striking than the little church of St. Fosca, with its
cupola designed but never finished. The elegant

BAPTISTERY, PADUA.

To face page 25.

gallery of Murano reappears in a clumsier form as
an addition—for good constructive reasons — to the
apse of St. Sophia at Padua, the only Romanesque
church of that city which has so much to show of other
kinds. The baptistery of its cathedral—the church
itself is worthless—shows us the same general type to
be seen in many other places, and the treatment of
the architectural design is fully worthy of the noble
paintings with which it is enriched.

Verona, so rich in Roman and again in later work,
has but little of Romanesque beyond its great minster
of St. Zeno. But that is a host in itself. Basilican in
its ground plan, it departs a good deal from the
basilican type in its architecture. The compound piers
of the Northern Romanesque alternate with the columns
of the basilica. The west front shows the Italian
Romanesque in perfection ; rich, but without the ex-
travagance into which the style sometimes ran in the
Tuscan cities. The gap between pier-arch and clerestory
is not more painful than in many German churches ; in
either case it calls for the mosaic of Ravenna to relieve
the bareness. To many this noble church will be the
first glimpse of Italian ecclesiastical architecture.
Even with Ravenna, Lucca, and Pisa to come, the first
fruits are worthy of what is to follow.

ANCIENT VERONA.

WE spoke casually of some of the buildings of Verona in speaking of Romanesque architecture in Northern Italy. But, like all the great Italian cities, Verona may be looked at in many ways, and in truth the only way truly to master any of them is to visit them again and again, looking at them each time with a special view to one class of subjects. As for objects of other classes, it will be well for the time being, we will not say to shut the eyes to them altogether, but certainly to look at them only as subordinate to what for the time is the main object of study. Taking Verona as an example, there is the classic Verona, the Verona of Catullus and Pliny; there is the Verona of the Nibelungen, the Bern of Theodoric; there is the mediæval Verona, the Verona of commonwealths and tyrants, the Verona of Eccelino and Can Grande; and there is the Verona of later times, under Venetian, French, and Austrian bondage, the Verona of Congresses and fortifications. Verona, like Le Mans, is an Ecbatana, spreading, circle beyond circle, each range having its own history and its own monuments. Of one of these ranges it is at first disappointing to find so little to remind us. When we think of the fame of Verona in Teutonic romance—how the city and the hero have each taken the name of the other, and how they have been fused together on Teutonic lips—we are tempted to mourn that "Dietrich von Bern" should have left such slight traces of himself in his own *Dietrichsbern*. But it is perhaps well that the surviving monuments of Theodoric and his age should be gathered together round the one spot which stands by itself in the whole world. It may be well that the city which boasts of his church, his palace, and his tomb should not be exposed to rivalry from another city which, though it has come to bear his name, was, after all, only his occasional sojourn. It is perhaps well that, as Ravenna has no share in the earlier and later glories of other cities, as it boasts no arches or amphitheatres of heathen days, no palaces and churches of the later Christian ages, it should have its own intermediate age wholly to itself. It may be well that neither Verona nor any other city should intrude on its special privilege as the bridge which joins together the two worlds which elsewhere are parted by so yawning a gap. Certain it is that, while Verona is so rich in remains of earlier and later times, it has not a single perfect building, nothing beyond doubtful pieces of wall, which even pretends to belong to the age of Theodoric or to the ages immediately before and after him. Of his palace on the further side of the river, looking down on the city and the surrounding lands, a contrast indeed to the site of his own home among the canals and marshes of Ravenna, the history can be traced down to our own century. But all traces both of the palace itself and of the many buildings which have succeeded it have vanished before the necessities of modern warfare and defence. The palace of the Goth has made way for the fortress of the Austrian.

As Theodoric has left no sign, we leap, as far as the great monuments of the city go, from Gallienus and Diocletian to Henry the Third. The intermediate ages give us only some fragments of wall, which, truly or falsely, bear the name of the Great Charles, and that single strange structure under the shadow of St. Zeno's minster, which calls itself the tomb of his son, the youngest Pippin, the first of the Frankish house who reigned over Italy as a separate kingdom. The series is not an uninstructive one; Diocletian, Charles, and Henry each mark stages in the history of the Empire; each was a restorer after a time in which its power and glory had fallen. It is well that the series should be formed by them, while Theodoric, with all the splendour and happiness of his

APSE OF ST. STEPHEN'S, VERONA.

To face page 29.

Italian reign, stands rather as a break than as a link in the Imperial series. And, when we reach the reign of Henry the Third, we cannot point with certainty to any monument of his time, except the unadorned lower stage of the great campanile of St. Zeno. All that gives that noble tower the character which it stamped on all the towers of the city for so many centuries comes from the stages which were carried up perhaps a hundred and thirty years later. Among the great buildings of Verona there is in truth a gap which spreads from the third century to the twelfth, and which carries us at a bound from the amphitheatre of the days of Diocletian to the church of the days of Frederick Barbarossa. To the architectural student indeed that church, the great example of what, in contrast to Pisa and Lucca, we may be tempted to call the barbaric form of Italian Romanesque, is alone worth a pilgrimage. St. Zeno ranks as an example of its own style with Durham and Pisa and Speyer and St. Sernin at Toulouse. And far less stately, but hardly less interesting, is the little church of St. Stephen on Theodoric's side of the river. Its main body is ruthlessly disfigured: but it still keeps its central octagon, its pillared crypt, the arcades of its upper and its lower apse, and the stone chair of the bishop still in its ancient place, a monument of the times when St. Stephen's disputed with the vaster

duomo on the other side of the river its right to hold
the first place among the churches of Verona, as the
seat of her bishops in life and their burying-place in
death.

No less full of associations in their own way are the
later buildings, the tall tower of the municipality,
the palaces and tombs of the tyrants, the house that
sheltered Dante, the castle looking forth so proudly on
the northern mountains, the broad arches of the bridge
that stems the rushing Adige, the long array of domestic
buildings which make Verona one of the chief schools
of architecture of its own type. For the admirers of
that type there is the *duomo* — containing also parts
of earlier and better work—and the more striking
pile of St. Anastasia. This last is one of those vast
churches whose pointed arches cry for this appropriate
detail, churches which we should welcome at Palermo
in the days of King Roger, but which we look on with
less respect when we remember that, when they arose,
Westminster and Köln and Amiens were already risen
or rising. But for the nonce we wish to take our leap
backwards to the earliest existing remains, to the
Verona, not indeed of Catullus, hardly of Pliny, but to
a Verona which was already beginning to be ancient
when Claudian sang of it. The theatre on the left—
on Theodoric's—side of the river, the theatre which
had become a licensed quarry in the days of King

Berengar, is so utterly shattered that we can hardly do more than judge from the noble capitals of the earlier and purer Ionic form how stately a pile it must have been in the days of its perfection. The amphitheatre all the world knows; perhaps it is less generally known how lately an Emperor sat there to behold the kind of spectacle for which the building was at first raised. Joseph the Second had so far forgotten who he was as to go to Rome and to come away without receiving the rite which would have enabled him to strike out the word *Erwählter* or *Electus* from his style. But he was reminded of his own existence by the popular voice both of Rome and of Verona. The Roman people welcomed *their* Emperor ("Imperatore *nostro*"): the people of Verona greeted him with a threefold clapping of hands, as he beheld a bull-fight in the old arena, and the magistrates duly commemorated the fact by an inscription in which "Imp. Cæs. Josephus II. P.F.A." took his place as naturally as if he had been Vespasian or Trajan. At first sight, while one laments the loss of nearly the whole of the outside range of arches, one is tempted to be displeased at the absolute perfection of the internal seats, and the new look of some of them. But when we find that the practice of keeping them in repair has gone on unbroken through all ages down to our own, the custom itself becomes a part of the history of the building, a part as well worth preserving as any other, and which helps in a forcible way to keep up the feeling of unbroken connexion with the past.

Looking to the building distinctly as a work of architects, the Veronese amphitheatre, like all other buildings of the same class, brings out in its full perfection the massive grandeur of the true Roman style of building. It is the arch, the true Roman feature, which gives the building its character. The Greek features, which in the more enriched Roman buildings act as a mask to the real construction, are either not there at all, or else they have so little prominence as not to interfere with the genuine Roman effect. They hardly count for more than the engaged shafts which surround the apses of Lucca and Speyer, or even than the pilaster buttresses of our own Norman buildings. And, if we go into the vast and cavernous recesses of the building, we learn another lesson in the history of the building art. Those who have not carried their studies beyond our own island are irresistibly tempted to attribute some of the characteristic features of our earliest towers to imitation of a timber construction in stone, to what has been ingeniously called "stone carpentry." But in this respect, as in every other, our primitive Romanesque buildings are built as their founders professed to build them. They are built *more Romano*. The stone carpentry, the long-and-short work, of our primitive towers, is thoroughly Roman; it may be seen on a gigantic scale in the dark places of the amphitheatre of Verona.

From the amphitheatre we turn to the gateways, and the great gate at Verona can hardly fail to suggest a comparison with the mighty *Porta Nigra* of Trier. Balancing the remains of the two cities, and setting aside the basilica of Trier, Verona as much surpasses Trier in its amphitheatre as Trier surpasses Verona in its gateway. The comparison may be thought unfair, as the Trier gate is all but perfect, while the Verona gate is simply the outside shell. Still the outer faces of the two may fairly be compared. Trier indeed has the advantage of outline, in the magnificent flanking towers on either side, while Verona has only a flat front on a single level. Trier too has the advantage of position, as standing free from other buildings, as still being the actual entrance to the city from its suburbs; while the gate at Verona suffers in architectural effect, though it really becomes more striking as an historical monument, by being no longer the entrance to anything, but spanning one of the busiest streets of a flourishing modern town. The doctrine may sound frightful in classic ears; but to our mind the comparison between the two gateways shows how far the real art of architecture had advanced between the days of Gallienus, or the days before Gallienus, and those days of Constantine or later which beheld the building of the sublime pile at

D

Trier. Between the two, in fact, architecture made its great step; the gate at Trier carries us to the days of Spálato, to the earliest days of Ravenna. In the Verona gate the Greek features are still there, masking the Roman construction; over the actual openings, over the windows above them, we get unmeaning entablatures and pediments, stone pictures, so to speak, of real entablatures and pediments, like the survivals of the shape of the old post-chaise carved or painted on the modern railway-carriage. This gives the front the appearance of a confusion of Greek and Roman ideas, while at Trier, as in the amphitheatres, indeed even more thoroughly than in the amphitheatres, the remains of the columnar system, the half-columns or pilasters, have sunk into the subordinate place which they hold in Romanesque buildings. In fact, according to our heretical view that classical Roman architecture is only a transitional stage between one consistent form of construction and decoration in the shape of Greek art and another consistent form of construction and decoration in the shape of Romanesque art, one might doubt whether the Trier gateway is not entitled to be called Romanesque rather than Roman. Whether Gallienus built the whole gate at Verona, or simply repaired and raised an earlier gate, is of no importance at all in this point of view. Both parts of the gateway show the same fault, the inherent fault of the classical Roman style; both, in a word, are *præ-Spala-*

tine. But at Trier, though, from the nature of the building, no arches actually rest on columns, we see the working of the same principle, the effect of that great architectural revolution of which the court of Diocletian was the beginning.

Still, with all this, the *Porta dei Borsari* of Verona is a striking object, the more striking, as we have already said, from the very position which takes away somewhat from its effect as a work of architecture. One wonders how it has lived through so many ages. At Trier, even if we did not know that the gateway was for nearly eight hundred years preserved by being used as a church, we do not for a moment wonder at its preservation. At Verona the preservation of the gateway itself is hardly so striking as the sight of the small inscribed stones which stand near it, remaining there in the crowded street untouched by the changes of sixteen hundred years. And it must always be remembered that the present gateway is simply one wall of the ancient structure; the place of its fellow may easily be marked some way back, where a small piece of the wall, which is still to be seen in the adjoining side street, marks the place where the other wall of the gateway spanned the main street.

Besides the gate of which so large a part has been preserved, the traveller should not fail to notice a fragment of one of the other gateways, that known as the *Arco dei Leoni,* where one half of the gateway has been preserved through the accident of a change in the direction of the street. In this gate the faults of the *Porta dei Borsari* are less strongly marked, and great lightness and elegance must have been given to the highest story of all by the small detached columns with their twisted flutings, like those in the Laurentian basilica at Rome, suggesting what was to come on a vaster scale at Waltham, Durham, Dunfermline, and Lindisfarne. One only remains, but it struck us that some of its fellows had been used up again among the columns of various kinds which are to be found in the apse of St. Stephen's. We have not local knowledge enough to identify the Triumvir Tiberius Flavius Noricus, the son of Spurius, whose name may still clearly be read on the architrave above the surviving arch. But we certainly think that, when the building was perfect, it must have formed a finer whole than the gate which is still preserved to us nearly entire. Both, along with the other Roman remains of the city, form a noble beginning of that series of buildings of all dates which gather, as round their centre, around the glorious pile of St. Zeno, the greatest of them all.

RAVENNA AND HER SISTERS.

RAVENNA.

If we seek through the world for a city which is absolutely unique in its character and interest, we shall find it at Ravenna. It is a city in which, as soon as we set foot, we at once find ourselves among the memorials of an age which has left but few memorials elsewhere. The sea which once gave Ravenna her greatness has fallen back and left the once Imperial city like a wreck in a wilderness. In the like sort, the memory of an age, strange if not glorious, full of great changes if not of great deeds, has passed away from other spots without leaving any visible memorial; at Ravenna the memorials of that age are well nigh all that is left. It is well that such a strange corner of history should still abide as a living thing in one forsaken corner of Europe. It is well that there should be one spot from which the monuments of heathen Rome and the monuments of mediæval Christendom are alike absent, where every relic breathes of the strange and almost forgotten time which comes between the two. At Ravenna the amphitheatre of Verona and the *duomo*

of Milan, nay even the more venerable temple which
covers the bones of Ambrose, would all be out of place.
We walk its streets, and we feel glad that we do not
walk among the stately arcades of Padua and Bologna,
that our eye is not met by such memories of municipal
freedom as we see at Pistoia and Piacenza, or by such
frowning relics of signorial and ducal rule as seem still
to keep their grasp on Milan and Verona. Ravenna, like
other cities, had its commonwealth and its tyrants; but a
single inconsiderable tower and a few not very conspicuous
tombs are the only traces left either of the commonwealth
or of the tyranny. Two or three mediæval churches do
not seriously interfere with the character of the city,
and the *Renaissance* cathedral, eyesore as it is, is well
nigh forgotten beside its own baptistery and campanile.
Indeed, when we casually enter its walls, and light on
a priest saying mass in ancient form, neither before the
altar nor on its north side, but looking westward alike on
altar and congregation, we feel that, if the bricks and
stones of the elder church have vanished, the usages of
primitive times still live in the home which may fittingly
be their last resting-place. So again, on two of the few
later monuments of Ravenna we look with other eyes.
Later in date, they do in fact carry on in a strange way
the traditions which, to a lover of the days of the latest
Roman and the earliest Teutonic powers, make Ravenna
the very goal of his pilgrimage, the very centre of the

earth. The Venetian column in the market-place tells
of the days of the greatest prosperity that Ravenna
has seen in later times; but it has also a strange fitness
that the spot where the elder Roman power lingered
on the longest should have become part of the possessions of the island city where the true Roman life
lived on when it had passed away from the mainland.
And the one object which to many minds will ever give
Ravenna its greatest charm, the tomb which contains
the most precious dust within its walls, in truth forms
another link in the same chain. We need not mourn
that Dante lies far away from his own Florence. A
whole of which Florence was but a part may truly
claim ten parts in him. The poet of the Empire
could nowhere sleep so well as among the Cæsars of
whom he dreamed.

With these exceptions, of which the two last and most
striking are no real exceptions, all the monuments of
Ravenna belong to the days of transition from Roman
to mediæval times, and the greater part of them come
within the fifth and sixth centuries. It was then that
Ravenna became, for a season, the head of Italy and of
the Western world. The sea had made Ravenna a
great haven; the falling back of the sea made her the
ruling city of the earth. Augustus had called into
being the port of Cæsarea as the Peiraieus of the
old Thessalian or Umbrian Ravenna. Haven and city

grew and became one; but the faithless element again
fell back; the haven of Augustus became dry land
covered by orchards, and Classis arose as the third
naval station, leaving Ravenna itself an inland city.
Again has the sea fallen back; Cæsarea has utterly
perished; Classis survives only in one venerable church;
the famous pine forest has grown up between the third
haven and the now distant Hadriatic. Out of all this
grew the momentary greatness of Ravenna. The city,
girded with the threefold zone of marshes, causeways,
and strong walls, became the impregnable shelter of
the later Emperors; and the earliest Teutonic Kings
naturally fixed their royal seat in the city of their
Imperial predecessors. When this immediate need had
passed away, the city naturally fell into insignificance,
and it plays hardly any part in the history of mediæval
Italy. Hence it is that the city is crowded with the
monuments of an age which has left hardly any monuments elsewhere. In Britain indeed, if Dr. Merivale
be right in the date which he gives to the great Northern
wall, we have a wonderful relic of those times; but it
is the work, not of the architect, but of the military
engineer. In other parts of Europe also works of this
date are found here and there; but nowhere save at
Ravenna is there a whole city, so to speak, made up of
them. Nowhere but at Ravenna can we find, thickly
scattered around us, the churches, the tombs, perhaps

the palaces, of the last Roman and the first Teutonic
rulers of Italy. In the Old and in the New Rome, and
in Milan also, works of the same date exist; but
either they do not form the chief objects of the city,
or they have lost their character and position through
later changes. If Ravenna boasts of the tombs of
Honorius and Theodoric, Milan boasts also, truly or
falsely, of the tombs of Stilicho and Athaulf. But at
Milan we have to seek for the so-called tomb of Athaulf
in a side-chapel of a church which has lost all ancient
character, and the so-called tomb of Stilicho, though
placed in the most venerable church of the city, stands
in a strange position as the support of a pulpit. At
Ravenna, on the other hand, the mighty mausoleum of
Theodoric, and the chapel which contains the tombs of
Galla Placidia, her brother, and her second husband,
are among the best known and best preserved monuments
of the city. Ravenna, in the days of its Exarchs, could
never have dared to set up its own St. Vital as a rival
to Imperial St. Sophia. But at St. Sophia, changed
into the temple of another faith, the most characteristic
ornaments have been hidden or torn away, while at St.
Vital Hebrew patriarchs and Christian saints, and the
Imperial forms of Justinian and his strangely-chosen
Empress, still look down, as they did thirteen hundred
years back, upon the altars of Christian worship.
Ravenna, in short, seems, as it were, to have been

preserved all but untouched to keep up the memory
of the days which were alike Roman, Christian, and
Imperial.

The great monuments of Ravenna all come within
less than a hundred and fifty years of each other, and
yet they fall naturally into three periods. First come
the monuments of the Christian Western Empire, the
churches and tombs of the family of Theodosius. Next
come the works of the Gothic kingdom, the churches
and the mausoleum of Theodoric. Lastly come the
buildings, St. Vital among the foremost, which are, in
part at least, later than the recovery of Italy under
Justinian. It follows then that two great historical
revolutions come within the range of the Ravenna
monuments. One of these revolutions clothes the
monuments of the second class with an interest which is
absolutely unique. The Gothic monuments of Ravenna
—at Ravenna we must call back the word "Gothic"
from its secondary to its primary meaning—are the
earliest civilized monuments of our own race. They are
the only monuments of that illustrious branch of our race
—a branch, be it ever remembered, nearer to us than
to our High-German kinsfolk—to whose lot it fell to
be the first Teutonic masters of Italy. The brilliant
episode of the Gothic kingdom—that most brilliant
time of it when Theodoric gave Italy such a season of
rest and prosperity as she had never had since the days of

the Antonines, such as she has never had again till our
own times—all this lives at Ravenna in brick and stone,
while from the rest of the world it has utterly passed
away. The churches of Theodoric too have an interest
of another kind, as the earliest monuments of religious
equality. In claiming them as the first monuments of
our own race, we may be inclined to forgive them
for being the first monuments of heresy. But as
such, the churches of Theodoric, raised for the worship
of his Arian Goths, mark one of those rare moments in
the history of the world when a wise and impartial ruler
compelled contending sects to live in peace side by
side. The policy of the great Goth was far wiser than
that of the Arian Emperors who had reigned before
him. Constantius and Valens were persecutors of the
Orthodox; Justina demanded of St. Ambrose the sur-
render of a church in Milan for the heretical worship.
Theodoric made no such mistakes; he gave no such
opportunities to his enemies. He in no way persecuted
the Catholics; he in no way disturbed them in their
possessions; but, with a wisdom the like of which was
not seen for ages after, he simply set up the worship
of his own sect on terms of perfect equality with theirs.

The reign of Theodoric—λόγῳ μὲν τύραννος, says
Prokopios, ἔργῳ δὲ βασιλεὺς ἀληθής—save the dark
events with which it begins and ends, is like a kind
of dream, like the romantic ideal of a beneficent ruler

turned by some spell into true history. But, great as were the events which lie within the range of the Ravenna monuments, all come together under one head; they are all Christian Roman. The architecture of the reign of Theodoric — the only existing Gothic architecture in the literal sense—does not differ from the style of the earlier and later buildings of the same class. There was no reason why it should. Theodoric was King of the Goths, but he ruled in Italy as a vicegerent of the absent Emperor, and throughout his reign the preservation and imitation of the works of earlier Roman art was a chief object of his care. So again we must remember that the recovery of Italy by Belisarius and Narses was strictly a Roman reconquest. Belisarius himself was Consul of the Republic when he sailed for Sicily. One of the Ravenna inscriptions speaks of the "Pax et Libertas" which were restored to Italy by the overthrow of the Gothic rule. We may perhaps think that the rule of a Gothic King was likely to be more favourable to peace and freedom than the rule of a Byzantine Exarch. Such was not the mind of the sixth century. Nothing had yet happened to give the Empire anything but a Roman character. Cæsar Augustus might dwell at the New Rome, not at the Old, but that was simply as in former times he had dwelled at Milan or at Ravenna itself. The Empire

was none the less Roman for any of those changes.
The official speech was still Latin, as the mighty volume
of the Civil Law remains to bear witness. At St. Mark's
we see the Byzantine influence after Byzantine influence
had become Greek influence. Greek inscriptions appear
over the heads of the holy personages in the mosaics.
But the walls of St. Vital and St. Apollinaris in Classe
speak no tongue but Latin. Whatever may have been
the native speech of the peasant from the foot of
Hæmus, Imperator Cæsar Flavius Justinianus Augustus
could acknowledge no tongue but the Roman tongue
of his predecessors.

And now for a few words on the monuments themselves. They are mainly ecclesiastical. There is indeed
one noble fragment of early domestic work in the so-
called Palace of Theodoric. Whether the existing building can claim to have really been the dwelling-place of
the great Goth has been strongly called in question, and
we must confess that we share the doubt. It is older
than Charles the Great—it served as a quarry for the
pillars which he carried off to adorn his palace at
Aachen; but we are inclined to attribute it to the days
of Lombard rather than of Gothic rule. The works of
Theodoric are Roman; this palace is not Roman, but
Romanesque, though undoubtedly a very early form of
Romanesque. We can hardly persuade ourselves that
the great arched-headed doorway can belong to Theod-

oric's age, an age when doorways were still square, and
when the tympanum itself had not begun to appear.
But we have its fellow at home; the tower-arch of
St. Bene't's at Cambridge is plainly a rougher example
of the same class. Still there is a sense in which we
may still fairly call it Theodoric's palace. It is in all
probability an addition to Theodoric's actual work, an
addition which has been left as the single remnant of
the building to which it was added. And, if we have
not reached the actual home of the great Goth,
we have at least reached a spot where we are driven
to look on the great Frank as a modern intruder and
destroyer. We have somewhat of the same feeling
when we walk through the room in the archiepiscopal palace where so many of the inscriptions of
Ravenna are carefully preserved. We pass by some
inscriptions of heathen times with less attention than
we should give them elsewhere; our eye is caught on
one side by a Latin inscription to a Chamberlain of the
Gothic King, and on the other by the Greek epitaph
of a later Byzantine Exarch, which tells us, truly or
falsely, how the army of the Italians (τὸ στράτευμα τῶν
Ἰταλῶν) wept for him. These are genuine memorials,
such as Ravenna alone could supply; but when we see
among them a dedication " Karolo Regi Francorum et
Langobardorum et Patricio Romanorum," the titles
which elsewhere would call forth reverence here raise a

certain feeling of incongruity; we are half inclined
to say, "Friend, thou hast no business here." We look
with more interest on the arcade in the market-place
formed of pillars and capitals strangely put together,
but on one of which is a monograph out of which
ingenious men have spelled the word "Theodoricus"
—a memorial, it may be, of the Gothic King; it may
be of some meaner craftsman.

The mention of the Archbishop's palace leads us to
an easy division of the ecclesiastical buildings of
Ravenna into two classes: those which follow the cruciform and domical type, and those which follow that of
the basilicas. But it must be added that in both classes
the glory of the Ravenna churches is to be sought for
wholly within. The early Christian buildings had no
means of producing a striking exterior. The elder
architecture produced it by means of the colonnade,
and the basilica had taken the colonnade indoors. The
Ravenna buildings, built mainly of brick, have but little
to show without; to make the outside worthy of what it
contains was reserved for the men of Lucca and Pisa at
a later day. But go within, and few things are more
striking than the long ranges of columns, the spoils of
heathendom, varying, it may be, slightly in height
and size, often supporting capitals of various forms,
but still joining in a true harmony to bear up those endless ranges of arches in which the lowest stage of the

E

mediæval minster already begins to be foreshadowed. The
triforium, clerestory, and vault are things yet to come,
or they are at most represented by a few windows
pierced in the upper part of the wall with but little
reference to the arches below. But the basilica has
its own substitute. We do not lack the triforium of
Modena or Norwich or Pisa or Durham itself, as we gaze
on the glorious series of mosaics which fill its place
in the basilica of Theodoric, the misnamed St. Apollinaris, the church which the Gothic lord of Ravenna
reared for his countrymen and fellow-believers, and to
which a later age and another form of faith added
what has become its chiefest ornament. Few of
man's works are more striking than that long procession of triumphant virgins headed by the Three
Kings—not stiff conventional forms, as in the later
Byzantine work, but living and moving human beings
—bearing their gifts to their Lord on the knees of His
Mother. This splendid church is indeed the noblest of
all; but it is only one out of the examples of this date
which Ravenna, alone among the cities of the earth,
sets before us in such abundance. One of the finest,
St. Apollinaris in Classe, lies far out of the city, a
witness to those changes in the relations of land and
water which form the history of Ravenna. The one
relic of Classis now is this magnificent abbey, with its
sixth century basilica, begun in the last days of Gothic

ST. APOLLINARIS IN CLASSE.

To face page 51.

rule, finished after Ravenna had become an outpost of
Byzantium. Parts of the conventual buildings seem
to be of the same date. For they are built of the
same genuine Roman brick as the church itself, while
the brick of the campanile is of a smaller and later kind.
The distinguishing campanile of Ravenna, as of Ireland
and East-Anglia, is round. The Ravenna towers have
a rougher and earlier look than the square towers, but
this may partly be owing to their shape, partly to the
practice of blocking up most of the windows. Their
date is uncertain ; but they are later than the days of
Charles the Great. The local writer Agnellus, writing
soon after his time, describes the churches of Ravenna
nearly as they still are; but he says not a word about
bell-towers. His description distinctly confirms the
early date commonly given to the Ravenna basilicas ;
but it is clear that in some places they contain portions
of buildings earlier still. In the church of St. Agatha,
towards the west end, arches of Roman brick have been
cut through to make way for the columnar arcades, and
though this change may have been made in the fifteenth
century, it marks the former existence of something
earlier than the existing basilican forms.

The baptisteries—at Ravenna alone we can use the
plural form—which, as elsewhere in Italy, stand distinct from the churches, form the natural transition to
the domical and cruciform buildings. The two cathe-

E 2

dral churches, Catholic and Arian, each had its baptistery, and each still survives. Of the domical churches
the archiepiscopal chapel, though the smallest, is not
the least interesting, by reason of its exquisite early
mosaics. The famous chapel and tomb of Galla
Placidia eminently illustrate the way in which at
Ravenna all attractions are to be looked for within.
From without, the building is hardly to be seen;
within it is rich with mosaics, and the interest of its
contents is not lessened by the personal insignificance
of the persons commemorated. We seek in vain for
the tomb of Constantine or Theodosius; but Honorius
sleeps undisturbed in his sister's chapel; so does
her Roman husband Constantius—her nobler Goth
lies far away, perhaps at Milan, perhaps rather at
Barcelona. In tombs of this date Ravenna is specially
rich. The sarcophagi of early Christian times lie
about uncared for in the churches and in the streets,
and they have often been freely used by men of
later ages as their own resting-places. The crowning
glory of this class of objects has been at least spared
this indignity; but the bones of Theodoric, as those of
a heretic—perhaps as those of a barbarian—were soon
cast out from beneath his mighty monolith dome. The
very name of the hero has been exchanged in popular
speech for one which simply describes the form of the
building. *La Rotonda* stands distinguished as the one

building of Ravenna built wholly of stone; but it is stone from distant Istria, whence came also the gigantic block, now unluckily broken, which covers the whole. Of domical churches proper, not being also tombs, the chief is of course the grand pile of St. Vital, the model of Aachen. This again, like St. Apollinaris in Classe, was begun under the Goth and finished under the restored rule of the Roman. This too, in its shapeless brick outside, gives little promise of its sublime interior, its cupola, its columnar galleries, and the glorious mosaics which look down on its high altar. One thing however is lacking; the wretched paintings which disfigure the cupola, and which, by imitating architectural forms, mislead the eye in following the lines of the building, may well be displaced, if possible, by mosaics, or, failing that, by honest whitewash. Outside the building stands a sepulchral monument such as could be found nowhere but at Ravenna. It is the tomb of an Exarch of Armenian birth, sent from Constantinople to bear rule over Italy. With this we will wind up our list of Ravennese antiquities. The place has associations of later date; but, in the presence of the tomb of Theodoric and the tomb of Dante, we have no mind to tarry by the column which commemorates the death and the useless victory of Gaston of Foix.

TRIER.

———◦◦◦———

THE ancient capital of the Treveri has the privilege of
being known by two modern names, native and foreign,
each of which preserves a letter of the ancient name
which is lost in its rival. *Treveris* is by its own people
contracted into *Trier*, while by its neighbours it is cut
short into *Trèves*. But one who looks out from the amphitheatre beyond its walls on the city which boasts itself to
have stood for thirteen hundred years longer than Rome,
will be inclined to hold' that the beauty of its position
and the interest of its long history cannot lose their
charm under any name. It was not without reason that
the mythical Trebetas, son of Ninus, after wandering
through all lands, pitched on the spot by the Mosel as
the loveliest and richest site that he could find for the
foundation of the first city which arose on European
soil. He might have chosen sites of greater sublimity;
he might have pitched his city among the high
mountains, like Trent or Innsbrück or Aosta. But
sites of this kind, less easily accessible according to
early modes of travelling, would have been less suited

than the actual site of Trier for a city which was to rule the nations. For we must remember that Trier is a city which, even in sober history, did for a while rule the nations, and in local legend it naturally does much more in that way than it does in sober history. The position of Trent, with high Alps on each side of it, is incomparably more majestic than the position of Trier. But, though Trent once incidentally did a good deal towards fixing the destinies of Christendom, yet it never became a seat of rule over anything beyond its immediate district. No Cæsar ever thought of fixing his throne in the Alpine valley. But, among cities whose surroundings are satisfied with the beauty of hills and do not aspire to the awfulness of mountains, it would not be easy to surpass the site of Trier. It is essentially a river city. It is not a hill fort, but a site on the stream with hills on each side. And, as we are told that, in the Imperial days of Trier, the Mosel brought thither all the riches of the earth, we must, even after making allowance for the smaller size of the vessels of old times, believe that its stream did not so often fail its ancient masters as it is apt to fail the modern traveller who wishes to use the river as his way from Trier to Coblenz. In the legend the city of Trebetas became, like the cities which its founder left behind him in the East, a ruling city from the beginning. In sober history we see in the Treveri one of the tribes of Rhenish Gaul, boasting, some thought untruly, of a German descent, whose chief post became a Roman colony in the early days of the Empire, and which, in the later days of the Empire, when Imperial colleagues and rivals divided the lands among them became the seat of a dominion which took in the Roman lands beyond the Alps, Spain, Gaul, and Britain.

Trier holds, north of the Alps, a position which is in some respects analogous to the position of Ravenna south of the Alps. The points both of likeness and of unlikeness between the two cities may be instructively compared. In physical position no two cities can well be more opposite. No two spots can be more unlike than Trier, with its hills, its river, and its bridge, and Ravenna, forsaken by the sea, left in its marshy flat, with its streets, which were once canals like those of Venice, now canals no longer. In their history the two cities have thus much in common, that each was a seat of the Imperial power of Rome in the days of its decline. Each too is remarkable for its rich store of buildings handed on from the days of its greatness, buildings which stamp upon each city an unique character of its own. But, when we more minutely compare either the history or the surviving antiquities of the two cities, when we compare the circumstances under which each city rose to greatness, we shall find on the whole less of likeness than of unlikeness. The difference may be summed up when we say that Trier is the city of Constantine, that Ravenna is the city of Honorius. Trier became a seat of Empire in days when the Teutonic enemy was already threatening, in days when the presence of an Emperor near the frontier was needed to drive back and to avenge Teutonic inroads, but still in days when Teutonic inroads could yet be driven back and could even be avenged. Trier was the seat of Emperors in days when the Roman pilum and broadsword could still win victories which supplied the materials for the bloodiest of all the butcheries that ever marked an Imperial victory. It was in the now grass-grown amphitheatre hewn out of the hill that Constantine made, as men then deemed, the proudest of Roman holidays by casting Frankish kings and thousands of their subjects to the wild beasts. At Ravenna we hear nothing of such shows; it was at Rome, in the Flavian amphitheatre, that the check which Stilicho gave to the Gothic arms at Pollentia was celebrated by that last show of gladiators when Telemachus, as we would fain believe, won the crown of martyrdom in the cause of humanity. In short, the Imperial days of Trier were days when the time of conquest was past, when the Empire had to put forth all its strength to maintain its frontiers, but when it was not yet trembling for its very being. It was a post chosen by great states-

men and soldiers, in obedience to the political and military
needs of their dominions. Ravenna became an Imperial
dwelling-place because an Emperor, more at home in
the poultry-yard than either in camp or council, sought
shelter in its impenetrable fortress for his own sacred
person. Yet, after the causes which made either city
a seat of Empire had passed away, Ravenna went on
being the seat of kings and rulers, and Trier did not.
After Gratian and his murderer Maximus, no Emperor
reigned in Trier, nor did Trier become one of the many
and shifting seats of Frankish kingship. The city which
had once been the head of Gaul, Spain, and Britain
became part of a kingdom whose place of dominion was at
Metz. Ravenna on the other hand, after it had ceased to
be the dwelling-place of Emperors, was still, for not far
short of three hundred years, the seat of Gothic Kings
and Byzantine Exarchs. In every detail then of the
history of the two cities there is unlikeliness; yet the
two form a class by themselves, as the two western seats
of Imperial power after Rome herself ceased to be the
dwelling-place of Emperors. In a strictly historical
view, Milan ranges with them as a third Imperial city;
but the overthrow of Milan by an Emperor of later
times hinders that city from keeping any such living
memorials of her own Imperial days as we see in either
of the other two cities. The single colonnade of St.
Lawrence and two or three tombs and other fragments

in its churches make up all that Milan has to set
against the varied stores of antiquities which still
remain to instruct us both at Ravenna and at Trier.

As far as the existing monuments are concerned, the
unique character of Ravenna comes out in the fact that
all its remains belong to one particular time, and that
a time of which there is hardly anything anywhere
else. Ravenna has nothing of any consequence belonging
either to heathen Roman or to mediæval times; its
monuments belong to the days of Honorius and Placidia,
to the days of the Gothic kingdom, to the very first days
of the restored Imperial rule. To these, except one or
two of the churches of Rome, there is nothing in the
West to answer. The monuments of Trier are spread
over a far wider space of time. They stretch from the
first days of Roman occupation to an advanced stage of
the middle ages. The mighty pile of the Black Gate,
the *Porta Nigra* or *Porta Martis*, a pile to which
Ravenna, and Rome herself, can supply no rival, is a
work which it is hard to believe can belong to any days
but those when the city was the dwelling-place of
Emperors. Yet scholars are not lacking who argue
that it really dates from the early days of the Roman
only, from a date earlier than that which some
other scholars assign to the first foundations of the
colony, from the days of Claudius. The amphitheatre
is said to date from the reign of Trajan. The basilica,

so strangely turned into a Protestant church by the late
King of Prussia, can hardly fail to be the work of
Constantine. But, after all, the building at Trier which
will most reward careful study is the metropolitan
church. At the first glimpse it seems less unique than
the Porta Nigra; its distant outline is massive and
picturesque, but it is an outline with which every one
who has seen many of the great churches of Germany
must be thoroughly familiar. Or, if it has a special
character of its own, it seems to come from the blending
of the four towers of the main buildings with a fifth,
the massive tower of the *Liebfrauenkirche*, which, in
the general view, none would fancy to be one of the
most perfect and graceful specimens of the early German
Gothic of the thirteenth century. It is only gradually
that the unique character of the building dawns on the
inquirer. What at first sight seemed to be a church of
the type of Mainz, Worms, and Speyer, and inferior
to them in lacking the central tower or cupola, turns
out to be something which has no parallel north of
the Alps, nor, we may add, south of them either. It
is a Roman building of the sixth century—none the
less Roman for being built under a Frankish king—
preserving large portions of a yet earlier building of
the fourth. The capitals of its mighty columns peep
out from amid the later work, and fragments of the
pillars lie about in the cloister and before the western

door, as the like fragments do in the Forum of Trajan.
Repaired and enlarged in the eleventh century in
remarkably close imitation of the original design, the
church has gone through a series of additions and
recastings, in order to change it into the likeness of an
ordinary mediæval German church. Had St. Vital at
Ravenna, had St. Sophia itself, stood where the *dom* of
Trier stands, the same misapplied labour would most
likely have been bestowed upon them. But, well pleased
as we should have been to have had such a building as
this kept to us in its original form, there is no denying
that those who enjoy spelling out the changes which a
great building has gone through, comparing the statements of the local chroniclers with the evidence of the
building itself—a process which, like every other
process of discovery, is not without its charm—will
find no more attractive problem of the kind than is
supplied by the venerable minster of Trier.

The student who visits Trier with the days of its
Imperial greatness chiefly in his mind will perhaps not
be inclined to tarry long over the memories of the days
when Trier still was a capital, though the capital only
of a German ecclesiastical electorate. The vast palace of
the Archbishops, degraded into barracks and cut short by
the strange whim of restoring the basilica, stands as a
record of what ecclesiastical potentates could grow into;
but, after all, it is not so much at Trier as at Coblenz

that the memorials of the archiepiscopal Electors are
to be looked for. There they lived as princes; their
duties as bishops were for the most part left to suf-
fragans, bishops *in partibus infidelium*, the name of
one of whom suggests a curious contrast just now.
One suffragan of Trier, the laborious local historian
Von Hontheim, was in the last century, under the
assumed name of Febronius, one of the most vigorous
champions of the rights of national churches against
the encroachments of Rome. All that is now past.
The Ultramontane system of the present day is no
more the same thing with the Roman Catholic system
of the last century than the Roman Catholic system
of the last century was the same thing with the
Church of the middle ages. Gallicanism, Febronianism,
every appeal to national and historical rights against
modern usurpations, is now set down as a heresy almost
worse than Protestantism itself. In the very city
where Von Hontheim asserted the rights of the
German nation, a modern bishop has suffered, or
deems himself to have suffered, in an exactly opposite
cause, a cause which would have been almost un-
intelligible to any one of the prelates whose mighty
work stands opposite to the prison which has become
for awhile the dwelling-place of their successor.

AACHEN REVISITED.

THOROUGHLY to get up any city or district in its historical relations is rather a long business. We believe
that, in order to be thoroughly master of any place, a
fourfold process is needed. The traveller should first
arm himself with a general knowledge of the history
of the place and of all that is to be seen in it. He
will thus be able to examine the objects themselves
in an intelligent way, to understand their history and
meaning, and to go through the process implied in the
Aristotelian phrase of τοῦτο ἐκεῖνο. Then let him go
home and study all his materials afresh by the light of
the local knowledge which he has thus gained. The
difference between reading the history of a place which
we have seen and reading that of one which we have not
seen is simply infinite. When we read of spots, buildings,
natural objects, which we have ourselves looked on and
examined, the story gains a force and depth and meaning which makes all the difference between a living
thing and a dead one. We feel at home in the place
of which we are reading; we feel as if the men of

whom we read were our personal acquaintance. Then
lastly, having done this, it is well to see the place a
second time by the light of the livelier knowledge thus
gained. We are now in a position to correct any
mistakes which we have made in our first visit, and
generally to bring our book-learning and the evidence
of our own eyes to illustrate and strengthen one
another. Every place, every part of every place, should,
whenever it may be done, be visited twice, even if the
two visits happen on the same day with only a few
hours' interval. There is something in the process of
recollection, another form of the τοῦτο ἐκεῖνο process,
which makes the impression far keener than if the
object be looked at only once. Even if a man has only
an hour to give to an object, he will learn more by
giving it in the form of two distinct half-hours. But
this work of revisiting reaches its highest form when
we come the second time charged with all the knowledge gained by a comparison of our earlier memories
with the written history of the place.

Sometimes again, a visit to one place makes it
almost a duty to make a second visit to another place.
Two or more places are often so closely connected that
the history of the one is imperfect without the history
of the other. The connexion may be of various kinds.
The same great names may be common to both; the
events which happened at one may have had a direct

influence on the events which happened at the other;
the two places may actually stand to one another either
in the relation of sisters or in that of child and parent.
Or again the connexion, though not so direct as this,
may be none the less true and instructive. The two
places may hold the same position in the history of
their several countries, or of the times when they were
severally most famous; the comparison may be instructive through the likeness or the unlikeness of the two
physical sites, or through the likeness or unlikeness of
the buildings which have been raised upon them. In
all these ways, whether by likeness or unlikeness, by
direct cause and effect or by mere analogy, one place
illustrates another, and the traveller is constantly led
to form the fruitless wish that he could suddenly spirit
himself away from one spot to another far distant. The
architectural inquirer would be well pleased if he could
place the apses of Köln and Amiens side by side. He
would be still better pleased if he could fly suddenly
from the banks of the Wear to the banks of the Arno,
and see the glories of Northern and Southern Romanesque, Durham and Pisa, in successive hours. And he
would be well pleased again on such an Utopian ramble
if he could stop on the way by the banks of the Rhine,
and compare the metropolitan church of Germany, the
stately and varied forms of the great minster of Mainz,
with the buildings on each side of it which have so

F

much in common with it and yet so much that is unlike.
Here the connexion is one only of analogy and of contrast. But when we stand in St. Mark's, we feel that
the survey is imperfect, because we see the intermediate building only, because we cannot see at the
same glance its parent church at Constantinople and
its daughter church at Périgueux. In all these ways
one spot illustrates another; and as, even in the days
of electric telegraphs, the laws of time and space cannot wholly be got rid of, the best thing is to take
every opportunity of seeing one of two places thus
mutually connected with a mind still full of the
memories of the other.

We have been led into this train of thought by a
comparison of the feelings aroused by three visits, under
three different sets of circumstances, to the city of the
Great Charles. *Aquæ Grani*, Aachen—*Aken*, as our
forefathers called it, with a nearer approach to the true
speech of the country—and its minster will be to many
travellers their first German city and their first German
church. There they may see for the first time on a gigantic scale the tall aisleless apse with windows of boundless height, which so clearly distinguishes the churches
of Germany alike from the square ends of England and
from the surrounding chapels of France. But, setting
aside this one feature, there is nothing about Aachen
which specially connects it with German buildings

rather than with the buildings of any other part of
Christendom. It is rather one of a class belonging to no
particular land, but scattered here and there through all
lands. The round or octagonal church, very commonly
with a choir added to the east and a tower added to the
west—three things which can never be brought into
real harmony with one another, but which, from their very
incongruity, always produce a striking effect—is found
scattered here and there from Jerusalem to Ludlow.
The form is more common in some countries than in
others; but everywhere it is rare enough for each particular example to have a kind of personal interest of its
own. The Temple Church in London and the renowned
St. Gereon at Köln are among the examples which will
occur to every one; but the peculiar effect of Aachen is
best realized on a humbler scale in the churches of
St. John at Liège, and of St. Sepulchre at Northampton.
Of this last we speak as we knew it years ago; we believe
that additions have lately been made to it. In all these
three, without any kind of likeness in any other point,
we find the three elements placed close together which
no art can really fuse into one whole, the western
tower, the central round, and the eastern choir. But the
city with which Aachen, and the church with which the
minster of Aachen, really connect themselves are not to
be looked for on either English or German soil. Aachen
can never be so well understood as with the mind fresh

from the memory of Ravenna; the Imperial minster
better takes its place in the general order of things if
we look at it with a constant reference to its parent
church of St. Vital.

The connexion between Ravenna and Aachen illustrates well nigh all those different forms of relation
which, as we have said, bind one building or city to
another. Among all the cities of earth these two stand
forth as the chosen homes of Teutonic dominion. To the
student of the general history of our race no spots can
speak like the city of Theodoric and the city of Charles.
Each is, as it were, the crowning-place of one of the two
great branches of our race; and we in our island cannot
forget that the elder and the nobler of the two was the
crowning-place of that branch whose kindred to our
selves was the nearer. We honour the Frank; we feel
our common blood stirred by the vision of his greatness;
but in the Goth we have our ten parts, as in one who
spoke that oldest form of the common tongue from which
we have, after all, changed less than Frank or Swabian.
But the Goth ruling over Italy in a Roman city, according to Roman law, and the Frank translating the
seat of the Roman power to a city of his own Northern
land, alike set forth the twofold and mutual conquest,
the way in which the Teuton bore rule over the
Roman, and the way in which, in return, the Roman
led captive his conqueror. The Goth who on Italian

ground remained king only of his own people, and the Frank who on German ground reigned as Cæsar and Augustus, each played his part in the same great work. But they severally mark two stages of it. In the state of things under Theodoric we see the stage when the Roman and the Teutonic elements stood distinct and side by side. In the state of things under Charles we see the stage when the two were fast fusing together into a third thing different from either. But of these several stages, and of the work in which they were stages, Ravenna and Aachen stand out as representatives beyond all other cities of the earth. Nowhere else do we feel so thoroughly in the presence of the Teutonic lords of Rome, lords who were at once conquerors and disciples. In the local Rome the names even of Theodoric and Charles are simply two in the long series of the mighty ones of her history. And in the local Rome neither Theodoric nor Charles ever dwelled. It was their highest glory to be its masters; they visited it as the venerable centre of their dominion; but it was not their home in life or their resting-place in death. For that end they chose Ravenna and Aachen; and, as such, Ravenna and Aachen stand together, apart from all other spots on earth, the cradles of the two mightiest forms that Teutonic dominion ever took.

As regards the buildings of the two cities, the connexion is of the closest possible kind. It is a connexion

of cause and effect, and indeed of something closer
still.   The greatest building of Aachen is a direct
copy of the greatest building of Ravenna, and for more
than one building in Aachen Ravenna actually supplied
the materials.   The round of the minster at Aachen
beyond all doubt reproduces the round of St. Vital;
and columns from Ravenna, though certainly not from
St. Vital, were used to adorn the churches and palaces
which Charles raised, both at Aachen and at Ingelheim.
The letter is well known in which Pope Hadrian gives
leave to the Frankish king and Roman patrician to
remove columns and marbles from the palace of
Ravenna, and there can be no doubt that some at least
of the monoliths which adorn the dome of Aachen,
which the eye now dimly sees through piles of scaffold-
ing, were once among the enrichments of the fallen
house of the great Goth.   The man whom at Aachen
we revere as a founder, we are tempted at Ravenna to
curse as a destroyer; but the spoliation of Theodoric's
palace has at least brought about what we might almost
call a material identity between the two most famous
spots in the transitional period of European history.

As regards the two men themselves, the kings who
each for a while raised his city to the second—or at
least the third—place on earth, their fate has in it a
strange mixture of likeness and of unlikeness. The work
of Theodoric died with him. No successor was found

worthy to fill his place, and the very name of his kingdom and dynasty soon perished from among men. The power founded by Charles lived on in name within the memory of men now living; but it was but in name that it lived on, and the noblest part of his work, the welding together of an united Germany, has been done over again, by other means, before our eyes. As for the mortal remains of the men themselves, they have gone the way of the mortal remains of most of the mightiest men of the world's history. As we seek in vain for the dust of Harold at Waltham or the dust of William at Caen, so we seek in vain for the dust of Theodoric in the resting-place reared on high beneath his own mighty monolith; and we seek no less in vain for the dust of Charles beneath the huge slab which bears his name within his own minster. Bigotry cast forth the bones of the barbarian and of the heretic; reverence translated the bones of the hero, the founder, the reputed saint, that his fragments might be exposed to the same degrading veneration as any stray relic to which fancy or legend might have attached a memorable name. In the view of what we venture to think a higher feeling of reverence, each is alike removed from his own place, each is alike cast forth from the sepulchre which he had himself wrought for his own resting-place.

As regards the present state of the two cities, no contrast can well be greater. At Ravenna we have

no temptation to think of aught but the past, of aught
but those few wondrous ages of the past of which Ravenna
has, as it were, the sole possession. The monuments of
those times meet us at every step; tombs and churches,
towers and palaces, such as no other spot on earth can
show, are strewed, as by a lavish hand, from one end of
the city to the other; there is hardly enough either
of modern life or of memorials of later times to disturb us
in their contemplation. From Aachen, as from Ravenna,
her dominion has passed away; she is no longer

> Urbs Aquensis, urbs regalis,
> Regni sedes principalis,
> Summa regum curia;

but in the general aspect of the city the present has
swept away the past. It is only while we keep within
the shadow of his minster, or look on the one surviving
fragment of domestic building which speaks of his age
or of the age of his early successors, that we really feel
that we are in the city of the Great Charles. Go where
we will, there is nothing to set against that one city
which seems preserved as a fossil fragment of a world
which has passed away, of a world which in some sort
had its own being within its walls. The true life of
Ravenna has been kept safe and sound by its abiding
death; at Aachen, as in a crowd of other places, the
life of the past is well-nigh choked by the continued or
revived life of the present.

GELNHAUSEN.

To the true student of universal history Rome is everywhere. The great result to which all Roman history led was the destruction of the exclusive pre-eminence of the Roman city, the extension of her citizen-ship to the whole civilized world, the state of things when the chief of the Roman commonwealth was as much at home at Milan or at Ravenna, at York or at Antioch, as if he had still stayed on the Seven Hills. And the strange revolution which transferred the name, if not the power, of Rome to the rulers of lands of which the elder Cæsars had never heard, has, as it were, carried Rome with it wherever the successor of Augustus marked his house or his tomb with the eagle of Caius Marius. Drusus and Varus strove in vain to carry Rome over the wide lands between the Rhine and the Elbe; but what was beyond the power of the Roman invaders of Germany was done in another sort by the German lords of Rome. As long as the connexion between Italy and the Empire remained more than a name, we may fairly say that, wherever Cæsar dwelled,

Rome went with him. Sometimes she contributed her
very stones, as when the marbles of Rome as well as of
Ravenna were carried off for the adornment of Ingelheim and Aachen. And elsewhere too, in the chosen
seats of early German royalty, we are ever lighting on
some touch, some architectural form, some exotic freak
of taste, which tells us that we are looking on the works,
not only of a German King, but of a Roman Emperor.
We enter the minster of Speyer, we pass along the vast
arcades of its nave, and we see in its huge piers and
round arches the impress of one, and that the most
characteristic, form of Roman workmanship. They
suggest such memories of Roman art as might have
lived on from the relics which the Roman himself had
left on German soil. The square piers and unadorned
arches of a great German church breathe rather of the
aqueduct and the amphitheatre than of the pillared
hall of the basilica. But turn aside from the main
body of the building, and we find ourselves among
forms which suggest the presence of craftsmen brought
thither not by a Roman lord of Germany, but by a
German lord of Rome. There is the famous *Afra
Capella*, a name which certain old associations make it
hard to utter without a smile, but which, as the hardly-
won resting-place of Henry the Fourth, is the spot, of
all spots within that gigantic building, which calls up
the longest and deepest train of thought. And on the

building itself the fact is legibly written that it was not a mere Frankish King, but a Roman Cæsar who raised it. No contrast can be greater than that which strikes us between the huge masses of wall which act as pillars in the nave and the delicate monolith columns, with their graceful Ionic capitals, carved out, some of them, into forms of more varied foliage than the elder Ionic deemed lawful, which stand free, row by row, in front of the walls of the Imperial chapel. We feel at once that these are the work of hands brought from a Southern land; that they rose at the bidding of a ruler who bore sway on both sides of the Alps, of a King who did penance at Canosa, of a Cæsar who wore his crown in Rome.

But let us go beyond the further bounds of the dominion of the elder Roman. Let us pass the stream, and the bulwark beyond the stream, which parted the free Germany over which the Roman city never ruled from the conquered Germany which Rome counted as part of its Gaulish province. The Rhine is fed by the Main, the Main is fed by the Kinzig, and we pass along by the meadows through which it flows, as the herons stalk unheeding by its banks, till we reach an island in the stream, lying near the foot of a bold height. The slopes are covered by the buildings of a small town, which a stately group of towers, both ecclesiastical and military, proclaims to have held in former times an importance which has now passed away from it. That is the free Imperial city of Gelnhausen, and in the island at its foot are the remains of the Imperial palace, a spot famous alike in history and in legend. There was the favourite dwelling-place of the Cæsars of Hohenstaufen, the house which rose at the bidding of the first Frederick, and for which his sterner son, Henry the conqueror of Sicily, professed a special love. Moved by that special love ("singulari ipsius loci amore inducti"), he confirmed the rights of its citizens, and ages after, in 1454, they were again confirmed by the last Frederick as they had been granted by the first. Within those now ruined walls were held some of the most important assemblies in the history of the German kingdom. There it was that its founder Frederick gathered that great meeting of his realm in which Henry the Lion was put under the ban of the Empire, and was presently driven to seek shelter at the court of his namesake and father-in-law in England. The great Saxon duchy was divided, and the archbishoprick of Köln, by the grant of a large share of the spoil, was raised to its high place among the principalities of the Empire. Fifteen years later, in 1195, after Frederick had been cut off on his second march for the deliverance of the holy places, Henry the Sixth held there another great assembly, in which a crowd of princes and others took the cross for another crusade.

In short, during the days of its founder and the days which immediately followed his, the palace in the island of the Kinzig, sheltered by its hill and surrounded by its meadows, was a special seat of the royal power of Germany and the Imperial power of Rome. The spot is one of such attraction in itself that it hardly needs the enrichment of legend. Yet a tale did not fail to arise how Gelnhausen derived its name and its being from the fair Gela; men sang how she turned aside from her royal lover, lest she should stand in the way of the great career of government and warfare to which he was called.

The remains of the palace are still considerable, though a good deal has been lost during the last forty years. A set of views of that date shows the chapel over the gateway, one of the most elegant portions of the building, perfect and roofed in; now it is a roof-less and broken-down ruin. But the gateway itself remains; the whole circuit of the outer walls is nearly perfect, and large portions of the most exquisite detail of which the Romanesque style is capable remain within. The building, lying low, without the town walls, and with no tower or other part of commanding height, does not enter at all into the general view of Gelnhausen. Its position and its whole air clearly mark the difference between a palace in whose neighbourhood a town has arisen—or at least has grown

through its neighbourhood into increased importance—
and a castle raised to overawe a town which already
existed. The gateway towers of the town itself still
form a striking feature in the general view, but the
home of Cæsar lies hidden in its island. It has to be
sought for by threading the winding paths of the little
village or suburb which has risen within its precinct,
and its whole air is that of a building where peaceful
habitation is the primary object, and defence something
wholly secondary. No contrast can be greater than
that between the royal house in the island of the Kinzig
and a robber castle on a peak by the Rhine. The
palace was not built for purposes of plunder, not even
for purposes of warfare. Its founder, at Gelnhausen at
least, had no mind to do harm to any man save by
sentence of law pronounced within its courts; he had
simply to put his house into such a degree of defence as
was needful in an age when men might be found both
willing and able to do harm even to a Roman Emperor.
And one thing at least is plain; it is written on the
walls of Gelnhausen, in characters which cannot be
mistaken, that it was a Roman Emperor who raised
them. They are built of massive stones, so thoroughly
Roman in their masonry that it needs something of an
effort to believe that it was in the twelfth century that
they were hewn, and not a thousand years sooner. The
gateway, though the chapel over it is broken down,

still remains; and, while the pillars which bear up its
vault have a more massive and Teutonic air, its inner
face is adorned with the same graceful monoliths as
Henry's chapel at Speyer, finished too with capitals one
of which distinctly carries us back to St. Michael at
Pavia and to St. Ambrose at Milan. At each corner of
the capital the Imperial bird bows his head and folds
his wings, so that he himself makes the Ionic volute
without the help of any strictly architectural forms.
A row of open arches on coupled columns, carved
and enriched with the most delicate art of the time,
shows us the cloisters of Arles and Zürich, both alike
cities of Frederick's Empire, wrought into the lighter
and more graceful forms which befitted the courtyard
of an Imperial palace. A yet more lavish display of
carving and surface ornament marks the fireplace of
the great hall, beside which that of our own Conings-
burgh seems a small matter. The whole shows how high
a degree, not only of richness, but even of elegance,
could be gained while the Romanesque form of arch and
the Romanesque form of ornament were still in use.
The graceful and airy palace of Frederick Barbarossa
seems removed by far more than a hundred years from
the stern and gloomy fortress of our own Conqueror.

But the palace is not all that Gelnhausen has to
show. The steep streets of the little town climb up to
one of the noblest churches of its own order in Germany,

a church which in the general view dwarfs not only
the island palace but the encircling towers of the town
wall, and which in variety and, to English eyes, strange-
ness of outline, is surpassed by few churches anywhere.
A parish church with four towers would be unique in
England; it would hardly have arisen in Germany
except in a place which enjoyed an unusual measure of
Imperial favour. And even here one would rather
have expected to find Imperial favour taking the form
of some great foundation, monastic or secular. Gelnhausen church is one of the most picturesque of
buildings. An earlier Romanesque church has been
transformed into the present stately pile of the thirteenth century. The western tower, of the earlier date,
is assigned by tradition to Charles the Great. Such
a tradition proves hardly more than what the tower
itself proves, namely, that Gelnhausen existed, though
perhaps as a mere village with its church, before it
became an object of the special love of the Swabian
Kings. There is a contrast indeed between the graceful forms of the palace and the massive and unadorned
Romanesque of the church. Yet the latter can hardly
be earlier than the later days of the eleventh century,
and it may well belong to the earlier days of the
twelfth. It should be noticed that it opens to the
church, not by an arch, but by a doorway. In this it
reminds us somewhat of St. Woollos at Newport, though

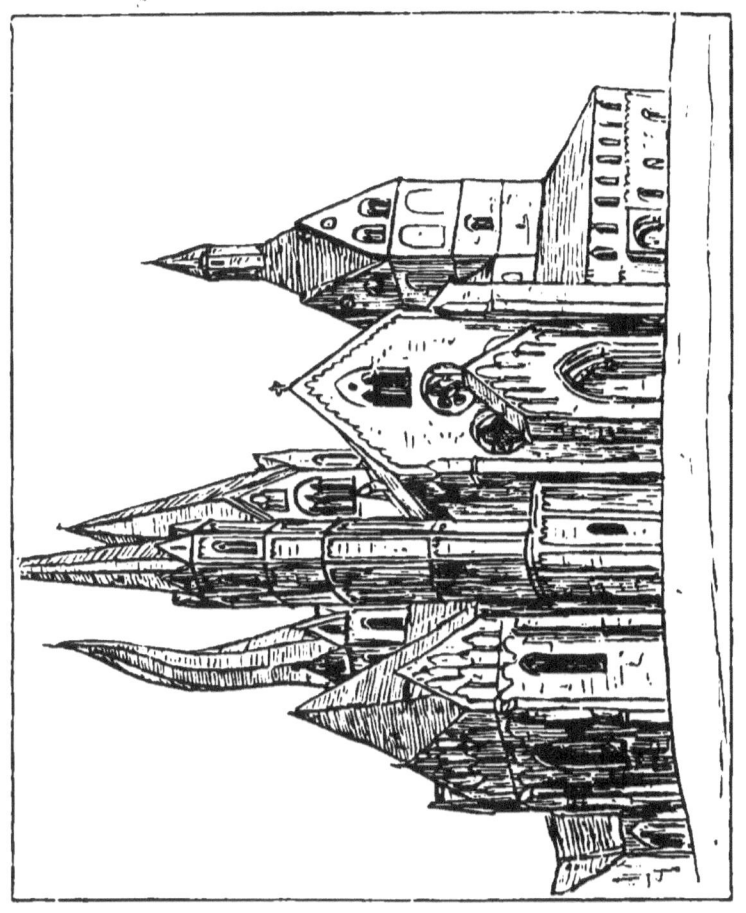

GELNHAUSEN CHURCH, N.E.

To face page 80.

it hardly rivals that perhaps unique example in Britain of the practice so common in Italy and southern Gaul, of using up classical columns a second time. The cruciform shape of the church gives the opportunity, an opportunity not always made the most of, for a central octagon, and two little apsidal chapels east of the transepts have been more ingeniously seized on and carried up into tall octagonal eastern towers. Nowhere does the German love of gables, spires, conical finishes of every kind, come out more strongly. All the towers, square and octagonal, have each of their faces gabled, and the eastern triad are carried up into lofty spires of wood, one of which has been for forty years as grievously twisted as those of Lübeck or Chesterfield. The chief apse too has all its faces gabled, and its roof is carried up high like a chapter-house. So many points and angles brought together in this way produce a whole unsurpassed for variety and picturesque effect. The interior also, especially the treatment of the choir and octagon, is as well worth studying as the general outline. But the nave is bare; the pillars are square, massive, with a single attached shaft, and a vast space crying for pictures.

But not the least attractive feature of Gelnhausen is that which it shares with most of those churches which have had what, for antiquarian purposes, is the good luck of falling into Lutheran hands. For it is in a Lutheran, not in a Roman or an Anglican, building that we learn what a mediæval church really looked like. A Lutheran church often looks squalid and uncared for; it is often choked up by pews and galleries; but it has neither been sacked by iconoclasts nor disfigured with trumpery of the days of Lewis the Great. At Gelnhausen the altars keep their splendid triptychs, so incomparably grander than the tinsel frippery of most Roman Catholic altars; and there still abides —at the expense, to be sure, of leaving the choir seemingly useless—one of the stateliest of roodlofts, still crowned by the crucifix. The roodloft is of stone, and projects westward like an apse, with pillars and vaulting and rich carving, representing in stone the subject which so often occupies an analogous place in painting, the awful scene of the Last Judgement. Altogether the church of Gelnhausen is a worthy companion to the palace. Spots like this, spots which do not, like the greater cities of history, leave their mark for ever on the world, are none the less worth studying, none the less fertile in suggesting instructive lines of thought. The greatness of Gelnhausen belongs to a single age, to a single family; but for that very reason it brings us more fully face to face with that age and that family. And it is something to see the destroyer of Milan, the defeated of Legnano,

the legislator of Constanz, the twice pilgrim of Jerusalem, far away in his Northern home, and to see that
even there everything still brings home to our minds
the truth that the German King was also "Cæsar
noster" and "mundi dominus."

CENTRAL ITALY.

LUCCA.

THE visitor to Ravenna will not do amiss if he carries himself as speedily as possible to the longest-lived among the Tuscan commonwealths. The city which formed the favourite winter-quarters of the first Cæsar, the city which, if enslaved, was also glorified by the genius of Castruccio Castracani, the city which preserved its republican independence for two centuries and a half after Florence and Siena had fallen, is a city rich in attractions both of nature and art. Lucca moreover has points both of likeness and unlikeness to the unique wonders of Ravenna which make it well to study the two cities in as close a connexion as possible. It is impossible not to feel an interest in the single inland Italian city—San Marino can hardly count as a city —which kept its independence alongside of Venice and Genoa, and which painted the word "Libertas" on its banner till the general overthrow of all things at the hands of revolutionary France. A cavil indeed may be raised as to the nature of such freedom and independence as could be kept on under an oligarchic rule; we may be asked to look how carefully, on the later monuments of Lucca, the word "Senatus" is made to appear alone, without the dangerous addition of "Populusque." But in this Lucca did but share the fate of her greater sisters; and the rule of a native oligarchy, with all its faults, may perhaps be deemed less degrading than the more modern destiny of the duchy, tossed to and fro between Spanish Infantas and Yorkshire grooms. The history of Lucca reminds one on a smaller scale of that of Sweden and Holland. Naturally one of the lesser states of Italy, she suddenly rose, for a few years in the early part of the fourteenth century, to a greatness which was beyond her real power. Lucca under Castruccio, like Sweden under Gustavus, held a position too brilliant to last. For a moment Lucca, under her illustrious tyrant, was the leading state of Italy, the more than equal of Florence and Milan. When the last Imperial Lewis came into Italy to win the crown which had been so worthily worn by the second, the lord of Lucca was the righthand man of the Bavarian Cæsar. Perhaps when he stooped to become a Duke, his fall prefigured that of his city. At all events Lucca paid for her momentary greatness in half a century of tossing to and fro between one master and another—now subject to Pisa, now to Florence, now receiving a somewhat illusory freedom at the hands of Charles the Fourth. From the fourteenth century onwards, the name of the city appears but seldom in Italian history, and never as holding a place in the first rank. Still, if the earlier history of Lucca is less splendid than that of Milan, if she has been less emphatically the home of popular freedom than Florence, the city may boast that in the days of tyranny she obeyed the greatest of Italian tyrants; she may boast that in the days of oligarchy its masters at least knew how to preserve the outward indepen- dence of the commonwealth down to the common havoc which swept away alike princes, oligarchies, and democracies, if they were found guilty of the common sin of antiquity.

The position and the architecture of the city are worthy of its history. Ravenna, in her marshy flat, can boast of no such girdle around her as the encircling Apen- nines which keep watch over Lucca. The traveller who walks the bulwarks looks out on a glorious view on either hand, the mountains without and the soaring towers of the city within. And the space of a night at the right season of the year may bring home to him the process by which

Jupiter hibernas cana nive conspuit Alpes.

The peaks and ridges which were dark at sunset may have put on the garb of winter before the morning light. Within, the walls compass a crowd of antiquities, mainly, as at Ravenna, of an ecclesiastical kind. Lucca is not wholly void either of Roman or of municipal remains, but both are of quite secondary importance. The amphitheatre is there; but it has to be looked for, and it has undergone the strange doom of being cut up into a circus of new houses. The old palace of the commonwealth was forsaken as unworthy of its use, and the home of the municipal government was transferred to the site of the castle reared by Castruccio. The fortress of the lord and the hall of the republic have alike given way to the dwelling-place of the later rulers of Lucca, and commonwealth and tyranny alike have left but scant architectural representatives. The chief attraction of the city is derived from the possession of a crowd of churches, whose interest is greatly increased if they are studied in their direct bearing on the earlier buildings of Ravenna.

The churches of Lucca are distinctly basilican. But they are basilican in a different sense from the churches of Ravenna. At Ravenna we have the thing itself, the unaltered primitive basilica, still Roman and not yet Romanesque. In the Lucchese churches a type is followed which is essentially the same as that of Ravenna; but, if their received date is accepted, it is followed after an interval of some ages, whether through uninterrupted tradition or through a conscious falling back on earlier forms. Some at least of the Lucchese churches belong to a period ranging from the latter half of the eleventh century to the former half of the thirteenth. We would not take upon ourselves to deny that some parts, at all events of the internal arcades, may be far earlier. But, in any case, the Lucchese buildings display, whether by retention or by falling back, a remarkable clinging to highly classical forms. They are a marked contrast to the distinctive Romanesque of Northern Italy, the style of Pavia and Milan, a style so much more nearly akin to the Romanesque of Northern Europe. In the great arcades of the interior the compound pier is absolutely unknown, and animal forms in the capitals are sparingly employed. Indeed in some of the cases where they are found, the appearance of the naked human form shows them to be of pagan date. The general effect of the arcades is as classical as anything at Ravenna. The columns are in many cases ancient columns used up again, and the vast majority of the capitals are either actually classical, or carved in close imitation of classical forms. In a few cases the columnar pier is replaced by a form almost as unlike the vast piers of the Northern Romanesque as the column itself. This is a square pier of proportions not very different from those of the columns, and which has nearly the same effect in a general view of the arcades. In one or two cases this pier is used throughout the church. In some others it is used only in a single arch, the first or second from the east end. This last peculiarity, there can be little doubt, is not without a reason. The flat form was preferred in this position, as giving a better backing for stalls; as in so many churches at Rome, it marks the beginning of the choir.

The churches of Lucca thus differ but little in the general effect of their internal arcades from the far earlier churches of Ravenna. The later group cleaves almost as closely to classical forms as the earlier. But then at Ravenna none but classical forms were possible, unless the architects employed by Placidia and Theodoric had invented something absolutely new out of their own heads. At Lucca, the use of the same forms betokens either a remarkable ignorance or a conscious contempt of other forms which had come into use in the meanwhile. Either the forms which came into use further north never made their way into Tuscany, or else the Tuscan architects deliberately passed them by and chose to follow the earlier models. This last theory seems the more probable, as the use of the campanile was adopted. But with regard to the main arcades of the interior, it was evidently thought good to follow the type of the basilicas of earlier days.

In so doing however features were introduced which at once set aside the Lucchese basilicas as forming a class by themselves, distinct from those of Ravenna.

In the arcades themselves there is a marked difference. The great invention of Spálato, but half adopted at Ravenna, has made its way into universal use at Lucca; the intermediate or secondary capital of Ravenna is cast aside, and the arches spring immediately from the abaci of the columns. These abaci too have a peculiar feeling of hardness and squareness which it is hard to describe in words, and which forcibly brings home to us the alleged origin of the abacus in a tile placed above the capital. The proportions of the arches also differ. The Lucchese builder had learned better to trust the constructive power of his own style. He trusted his columns to stand further apart, and to support arches of wider span, the beginning, it must be confessed, of the broad sprawling arches of the later Italian style. The triforium, whether in the ruder form of Modena or in the more developed shape of Pisa, is as unknown at Lucca as it is at Ravenna; but the wonderful application of the subsidiary arts which is so glorious at Ravenna finds no parallel at Lucca. No procession of triumphant virgins leads the eye along the full length of any Lucchese basilica. The alternation of dark and light stone—brick is not used in the genuine style of Lucca—is the only substitute to relieve the bare space above the arcades, and a mere string-course—a slight approach to Northern models—alone represents the rich cornice of the basilica of Theodoric.

On the other hand, there are some not unimportant points in which Lucca has decidedly advanced on Ravenna. The Ravennese buildings, all glorious within, are absolutely without any pretence to artistic exteriors ; the Lucchese architects had found out that the outside of a church might be made rich and graceful as well as its inside. They devised ornamental and most characteristic forms for the two most necessary features of an exterior, the windows and doorways, features which at Ravenna were pretty well left to shift for themselves. They also made free application of arcades, both blank and detached, as decorative features, and thus produced some of the most gorgeous western fronts, and some of the really finest apsidal east ends, which the Romanesque style has ever developed. The campanile too was introduced, not in the round form of Ravenna, but in a quadrangular shape—we say quadrangular advisedly, as several of the Lucchese towers are not square but oblong —and enriched with special lavishness in the way of arcades and windows. It is seldom that we find a single city containing so many churches as Lucca does, varying greatly in scale and in degree of ornament, but all conceived on one common and distinctive type. Setting aside some of the large unsightly Friars' churches of later times—one of which however was the burying-place of Castruccio—and setting aside also the changes which we shall presently have to mention in one or two of the principal churches, the Lucchese buildings belong essentially to a single type and to a single period, even though we should hold that period to have been spread over several ages.

But as the period of Lucchese architecture is spread over two, perhaps three centuries, it is not wonderful that, with all the close general resemblance of the Lucchese churches, more than one type may be recognized among them. The *duomo*, the cathedral church, raised in the last century to metropolitan rank, is an instructive lesson in the differences between the earliest and latest stages of the local style. It is perhaps hardly straining a point to say that this church has a certain indirect connexion with English history. It was begun in 1063 by Bishop Anselm, who, three years later, as Pope Alexander the Second, blessed the enterprise of the Norman invader of England. The great apse is clearly the oldest part of the church, and it is doubtless a remnant, the only remaining remnant, of the church begun by Anselm. Nothing can show more clearly how much faster architecture had advanced in Tuscany than in England or even in Normandy. The style is a not very rich, but a very highly finished, Romanesque, such as in any Northern country would belong to the twelfth century, and not to its earliest years. The design is thoroughly Italian, and has very little in common with Lessay or Peterborough. A range of

tall columnar arcades, of which the alternate members
are pierced for windows, supports an open gallery after
the Italian and German fashion. This apse is a grand
and stately work, and it supplies a striking contrast
to the minute, elaborate, and even fantastic, ornament
of the west front. This last, as the dated inscriptions
bear witness, was built during the first forty years of
the thirteenth century, and it shows what the Italian
Romanesque could grow into without any foreign inter-
mixture. In the lowest stage three magnificent arches
form a vast portico, within which are the actual
doorways ; above are three ranges of open galleries,
covered, in their capitals, shafts, and cornices, with all
the devices of an exuberant fancy. This type of front,
with the omission of the portico, is the form which is
followed in a large class of west fronts in Lucca, and
it appears again in a form of yet higher dignity,
in the glory of all Italian architecture, the metropolitan church of Pisa. It is distinguished from
such fronts as that of St. Zeno by the absence of any
prominent window. At Zeno the great wheel is a noble
feature, but its presence forbids the arcades to take any
form but that of blank panelling. On the other hand
the wheel has a grand effect within as well as without,
while in the Lucchese type, as we feel even at Pisa, the
inside of the west end is wholly sacrificed to the outside.
The Lucchese type again supplies the temptation of

ST. MICHAEL, LUCCA, S.W.

To face page 97.

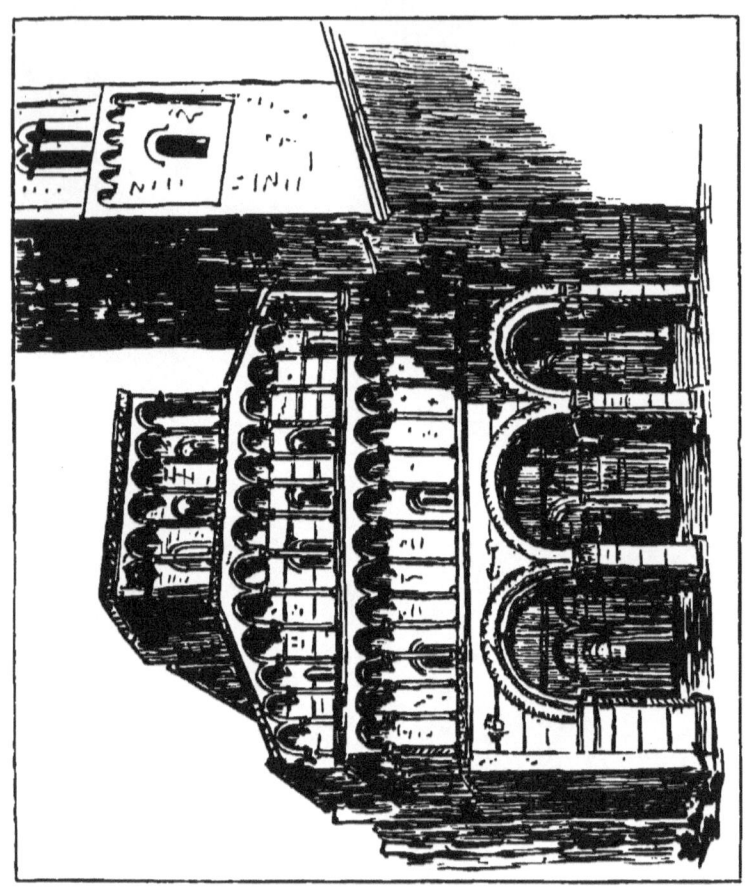

WEST FRONT OF THE DUOMO, LUCCA.

To face page 97.

turning the west front into a sham, by carrying it up as a mere screen covered with arcades to a height far greater than that of the building. The front of Pisa, like that of St. Zeno, is a real thing no less than the fronts of York and Abbeville; but the front of St. Michael at Lucca, which, looked at from the due west, is the most magnificent thing in the city, is a worse sham than anything at Brunswick or Strassburg, at Wells or Lincoln. Whether the front of the cathedral itself was not at one time equally a make-believe we do not feel quite certain. At present it does not rise above the height of the building; but it looks very much as if this was simply because everything between the apse and the west front has been rebuilt at a greater height than the original design. This later work is in the Italian Gothic, making a stately building in its way, though of course unsatisfactory when compared either with Italian Romanesque or with Northern Gothic. The great beauty of the cathedral front, which is lacking at St. Michael's, is undoubtedly the portico. The soaring arches of Peterborough are of course unique; but this front at Lucca has really far more in common with them than the doorways of Rheims and Amiens, with which they have sometimes been strangely compared.

But there are other west fronts in Lucca which do not follow this type. The second church in the city,

H

the great abbey of St. Frediano or Frigidian, is remarkable for having been turned round, like St. Agnes at
Rome and the metropolitan church at Besançon. Its
front is where its apse was once. The general design of
that front is bare and awkward, but its central compart-
ment deserves notice. There are neither arcades nor
wheel window. Over a small blank colonnade—not an
arcade—is a single small window, and above that a
magnificent mosaic picture, reminding one of those
at St. Mark's, to which the whole design of the front
is evidently sacrificed. A less striking, but far more
satisfactory, front is to be found at St. Christopher's.
A tall, bold, columnar arcade below, of which the central
arch forms a magnificent western doorway, and a wheel
window above, are its chief features. The details show
that its date must be far advanced in the thirteenth
century; they remind us in a strange way of some
of those English buildings, Chichester for instance and
several churches in Northamptonshire, where the
mouldings of that age are used in combination with
the round arch of an earlier day. But the whole conception of this front is thoroughly that of the Italian
Romanesque, and it shows, like Trent, though in a
different way from Trent, of what grace and delicacy
that style is capable.

Other fronts of various types will be found scattered
among the small churches of the city; but almost all

ST. FREDIANO, LUCCA.

To face page 98.

agree in their doorways, that of St. Christopher being in no way typical. A Lucchese doorway has a character of its own. It is very flat; it but seldom shows any projecting columns or mouldings; the lions of Trent and Verona, of Modena and Parma, were not, it would seem, to the taste of Lucca. A flat pilaster on each side supports a sculptured stone, over which is again an open tympanum. The narrow Lucchese window, often with a kind of indescribable twist in the head, is no less characteristic.

We have spoken of the *duomo*, of St. Frediano, and of St. Michael. The latter stands in the square which was of old the centre of the political life of Lucca, the square where the city received its last grant of freedom from the Bohemian Emperor. The building, as a whole, is worthy of its site. Like St. Frediano, it has a grand campanile of the oblong local type, and it has also a noble apse of the same type as that of the *duomo*. The campaniles of Lucca, it may be remarked, do not stand quite apart, but are worked into the general outline of the churches. Another church to be noticed— though all the churches of Lucca deserve notice in their several degrees—is that of St. John, near the *duomo*, where a basilica and a baptistery seem to have been rolled into one. The baptistery here is square; yet it reminds one even more forcibly than other baptisteries of the kitchens of Fontevrault and Glastonbury.

Such is a hurried sketch of the contributions of one Italian city to the history of Romanesque architecture. Lucca is remarkable for the prodigious number of objects, all of more or less importance, which it presents, without possessing any one building absolutely of the first rank. And it shows the wealth of Italian architecture that a city so attractive both for its history and for its existing remains seems almost as nothing bes'de a not distant neighbour. For the crowning work of Italian art, for the building which claims in the South the same place which belongs to our own Durham in the North, we have still to go on to Pisa.

PISA.

THE changes in the coast-line which, on one side of the Italian peninsula, in one sense destroyed, in another sense called into being, the renowned city of Ravenna, have on the other side dealt in nearly the same way with the no less renowned city of Pisa. It is but a glimpse of the Hadriatic which is to be had from the tower of St. Apollinaris in Classe, and it is a fainter glimpse still of the Tyrrhenian sea which rewards the traveller who climbs the more famous tower of Pisa. It is hard, as we look on that slight streak in the distance, to call up the days, days spreading over a long series of ages, in which the city in which we stand was one of the great havens of Italy, nay, whenever political circumstances allowed, one of the great seafaring powers of the earth. Our first glimpses of the old Etruscan city set her before us as

> The proud mart of Pisæ,
> Queen of the western waves,
> Where ride Massilia's triremes,
> Heavy with fair-haired slaves.

And when the power of the local Rome had passed

away, when her Empire had split up again into countless
principalities and commonwealths, Pisa again appears,
in the new birth of Italy, as one of those great maritime
cities which disputed the dominion of the Mediterranean
alike with the Saracen rovers of Spain and Africa
and with the Cæsars who still held the straits of the
Bosporos and the Hellespont. It is hard to believe
that the thoroughly inland city on which we look down
was once the rival of Venice and Genoa, alike in naval
warfare and in naval traffic. But Pisa, unlike Venice
and Genoa, depended on a river as the immediate highway for her fleets, and the river proved a less trustworthy stay of naval power than either the open sea or
the lagoon. The change in the coast doomed Ravenna
to final insignificance; but, before that day came, it
gave her first a moment of unrivalled greatness. To
Pisa it caused a gradual fall from the height of
power and glory to the most bitter form of bondage.
The rival of Venice and Genoa became the subject
city of inland Florence. But there is a cycle in human
things. New modes of communication are opened by
the discoveries of modern skill; and, as new cities rise,
old ones sometimes rise again. Pisa, shorn for ages of her
traffic by sea, looks forward, under the developement of
the Italian railway system, to become one of the great
centres of communication by land. She looks to reap
at last the reward of her ten years' struggle; she

trusts that this new tide in the affairs of men may again raise her above the city which was once her local tyrant, and to which she has had so long to look up, first as her provincial and then as her national capital.

The great architectural works which now form the chief glory of Pisa are closely connected with the early history and the early triumphs of the commonwealth. The great metropolitan church, the noblest pile reared by the native art of Italy, is emphatically a trophy of the warfare to which Pisa owed her ancient glory. The foundations of the mighty *duomo* were laid out of treasures won in naval warfare with the Saracen. To take in the position of Pisa in the eleventh and twelfth centuries, the time when the city on the Arno stood forth as a great European power, we must bear in mind how completely the sea had been up to that time the dominion of the two powers whose existence in European history men are apt to forget. The Western Empire and the kingdoms into which it split up were essentially land powers. They were like France under the elder Buonaparte, or like the new German Empire at this moment. Their rulers were lords of the mainland, but they were not lords of the sea, and therefore they were not lords of the islands. The dominion of the Mediterranean was disputed between the Eastern Emperors and the various Saracenic powers which grew out of the division of the Caliphate. The great islands of Sicily and Crete obeyed alternately a Byzantine and a Mahometan master : they paid no homage to Rome, Pavia, or Aachen. It was the maritime commonwealths of Italy which first won for Western Christendom any share in the dominion of the great inland sea. Such at least was the work of Genoa and Pisa ; Venice, the outpost of the Eastern Rome, can as yet hardly be looked on as part of Western Christendom. And, of the three, we can hardly doubt as to giving to Pisa the highest place as a worker for the general interests of Europe. Pisa was in the eleventh century what Venice became long after, the bulwark of Christendom against the Moslem. No power took a more active share in the real crusades against the infidel ; and Pisa, unlike Venice, was free from any share in that mock crusade which overthrew the Roman Empire of the East, and paved the way for the coming of the Ottoman into Europe. But Pisa, like the Christians of the far East and of the far West, was already a crusading power before crusades were preached to Western Christendom at large. The maritime commonwealth did what Emperors and Kings had failed to do, and won back the great island of Sardinia from the Saracen. Within that her insular realm Pisa had Judges and even Kings to her vassals, and, when her episcopal church was raised to metropolitan rank, the land which she had won back for Christendom was fittingly made part of the new ecclesiastical province. With the Saracens of Spain, of Africa, and of Sicily the warfare of the republic was never-ceasing, and it was a warfare in which her citizens had as often to defend their own homes as to invade those of the misbelievers. The alternations of the struggle are well marked in the meagre entries of the national chronicle :—

Anno 1005. "Fuit capta Pisa a Saracenis."

Anno 1006. "Pisani devicerunt Saracenos ad Regium die Sancti Sixti."

Anno 1012. "Stolus Saracenorum de Hispania venit Pisas et destruxit eas."

Later on, in 1035, 1050, and 1075 we read how Pisan fleets took Bona and what the chronicler is pleased to call Carthage, how they drove back a Saracen prince who had again established himself in Sardinia, and how, after each victory, the loyal commonwealth— Ghibeline before Guelf and Ghibeline were heard of— dutifully sent the crown of the vanquished prince to the Emperor. At last, in 1063, we come to the entry which most concerns us, an entry which may still be read on the front of the pile whose foundation it records :—

Anno 1063. "Pisani fuerunt Panormum et fractis catenis portus civitatem ipsam ceperunt, ibique sex naves ditissimas ceperunt, Saracenis plurimis interfectis, et combusserunt naves quinque ; unam Pisas duxerunt mirabili thesauro plenam, de quo thesauro eodem anno majorem Pisanam ecclesiam incœperunt."

These entries set before us the loftier character of

the Pisan commonwealth, at once maritime, crusading, and imperialist; but they are mixed up with other entries pointing to the causes which in the end brought the commonwealth to its fall. Along with the records of the great strife with the Infidel we light on the records of local warfare by land with Lucca and by sea with Genoa. The never-ending rivalry with Genoa led in the thirteenth century to the two sea-fights of Meloria, the first where the Ghibeline commonwealth made prey of the prelates bound for the Papal Council, the other that crushing overthrow in which history, as commonly read, sees the main cause of the downfall of the commonwealth. But perhaps a single defeat, however overwhelming for the moment, would not have crushed Pisa for ever, had not physical causes already determined that maritime rule was to pass away from the city on the Arno. Be this as it may, the history of Pisa, when forced to struggle on as a purely inland power, is a sad contrast to the earlier days of her naval greatness. One fearful tale, the tale of the most fearful doom which ever fell on convicted traitor, has made the name of Pisa and her Tower of Hunger familiar to every ear. But the course of later Pisan history is on the whole a dull one. Pisa, like Venice, had been transferred from the scene of her ancient glory to a scene on which little glory was to be won by her. But, unlike Venice, it was not wholly by her own act. At one moment the stern tyrant of Lucca, at another the oppressed bond-slave of Florence, engulfed at last in the common humiliation of Medicean dominion, chosen on account of her desolation as the theatre of an Œcumenical Council, twice only do the fortunes of Pisa call forth any real interest or sympathy. The Ghibeline city, true to her old faith, wakes into life when the Cæsar from Lüzelburg, the last real restorer of the Empire, comes to do honour to her loyalty, and at last to lay his dust within her mighty temple. She wakes again to a yet truer life in her last struggle with the revived democracy of Florence, that democracy so zealous of freedom for herself, so chary of letting others share with her in the gift. But, at least after the death of Henry the Seventh, the old Pisan commonwealth, the commonwealth which checked the advance of Saracen and Turk, the commonwealth which filled the East with her merchants and her warriors, and which raised as her trophies the noblest monuments of Italian skill, must be reckoned among the things which have passed away for ever.

We have quoted the entry from one of the Pisan chronicles which assigns the beginning of the metropolitan church to the year 1063. Another chronicle, also in the great collection of Muratori, places the date twenty-six years later. To a Northern inquirer the difference is of no great consequence. In either case the building is contemporary with Durham ; if we accept the earlier date, it is also contemporary with Eadward's work at Westminster and with Ealdwine's work at Jarrow. In the history of art the difference made by the few years between Jarrow and Durham bridges over one of the greatest gaps on record. But, after all, Jarrow is a rude specimen of the style of which Pisa is the noblest monument, while Durham is the equal rival of Pisa in a distinct style. As a group, the buildings of Pisa are probably unrivalled in the world. Nothing can be more unlike the usual way in which the great churches of continental cities are crowded and jostled by inferior buildings than the broad space which holds the four great ecclesiastical structures of Pisa. The *duomo*, the baptistery, the campanile, and the *campo santo*, all stand close together, apart from all other buildings, except the wall of the city itself, in a corner of whose circuit the wonderful group is placed. But it is hardly more unlike the position of those Italian churches — Venice, of course, being the crowning example of all — in which an attempt has been made to give effect to the building by making the front look out on a wide open *piazza*. At Venice indeed St. Mark's is a mere appendage to the secular buildings of the commonwealth; it is the *prytaneion* which hallowed the home of its rulers. But even where the *duomo* or other great

church stands more independently than it does at
Venice, there is not often the same air of an ecclesiastical quarter which there is at Pisa. But, though
there is at Pisa a distinct ecclesiastical quarter, its
feeling is as unlike as possible to that of an English
cathedral close. In England the close is commonly
something cut off from the city; in some cases the
city itself is simply something which has grown up
outside the close. At Pisa, though we are in as
ecclesiastical quarter of the city, we still feel that we
are within the city, that the great church and its
satellites were the work and the possession of its citizens,
and not the separate domain of an ecclesiastical prince.
So unusual a site was beyond doubt chosen advisedly.
The metropolitan church was built on ground which
had been occupied by a humbler church of St. Reparata;
the original cathedral must therefore have stood on
some other spot, most likely, as in most other cases, in
the heart of the city.

As a matter of mere style, of mere architectural
detail, the *duomo* of Pisa differs but little from the
forms which we have already seen at Lucca. We must
remember that the *duomo* of Lucca was rising at the
same time as the *duomo* of Pisa, and that, according to
one account, these two great works were begun in the
same year. The original design of the Lucchese church
has been lost among later additions and rebuildings.

At Pisa, just as at Salisbury, though the west front must in actual age be many years later than the apse, we still see one design, the creation of one master mind, harmoniously carried out from one end of the building to the other. It is easy to see breaks where the work has stopped and has begun again; but there is no change in style, no change in design. It is an abuse of words to speak of the western part of the church as an addition. The name of the architect of Pisa is handed down to us as Busketus or Buschetto, and he must have been a man worthy to rank beside Iktinos and Anthemios, beside the designer of Spálato and the designer of Durham. His work shows that he had thoughtfully studied all the forms of architecture which had arisen in his age. His work was the trophy of victories in a land which Normans as well as Saracens were striving to free from the yoke of the misbeliever. It was the work of a city which rivalled Venice in its commercial intercourse with the East. Is it too much to think that the designer of the great church of Pisa drew ideas from each of so many enemies, rivals, and allies? The apse and the west front, if they stood at Lucca, would simply be remarked as the greatest among many kindred works. But the ground-plan and the design of the interior introduce us to something which, in its fulness, has no parallel at Lucca, at Ravenna, or any other city. We see plainly the influence of the

basilica, but we see no less plainly the influence of the
domical churches of Constantinople and Venice; we
see also, we venture to think, the influence of the
mosques of Palermo, and of the churches, if not of
Northern Europe, at least of Northern Italy. From the
East came the central cupola; from the North surely
came the spreading transepts; and these two features
Buschetto strove to work into harmony with the central
body, whose general design was to be that of a vast
basilica, but not without touches which must have
come from a Northern source. St. Sophia, St. Vital,
and St. Mark had no long-drawn nave; the basilicas
had no central cupola; the church of Pisa was to have
both. The attempt was not wholly successful. Nothing
can be more glorious than the Pisan interior looking
directly east and west, than the long ranges of
mighty columns, the double aisles, all leading on to
the vast mosaic which looks down from over the high
altar. The general effect is that of a basilica of
the highest order. But to this effect the cupola
and the transepts are sacrificed; they are denied
their proper prominence, while they have prominence
enough to disturb in some degree the perfect basilican
ideal. The architect was evidently afraid to break
in on the direct eastern and western range by giving
the cupola its proper constructive and æsthetical
support. We miss the four great lantern arches

which should form the main feature in any church which has a central cupola or tower of any form. The Pisan cupola is, as it were, thrust in so as to interrupt the direct view as little as may be; its supports are thrown into the background; its scale is insignificant, and instead of the round resting on the square, its form is that of an awkward ellipse. Some of its faults may well be owing to its reconstruction in the days of Medicean tyranny; but the main fault, the attempt to combine two arrangements, each noble in itself, but which are inconsistent with one another, was inherent in the original design. It was also, no doubt, for the same reason, not to interrupt the direct range, perhaps also with some memory of the tribunes of St. Mark, that the arcades are carried, though with some change of design, across the openings of the transepts. The transepts are thus cut off from the main body of the building in a way which is most unusual, but which appears again, where we should not have looked for any special likeness to Pisa, in the two great churches of Strassburg.

The *duomo* then has some manifest faults; the architect had several conflicting ideas in his head, which it was hard to work into an harmonious whole. But the merits of the building far outshine its defects. The arcades are the very glory of the basilican idea. And they carry, what is not to be seen at Ravenna or

Lucca, a real triforium. The form of a Northern triforium is here skilfully translated into Italian language, more skilfully than in those examples at Modena and Pavia which come actually nearer to the thing itself. The triforium is here made flat; there is no recessing; ornament is sought for, in Italian fashion, by alternation of colours. The arcades and triforium are worked well together; but the architect was less successful with his clerestory, which still remains disjointed, with a gap between itself and the triforium, just as we see over the arcades of the basilicas from which the triforium is absent. The double aisles, as ever, help to heighten the feeling of vastness and infinity. And moreover, in order that their arches may reach the level of the main arcades, they have taken the pointed form. Let no one think that this is a sign of approaching Gothic. The pointed form is here the tribute of the vanquished Saracen, as in the triforium and the transepts we see the contributions of the Norman ally.

Such is the great church of Pisa, the glory of Italian Romanesque. Strange to say, some of its faults are avoided in a smaller church essentially of the same type on the other side of the Arno. But the few moments that we have left to speak of Pisa must be given to the satellites which surround the *duomo*. The lower stage of the baptistery is admirable work of the twelfth century; but the upper portion, which was not

finished till late in the next age, suffers a good deal
from the introduction of pseudo-Gothic detail. The
campanile is far more satisfactory. It is perhaps more
famous for the accident which has thrown it out of
the perpendicular than from its own merits. Yet the
tower of Pisa may claim to be—at least on its own
side of the Hadriatic—the noblest tower of the Southern
Romanesque. The round form doubtless comes from
Ravenna; but the Pisan tower is a Ravenna tower
glorified. At Ravenna, as in East-Anglia, the round
form may have been adopted in order to avoid the
necessity of ashlar quoins in a building of brick or
flint. At Pisa, as in Ireland, the form was chosen out
of deliberate preference. And the preference was a
wise one. The square form could hardly have borne
the endless ranges of arcade upon arcade which perfectly suit the shape of the Pisan campanile, and which
make it one of the noblest works of human skill.

The *Campo Santo*, the cloister which seems to have
supplanted an earlier one attached to the church itself,
hardly claims our notice as a specimen of the Italian
Gothic; nor do its painted decorations belong to our
subject. But nowhere else in the Ghibeline city does
the student of Imperial history find himself more
thoroughly at home. In one walk is the statue which
loyal Pisa reared in honour of the first Frederick, a
witness, we must confess, which says more for the loyalty
of the citizens than for their artistic skill. The sculpture

of the Imperial effigy at Pisa hardly ranks above that in which his enemies at Milan have recorded their triumphs over him. We turn to another walk, and there, at perfect contrast in its noble workmanship, is the effigy of the last Cæsar who found a resting-place in Italian soil. Moved from its earlier place in the church, the tomb of Henry the Seventh now fills a place in which the inquirer has to search carefully for the Imperial monument among the records of the meaner dead. Our thoughts fly back to the last Imperial tomb on which we have gazed. The gap between Honorius and Henry of Lüzelburg seems to us a wide one. In the eyes of Dante there was no gap, no break, between two lawful possessors of the throne of the world. Our thoughts may perhaps flit away from both to the true Imperial King of Italy, to the Karling Lewis who sleeps at Milan. The gap is hardly filled up by an intermediate stage so unlike either. But it is in truth in contrasts of this kind that we best learn the strength of the abiding Imperial idea. The difference between Honorius, Lewis, and Henry, seemed as nothing in the eyes of those who believed that the Roman Cæsar, in whatever form, was God's temporal Vicar upon earth. And to those who fail thoroughly to understand the full force and depth of that belief, how men were ready to spend and be spent for what seems to us the most shadowy of shadows, mediæval history must ever remain an utter blank.

FÆSULÆ.

———•◦•———

ALL the world goes to Florence; so we suppose that all
the world climbs up to the Etruscan hill-city which
looks down upon it. Mr. Dennis at least, when describing the Cities and Cemeteries of Etruria, seems to make
a kind of apology for speaking of Fæsulæ at all. He
takes for granted that every one who has gone to the
modern city has gone to the ancient one also, and he
speaks of the old fortress as "the Hampstead or
Highgate of the Tuscan capital—the Sunday resort of
Florentine Cockneyism." We cannot speak from experience of Fiesole on Sunday; on Saturday it may
be explored without any annoyance from Cockneyism,
Florentine or British, and with perhaps a trifle less
than the usual amount of worry from local guides and
touters. The chances are rather against the traveller
finding the chief antiquity of the place without the help
of a guide of some kind; but bright-eyed little boys
will be found ready to do all that is really needed quite
as well as any professional showman. The only drawback is the difficulty of getting anything to eat which

is likely to be felt by those visitors to whom a swift recital of the names of modern Italian dishes conveys just as clear an idea as if they were described in ancient Etruscan. But at Fiesole, as at other places, it is possible to fall back upon the staff of life; and the staff of life may perhaps be enough to stay a man through so small a piece of mountaineering as that which leads by either the shorter and steeper or the longer and easier road from Florence to her venerable metropolis.

Perhaps however in these days we may be taken to task for taking the ancient Etruscan tongue as the type of a tongue not easy to be understood. One inquirer has not perhaps much mended the matter, if he be right in ruling that the speech of Lars Porsena was something of the nature of Turkish or Finnish. To be sure another inquirer has found out that the mysterious tongue is nothing but very good High-Dutch; but this doctrine puts up our backs even more than the other, as we had always lived in the fond belief that the Low forms of the common speech were more ancient than the High. But if we are to believe the local history of Fiesole, we need hardly trouble ourselves with such modern questions. Trier, far more ancient than Rome, claimed to be the eldest city of Europe; Fiesole, with a higher flight still, claimed to be the eldest city of the world. If we trust Ricordano Malespini, the founders of Fiesole were Atlas, other-

wise called Jupiter, and his wife Electra. Their eldest
son Italus gave his name to the land of Italy, while
their second son Dardanus set forth to conquer the
world in general. This Dardanus was not only the
first to coin money, but also to tame horses, and to
invent saddles and bridles. These last are inventions
which we may suppose that he did not light on till he
had migrated to the plains of the Troad; for, except
Venice, we can conceive no city in which it would
be easier to do without horses than at Fiesole. The
ingenuity of this odd tale is obvious. When Æneas
comes to Italy, he is simply returning to the land
of his forefathers. The tale is of a piece with the
Egyptian tale which gave an Egyptian descent to
Cambyses, with the Persian tale which gave a Persian
descent to Alexander, with the English tale which
made the mother of the Norman Conqueror a daughter
of a daughter of Eadmund Ironside. Nothing better
shows how Roman memories, and among them the
great Trojan legend, had supplanted all true local
legend and tradition, than that this should be all
that the current tale has to tell us of the old Etruscan
stronghold, around the fragments of whose mighty
walls one would have thought that some traces of
national Etruscan tradition might have lingered.

But the life of Fæsulæ has been so long and so
strange that we can forgive its citizens for having

dreamed that their city was the oldest upon earth.
Other cities have lived on through all ages and all
revolutions by virtue of their greatness; Fæsulæ
seems to have weathered all storms by virtue of its
littleness. In its legendary history it has been so
often destroyed and so often restored that we begin
to doubt all the stories of destruction and restora-
tion, and to think that Fæsulæ has most likely lived
on as continuously as Rome, Gades, and Massalia,
though from an opposite reason to Rome, Gades, and
Massalia. Etruscan antiquaries tell us that it was at no
time one of the great cities of the Confederation; but
an Etruscan city it was; the walls are there to speak
for themselves. We hear of its destruction by Sulla;
but, as it presently appears as one of his Roman
colonies, the destruction was most likely a destruction
of the inhabitants rather than of the city itself. We
hear of its destruction by the Florentines in the eleventh
century; yet it has lived on to our own time, and it
has always kept the ecclesiastical and municipal rank
of a city, though now at least it is a city of much the
same class as Llandaff and St. David's. We meet with
its name at all dates; in Polybios, in Sallust, in Prokopios,
but we never, except in its mythical early days, find it
playing a leading part in history. The cause is obvious.
The strong height commanding the plain needed at all
times to be occupied as a military post, but there was

nothing in the spot which could at any time lead to its becoming the dwelling-place of any great multitude of men. Fæsulæ then has always been a city; it has never been a great city. Fæsulæ and Florence are as Dardaniê and Ilios; we might say that they were as our own Old and New Salisbury. The ditches of Old Sarum are as wonderful in their way as the Etruscan walls of Fiesole; but we cannot venture to compare the English with the Tuscan hill; and, while Fiesole is still a dwelling-place of man, the seat of the Earls and Bishops of the elder Salisbury is utterly desolate.

The point in Fæsulan history which local fancy has seized on to trick out with the wildest imaginings is that when the city comes prominently into notice in the days of Sulla and Catilina. The true history is simple enough. When Sulla finally smote Etruria after the Social War, the Etruscan city became a Roman colony. The discontented colonists joined the party of Catilina, and a nameless citizen of Fæsulæ held one of the chief commands in the rebel army when Catilina was overthrown at Pistoria. At this same time, or soon after, Florence came into being, and she gradually outstripped her ancient neighbour, and, in some sort, parent. On this foundation local imagination has built up one of the most amazing of legends. Fæsulan patriots, forestalling Mr. Beesly, have made a hero of Catilina, only changing him into the more

graceful-sounding *Catellino*. The party divisions at
Rome are indeed somewhat strangely turned about;
for Marius appears as an aristocratic leader, and Sulla,
under the form of Assilla, becomes the chief of the
lower people (*capo del minuto popolo*). The conspiracy
of Catellino is described, with some approach to the
true story, only with the curious turning about that
Giulio Cesare appears as the leader of the Senators by
whom the conspirators were put to death. Catellino
escapes to Fæsulæ, and, at the head of the local army,
wages war against Rome. A wonderful romance then
follows about Fiorino, King of Rome, and his death
in battle, about his widow Bellisea and his daughter
Teverina, and their dealings with Catellino and with
a centurion named Pravus. Malespini, accustomed to
Kings of the Romans in his own age, found no difficulty
in conceiving a King of Rome in the age of Cicero.
In a later, but clearly less genuine, form of the legend,
Fiorino is cut down from King to Prætor. The upshot
of the whole story is that Fæsulæ is destroyed by
Cæsar, and a new city is founded in the plain. This
the conqueror wishes to name, after his own name,
Cæsarea—a remembrance doubtless of the Cæsarea of
Frederick Barbarossa rather than of the Cæsarea by
Ravenna. But the Senate, disliking such personal
assumption, decreed to call it, in honour of the slain
King Fiorino, *Fiorenza Magna*, it being also called *La*

Piccola Roma. Presently a son of Catellino appears, who bears the name, remarkable in a member of the Sergian *gens*, of Uberto Cesare. His namesake Giulio spares him, and he is allowed to settle in the new city, and to surround it with its earliest and narrowest circle of walls. He leaves descendants behind him; but, oddly enough, he himself, with divers followers, goes away into Saxony, and becomes the forefather of the Imperial Ottos. Meanwhile the old city finds a friend, and the new one an enemy, in the scourge of God, Attila or Totilas (the one name is used as an *alias* for the other), who destroys Florence and rebuilds Fiesole. Later on we come to the almost equally mythical destruction of Fiesole by the Florentines in the eleventh century.

In the latter part of the legend we see a clear memory of the long siege of Fiesole recorded by Prokopios, when the troops of Witiges held out against Belisarius' lieutenants Cyprian and Justin, till they were starved out and saw no chance of help from Ravenna. That Radagaisus, Attila, Witiges, and Totilas are all jumbled together is not very wonderful. How should we wonder at it when we have heard men of our own day, in Parliament and out of Parliament, chatter about "Goths, Huns, and Vandals" as if they were all much the same kind of people? And the whole story of Catellino, wild as it is, is not wilder than many other

tales which were current in the same age; it is hardly
so wild as an incidental statement of Malespini himself
that the church of St. Peter at Rome was founded by
"Attaviano Cesare Augusto." But one would like to
know whether, in the belief of Malespini, the Etruscan
wall and the neighbouring theatre or amphitheatre
were the original work of Atlas, *alias* Jupiter, or only
of the second founder Attila. The wall, with its great
stones, mainly quadrangular, but with the vacant spaces
filled up in various irregular ways, still stands on the
northern slope of the hill, a memorial of days, perhaps
before Rome was, at all events before any man in Rome
could have dreamed that his city would ever bear rule
on the banks of the Arno. Its construction is minutely
described and compared with other Etruscan remains
by Mr. Dennis. The greater part of the extent of the
fortifications must be taken on faith by any one who is
not inquiring with the minuteness needed by one who
is going to write a topography of Fiesole; but this
mighty fragment speaks for itself, and there can be no
doubt that the Franciscan church, rising far above the
cathedral and the rest of the city, marks the site of
the Etruscan *arx*, though Mr. Dennis warns us that
the triple line of wall which once defended it is no
longer to be seen. One of the stages of the threefold
enclosure is doubtless marked by the somewhat lower
church of St. Alexander, a small basilica, with ancient

columns said to have come from a neighbouring temple of Bacchus.

But the two chief monuments of Fiesole, ancient and mediæval, stand on a lower level. Just within the Etruscan wall men were, in November 1874, digging out the remains of the famous theatre on which Niebuhr found so much to say, both as a witness to the greatness of ancient Fæsulæ, and as a witness to the high developement of the arts in dependent Etruria. Mr. Dennis however rules it to be only Roman work, and he hints that people who write histories on the scale of Niebuhr would do better not to meddle with local archæology. To this doctrine we must demur; but we will keep ourselves out of danger by not venturing any judgement either way, for which the fact that the diggings were unfinished when we saw them may supply a decent excuse. We will move to the surer ground of the *duomo*. It is indeed amazing, within sight of the great city below and of the mighty cupola of the metropolitan church, to find the little city on the height —some might feel inclined to call it the little village —still the seat of an independent bishopric, with its cathedral church and all the other appurtenances of an episcopal see. The tall, slender bell-tower, with its crenellated top, forms a striking object in every distant view; but, when we come near, it is disappointing in its utter absence of all architectural features. But the little *duomo* is a real study ; it forms a good companion-piece to the more famous church of St. Miniato on the other side of the famous city which lies in the plain between them. But, as a piece of Italian Romanesque, · it has nothing in common with the history of the old Etruscan fortress, or with the legend of Catellino. It may be well to say a few words about it in company with its neighbour.

THE NEIGHBOUR CHURCHES OF
FLORENCE.

———◦✦◦———

A TRAVELLER in Italy was lately much jeered at by
his friends for saying that, for his purposes, Florence
was chiefly the way to get to Fiesole and St. Miniato.
If he had said that Florence was in itself less worthy
of study than Fiesole and St. Miniato, the jeers would
have been well deserved.   But as the purposes for
which Italian travel may be undertaken are almost
endless; and, as it is wise to chalk out each journey
with a view to some special class or classes of objects
only, there is nothing absurd in looking at Florence
as, for certain purposes, the Fiesole-St.-Miniato station.
There are certain rational purposes of study for which
the illustrious city in the plain supplies less material
than the comparatively obscure spots which crown the
heights on either side of her.   As the most renowned
and the most abiding seat of mediæval civic democracy,
as the great home of Italian literature, as one of the
great homes of Italian art, as the city which has given
birth to a longer list of great men than any city since

the old days of Athens or Rome, Florence stands forth
illustrious above the cities of Italy and of the world.
For some centuries Florence was the centre of Italian
history; and those were centuries when the history of
Italy was the centre of the history of the world. Yet
many important ages of Italian history had passed away
before Florence rose to fill any leading place in Italy.
It is not till the thirteenth century that she begins to
step into the position which in earlier times had been
held by Milan. Few spots in the world call up nobler
associations than the open place where her citizens
came together under the shadow of the stately palace
of her magistrates. But both the historical associations
and the material fabrics belong to a comparatively late
time. The man who seeks for memorials of classic, or
even of early mediæval, days must not go to Florence
to look for them. The Roman city founded on Etruscan
soil has no traces to show of Etruscan art, and only very
feeble traces of Roman art. She has nothing to set
against the amphitheatre or the gateways of Verona,
against the unique wonders of Ravenna, against the
basilicas of Lucca, even against the few relics of ancient
Milan which escaped the hand of the Swabian conqueror, against the colonnade of Maximian and the
minster of St. Ambrose. Her baptistery stands as her
one relic which has lived on from the days of the truest
art of Italy. Her greater buildings belong to the days

when Italy had forsaken her native style, and had given herself to the vain attempt of reproducing the forms of Northern architecture on unkindly soil. Florence, in short, soars above all rivals within her own world; but there is an earlier world in which she has hardly any share. And those whose immediate studies lie within that earlier world may well, for the while, look on Florence the Fair as a spot which has less to set before them than her humbler satellites.

From the height of St. Miniato on the southern bank of the Arno we look down on the great city itself; we look out on the hill, crowned by the elder Etruscan settlement, where the slender tower of the little *duomo* of Fiesole lifts its head to mark the city which has been almost as eternal in her littleness as Rome has been in her greatness. We look too on the walls and forts and gates spread around us on every side, and we then feel that the greatest deed of the fair city's greatest artist was that which is not recorded in the list of his works on his monument in Santa Croce. Under grand-ducal rule it was safe to tell how Michael Angelo painted pictures and carved statues and raised the Pantheon upon the basilica of Constantine. It was not safe to tell how he wrought a yet nobler work in strengthening the walls of his native city, when she stood forth in her last days, a spectacle to heaven and earth, the one spot of free Italian ground which defied the united powers of Pope and Cæsar. But to the traveller whose immediate business lies among earlier days, his chief spot of pilgrimage on the left bank of the Arno will be the church of St. Miniato itself.

The hill monastery of St. Miniato has one point, and perhaps only one, in common with the metropolitan church of the city which lies at its feet. The *duomo* of Florence is one of the few Italian buildings where the outside so far surpasses the inside that we cannot enter one of its doors without a feeling of disappointment. This is most certainly not the case at St. Miniato. Yet the general outline of the church and its attendant buildings is decidedly striking, and it is especially so to an eye fresh from Rome, where the basilicas, of no very striking outline in themselves, have been so hopelessly disfigured by the vagaries of successive Popes. The traveller in Italy constantly sees some noble hill crest or peak crowned by a town or village, and almost the first thought is how much a picturesque site loses from the utter lack of picturesque effect in the buildings with which it is crowned. He cannot help thinking how different the landscape would be, if the successive architects of a German town had crowned such a site with walls, gates, towers, and spires, with the ever-shifting grouping of church, castle, and council-house. At St. Miniato, and at Fiesole too, we are less tempted to make this complaint than usual. Neither the monastery

K

of St. Miniato nor the *duomo* of Fiesole makes the least approach to the picturesque grouping of a German building; but they have more of outline than is to be found in most churches in Italy. Both perhaps have about as much outline as an Italian church without a cupola can have. Each has a real west front, not merely a rough wall to which a west front was to be added some time or other. In each the long line of narrow windows remains untouched, at least in the clerestory. In each the bell-tower, though in itself of no architectural value, has its share in the general effect of the whole. And at St. Miniato the castellated monastic buildings adjoining the church, though they have been a good deal disfigured in detail, stand out with more of distinctness and character than is common in Italian buildings of the kind, and they certainly have their share in the general effect which strikes the eye of the traveller as he climbs the hill from the St. Miniato gate of Florence.

Yet, after all, it is the inside of St. Miniato, or at all events the inside together with the west front, which most deserves our study. The visitor to St. Miniato, unless indeed he happens to be looking directly on the campanile, finds his thoughts at once carried back to St. Zeno at Verona. In both the long arcades of the basilica are broken by the great arches spanning the nave; and in both the effect of those spanning arches

is to make the column, the natural feature of Italian
architecture, alternate with the clustered pier or group
of half-columns which carries the thoughts to buildings
north of the Alps. In both the lofty choir is borne up
upon the open pillared crypt below, an arrangement
whose effect differs almost as much from the dark crypt
of an English minster as it does from the confessional of
a Roman basilica. Thus far St. Zeno and St. Miniata
agree in their main features of construction and arrangement. Where they differ is in the treatment of the
material of which each church is built. In St. Zeno
the alternation of bands of stone and brick, so as to
produce a variety of colour—an alternation which was
perhaps suggested by some of the later forms of Roman
masonry—is introduced in some slight degree, but not
enough to perplex the eye, still less to interfere with
any of the architectural features of the building. At
St. Miniato that alternation of black and white, which,
when carried to extreme, makes a building look like a
piece of Tunbridge ware, is applied both to a large part
of the inside and also to the west front. This last, as so
often happens, is plainly the last finish of the original
building, a finish which might be almost called an addition. The good or bad effect of this kind of ornament
is one of those things which are very largely a matter
of taste about which it is useless to argue. To cover a
wall with mathematical figures, traced out in black and

K 2

white, may be better than leaving it quite blank; but it is surely a poor substitute either for strictly architectural ornament or for mosaic or painted enrichments of any kind. It may be endured when it fills up the blank space which in a Northern church would be occupied by the triforium; but it has a strange effect when the round-headed windows of the clerestory peep out from between figures of this kind which look like a geometrical puzzle. In the inside this ornament seems to have been an afterthought; but in the west front, where it was evidently planned from the beginning, it has clearly affected the architectural design, and that not for the better. The wheel of fortune at St. Zeno, the arched windows of Pisa and Lucca, could hardly have found a place where the front was to be cut up into a series of squares and lozenges. Even in the lowest stage, where the range of five arches does suggest the lowest stage of Pisa, the passion for this kind of decoration has quite cut off the arcade from the doorways, leaving the latter simply square-headed, without any attempt to work the arches and doorways together in the manner of a tympanum. Within, the capitals are, as everywhere, a study. In the nave the columns have classical capitals; the clustered piers and the columns in the crypt have various kinds, classical, quasi-classical, and rude forms which might be cut out into something more enriched. As often happens, a strictly classical feature preserves its classical character, while a greater licence is allowed when the feature itself departs from classical precedent.

The abbey of St. Miniato, within and without, is now set apart for the use of the dead, as a burying-ground and a funeral church. The *duomo* of Fiesole, to which its tower seems to beckon us from the opposite height, is still in the hands of the living. It is a small basilica, with narrow aisles and with cross-arms which are something between a Roman *chalcidice* and a Northern transept. It has the same kind of crypt and raised choir as St. Miniato, but it lacks the arches spanning the nave. The capitals of the crypt are specially worthy of study, on account of their utter departure from any of the common Italian types. Some of them are by no means lacking in ornament, such as it is; but it is ornament which altogether departs from classical models, and which yet does not bring in the animal forms of Milan and Pavia. They approach nearer to our own primitive Romanesque; some of them seem to have a near kindred with the strange capitals in the slype at Worcester. Others, especially in the clustered piers of what we might almost call the lantern, present a rich variety of the Composite type, but a type which we suspect that a classical purist would be far from admitting as orthodox. Everywhere the transition takes different paths. Everywhere the classical types, which

are the common models of all, show their influence;
but they show it in different ways, and architectural
specialists could hardly hit upon a better subject than
an historical study of the various forms of capital to be
seen in the Roman and Romanesque buildings of Italy.
We can only suggest such a subject without following
it into detail; but we may add that, though the subject
may seem a small one, it is one which, like every other
subject of the kind, calls for real historical knowledge.
The man who tries to fix the dates of buildings without
knowing what the dates mean—that is, without knowing
what the state of things was when the buildings were
set up—can never reach to an accurate understanding
even of his own special walk.

ARIMINUM.

THE towns of Romagna lie thickly set along one of the main roads of the world, but we fancy that they lie out of the ordinary tourist range. Most of those, we fancy, who make the modern " iter ad Brundisium " have the best possible reasons for getting over the ground as fast as they can ; people stop at Bologna be-cause they must stop somewhere, but it does not come into their heads to stop at Pesaro or Fano. A most interesting line of country is therefore left pretty well undisturbed. No part of the world brings more thoroughly home to us one side both of ancient and mediæval history. At no time, save during the short dominion of Ravenna, has the Hadriatic coast of Italy held the same position as the Etruscan, Latin, and Campanian coasts. Neither in the days before the establishment of the Roman dominion in the peninsula, nor in the days after that dominion had fallen to pieces, did any of the cities on that side of the peninsula hold the same place as the great cities of the other side. The land too was less purely Italian than some other districts. .We must remember how far down the Gaulish occupation reached. Even in Cæsar's day, Ravenna, like Lucca on the other side, was still within his Gaulish province, and, in the third century before Christ, the Sena on the Hadriatic coast still deserved the epithet of *Gallica,* which it has kept in its corrupted form of Sinigaglia. Greek colonists too were believed to have settled on this coast in early times. Various legends were told of the origin both of Ravenna and of Spina; and Ancona has not yet forgotten the days when it claimed to be the Dorian Ankôn. But none of these real or pretended Greek settlements ever reached anything like the greatness of the famous Greek cities of the South of Italy. In later times too the cities which played a great part in mediæval history either lie further to the north, in the old Gaulish land, like Milan and her Lombard sisters, or else, like Genoa, Pisa, and Florence, to say nothing of Rome herself, they lie on the western side of the Apennines. It is by a kind of irony of fortune that the Roman name was doomed to cleave in a special way to this comparatively obscure district of Italy. It was by another freak of the same irony that it owed its name of Romagna, not to any special connexion with the Old Rome, but to its being the dwelling-place of the Exarchs who represented in Italy the majesty of the New.

Yet it is perhaps in some measure owing to this

very lack of cities of great and historic fame that the
upper coast of the Hadriatic has been enabled to show
forth the characteristics of Italian history in an almost
exaggerated form. The passenger by the railway which
has become one of the great roads of Europe has his ear
greeted at almost every station by the name of towns
which, if they never ranked alongside of Milan and
Florence and Genoa, still had each one its history, each
one its revolutions, each one its short-lived commonwealth and its often short-lived tyranny. Nowhere is
the state of things more forcibly brought home to
us in which it was the first principle of political life
that every town, whether commonwealth or principality,
should form an independent state, enjoying the same
attributes of sovereignty as those great cities which
might rank as the peers of kingdoms. Among these
towns one stands out as more truly claiming to have
played a part in the general history of the world than
most of its fellows. The name of Rimini will to most
minds first suggest the most pathetic passage in the
whole range of the *Inferno* of Dante; but, whether as
classical Ariminum or as mediæval Rimini, the city has
higher historic claims to notice than to have been the
birth-place of the erring Francesca. The first strictly
Italian city where Cæsar appeared in arms after crossing
the borders of his own province, the city which was the
scene of the Council after which the world was said to

have mourned and wondered to find itself Arian, certainly stands out in historic importance above its neighbours. Its later tyrants too of the house of Malatesta bear a more famous name than most of their neighbours. These last we chiefly remember, if we remember them at all, as falling into the common gulf of ecclesiastical dominion, either in the days of the Borgia or in the earlier days when Robert of Geneva, the future Antipope, wrought the great slaughter of Cesena. In the Forum of Ariminum we may see the stone which marks the spot where, according to local belief, Cæsar addressed his soldiers. But the inscription speaks of the speech as having been made "superato Rubicone," a phrase which savours rather of the rhetoric of Lucan than of the simple narrative of the great rebel himself, who did not think the crossing of the border streamlet worth recording. The momentary triumph of Arianism at Ariminum has left its memory in 'the name of the neighbouring *La Cattolica,* a spot which legend points out as the place of dwelling or shelter for the Orthodox minority in the famous Synod. In the general course of events, there may seem to be a certain kind of propriety in the formal promulgation of the heretical faith in this particular district, as a kind of foreshadowing of the coming rule of the Arian Goth in not far distant Ravenna. As for the tyrants, one at least among them has taken care that neither himself nor his wife shall be forgotten by any visitor to Rimini. Sigismund and Isotta appear on church and fortress as the chief later adorners of the city; and in the nomenclature of the modern streets, while the Dictator himself claims the great square of the ancient Forum, other and lowlier portions of the city bear the names of the most famous of the house of Malatesta.

If it be true that the voices of the sea and of the mountains are two voices which call men to freedom, Rimini ought never to have fallen under the power of tyrants. The Hadriatic has gone back from Rimini, as it has gone back from Ravenna; but it has not left the city so utterly stranded. It still keeps up somewhat of a seafaring character, both in the form of a haven and in the more modern form of a watering-place. But both haven and watering-place lie beyond the walls alike of the ancient and of the mediæval city; the city itself, like Chester, has at some points spread beyond the walls, and at others shrunk up within them. As we enter from the sea, from the port or from the station, the wall crosses the modern street, while at other points, as at Rome and Soest, large tracts of cultivated ground are found within the walls even of the sixteenth century. And while there is the sea on one side, there are the mountains on the other. Some of the noblest peaks of the Apennines rise in the distant view; and almost every child in the street is ready

to point out to the passer-by the site of the Commonwealth of St. Marino, the last surviving Italian
commonwealth, the sharer in the ancient freedom of
Andorra and of Uri. It is something to look out on
this abiding stronghold of freedom, whether it be from
the bridge of Tiberius, from the castle of the Malatesta, or from the walls of Pope Paul the Fifth.   If
we add to these the arch of Augustus and the church
of St. Francis, the later *duomo*, we shall have gone
through the list of the chief antiquities of Rimini.
The list is certainly scanty as compared with the
wealth of many other Italian cities, but it is spread
over nearly the whole range of Italian history.   Where
there is a gap at Rimini, it is the same gap which we
see at Rome itself, the gap which at Verona is so nobly
filled by St. Zeno, and at Venice by St. Mark's and the
range of Romanesque palaces by the Grand Canal. We
leap from the days of the Cæsars—in this case from
the Julian House itself—to works of the fourteenth
and fifteenth centuries.

The two works of the early Imperial age which
remain at Rimini are both striking in their grand
simplicity. The bridge is especially so; in a structure
of that kind there was hardly any scope for the ever-
recurring fault of Roman architecture, the masking of
a body built according to the native Italian arched
construction with a veil borrowed from the entablature

system of the Greeks. The stream is spanned by bold and simple arches of the best Roman masonry, with but little attempt at ornament. The general preservation is wonderful, though more than one of the arches has been partly patched, if not set up afresh. And to more than one of the piers it has been thought needful at some later time to add buttresses of brickwork, to which a mediæval architect might perhaps point with some triumph as a sign that his system of construction was after all better than that of the ancient engineers. The inscription on the bridge is not quite perfect; but it is striking, when crossing a thickly crowded thoroughfare between two parts of a modern city, to light on words forming a contemporary record of the names and offices of Augustus and his stepson. In Rome itself we soon cease to be startled as we stumble on fragments of this kind at every step. Their presence, or rather their abundance, is in truth what makes Rome Rome. But elsewhere, even in Italy, every fragment has a distinct being of its own, and makes its own distinct impression. We are tempted to wish that the stream spanned by the noble bridge was the Rubicon itself. But the traveller passes as lightly over the border stream in his actual journey as he does in the narrative of Cæsar. The bridge however at least marks the course by which the arch rebel must have entered his native land in his new character of invader.

From the bridge we follow the main street of the town; we pass through the square which bears the name of Cæsar, and at the further end of Rimini, hard by one of the gates of the Papal fortifications, we pass under the arch of Augustus. Spanning the street as it now does, it needs a slight effort to keep in mind that it is not the gate of the city, but simply a commemorative arch, one which, like all others of the class, was in its original object simply commemorative, which served no practical use, and never fulfilled the purpose of a gateway by being furnished with a gate. Later ages however turned the arch of Rimini, as they turned the arches of Rome, to their own purposes. A mass of brickwork on each side and above the arch, crowned with a double row of the so-called Scala battlement, shows that the arch raised in the seventh consulship of Augustus to commemorate no warlike triumph, but the peaceful work of mending the roads, was found convenient for the purposes of a fortress. We will remark in passing that this change is part of the history of the building and of the city, and we trust that no reformer or restorer will ever wipe out this small page of Italian history by pulling down the mediæval crest of the Roman arch. The arch, as we have said, is wide, and spans the street; and the arch itself takes up nearly the whole width of the building, leaving room only for

ARCH AT RIMINI.

To face page 142.

a single Corinthian column on each side. It has therefore little in common in point of effect with its neighbour at Ancona'; but it has still less likeness to such
massive structures as the later arches of Severus and
Constantine. It shows the usual faults of Roman
architecture in columns which support nothing except the projecting bits of entablature upon them,
and in a sham pediment which not only ends no
real roof, but does not even pretend to rest upon
the columns. Above this pediment is the inscription which records the date and object of the monument. These confusions of the constructive and
decorative system must be taken for granted in every
Roman building, till Diocletian taught men that the
Roman arch answered to the Greek entablature, and
that the column, used first as a support for the entablature, was equally fitted to become the support of the
arch. Still the arch of Rimini is a simple, stately,
and noble structure, all the better because it stands
out boldly in the simple dignity of its main architectural features, the arch itself and its attendant
columns, and is not overloaded with sculpture or with
exaggerated detail of any kind.

The visitor who reaches the arch can hardly fail to
turn one way or the other along the fortifications of
Pope Paul. On the side nearest the sea a hand set
up by authority of the Senate of Ariminum points to

the spot where he is to see the remains of an amphitheatre. The spot is within the papal walls; but it
was doubtless, as is the case well nigh everywhere but
in Rome itself, outside the gates of the ancient city.
We will not dispute a fact stated on such authority;
we will only say that to make out the extent, or even
the position, of the amphitheatre of Ariminum must
be the work of some one to whom Jupiter or Mars,
or whoever presides over such buildings, has given a
keener sight than we can pretend to. The fortifications
of Pope Paul, which reach in many parts far beyond
the extent of the modern town, are well preserved
through a great part of their extent; they jut in and
out so as to form a most irregular outline; and they
form a walk commanding fine points of view both
towards the mountains and towards the sea. The huge
brick castle of Sigismund Malatesta looks mountain-
wards; the great church which owes its present form
to him bears locally the name of the Temple of the
Malatesta. Its date is 1450, a few years before the
building of the castle. It is remarkable as a case in
which infinite pains have been taken to turn a church
of the Italian Gothic, with windows better deserving
the name of Gothic than most which are to be found
in Italy, into a building of the *Renaissance*. The
effect is strange, but it is striking in its way; the
initials of Sigismund and Isotta appear everywhere;

so does the Malatesta badge of the elephant; and the huge earth-shaking beast is everywhere shown of the African species, with the vast ears, an abiding remembrance, it may be, of the Gœtulian beast of Hannibal. The other churches of Rimini are of no great moment, nor is there anything very striking in its domestic architecture, though, as in every Italian city except Rome, graceful fragments are here and there scattered up and down its streets. Altogether, while neither in its history nor its architecture can Rimini at all claim to be a city of the first rank, it is a spot well worth turning aside to visit, and one, it may not be out of place to add, where better quarters may be had, and at lower cost, than in some cities of greater fame.

ANCONA.

THE wayfarer through the streets of Rome has his eye struck, in many of the open places of the city, by some monument of the old days of Paganism crowned with Christian emblems, and inscribed with the legend which tells how this or that Pope—stout Sixtus the Fifth perhaps oftener than any other—cleansed the heathen structure from all impiety and dedicated it to the service of the true faith. Such a christening of Trajan's column more than twelve hundred years after the conversion of Constantine awakens amusement rather than sympathy; but there are cases where the feeling is very different. It is very different when we come to works which underwent the like change when the new faith was still in the full glow of its first triumphs, when Paganism was still a real and living enemy, an enemy decaying perhaps and trodden down, but an enemy which was not dead, and which, as one great example showed, might spring up again with renewed strength at least for a season. In those days we can fully go along with the spirit which changed the basilica into the church, the throne of the judge into the chair of the bishop, the spirit which turned the Temple of all the Gods into the Church of all the Martyrs—nay, even with the spirit which bore away the marble columns as trophies from the vanquished heathen, and reared them again, in new forms and for new uses, in the long-drawn arcades of the earliest churches of Rome and of Ravenna. But there are cases in which nature seems to have done the work without the help of man, or rather cases in which man has done the work by a happy choice of sites which of themselves seem to proclaim the triumph of the new creed over the old. Let us stand on the quay of Ancona, and turn our eyes inland from its noble bay. From several happily chosen spots the view immediately before us seems a worthier symbol of the great change that has come over the world than the half-spiteful device of surmounting the monuments of Trajan and Antoninus with objects of Christian reverence. Close before us rises the arch of the prince to whom his own and later ages decreed the title of the Best. But here Trajan is celebrated, not for any of his warlike exploits, not for adding provinces beyond the Danube and the Tigris, but for the more useful task of finishing the work on which we are standing, the great mole of the harbour of Ancona. From a well-chosen spot we may look through the narrow arch, and see the peninsular

L 2

hill which rises above the port and city, itself crowned by the stately *duomo* of Ancona, the church of the martyr Cyriacus. From a spot still better chosen we may see hill and church soaring directly above the arch and all that it supports. The Christian temple seated on its lordly height seems to look down with an eye of silent rebuke upon the monument of the prince who condemned Ignatius to the lions. The moral of the group is perhaps disturbed rather than heightened when we carry our inquiries further, when we learn that the church of St. Cyriacus is itself an example of the less noble form of Christian triumph, that it has taken the place and grown out of the materials of the chief temple of heathen times. We could perhaps rather have wished that the triumph of the new faith on such a site had been embodied in some building which might be wholly the design of Christian skill and the work of Christian hands, some building which owed nothing to the despoiling of the holy places of the fallen creed. But from the points of which we speak thoughts of this kind cannot suggest themselves. The *duomo* of Ancona, as seen from the mole, as seen any-where from the outside, is a building whose forms are purely and eloquently Christian. Unlike the earlier basilicas of Ravenna and Rome, it is not satisfied to be all glorious within; it has its external outline, the outline of the now triumphant cross; the four arms

join to support the cupola as the crown of the whole, as
distinctly as in any minster of England or Normandy.
The cupola, instead of the massive tower, the detached
campanile, unworthy as it is of the building to which
it belongs, tells us that we are not in Normandy or in
England, but in Italy. But another feature of the
building tells us that we are in one of those spots of
Italy on which influences from the other side of the
Hadriatic have left a lasting impress. The city which
had once been the Dorian Ankôn, the city which was
to be the last fortress in Italy held by the troops
of a Byzantine Emperor, not unfittingly shows the
sign of kindred with the East in the form of the chief
monument of its intermediate days. The *duomo* of
Ancona follows neither the oblong type of the basilicas
nor the Latin cross of Pisa. The church which contains the plundered columns of the Dorian Aphroditê
is still so far Greek as to follow the Greek cross in
its general ground plan. The main plan is that of
St. Mark's: but it appears at Ancona without that
further accumulation of many cupolas which makes
the ducal church of Venice one of the many reminders
that in the city of the lagoons we are in the Eastern
and not in the Western world.

The city itself stands nobly, climbing the sides of the
steep hill, the peninsular projection, the very *elbow*
from which the place takes its name. Of that

peninsula the church of St. Cyriacus occupies, not
indeed the highest, but the most striking point.
Modern fortifications are spread over the heights, but
the precinct, first of the heathen and then of the
Christian temple, remains free of access as when in
ages past the seamen far away on the Hadriatic
greeted the first glimpse of the house of the patron
goddess. From the porch of the church the eye
ranges over the long line of coast, thickly strewed
with towns and castles and villages, and sheltered
as it were by the mountain wall further inland, the
barrier between the comparatively obscure shores of
the great gulf and the more historic lands beyond the
Apennines. We can well understand how attractive
the bay with its sheltering hills must have seemed to
colonists of early times; we can picture to ourselves the struggles, the ups and downs, the abiding
growth and the momentary checks, which must have
been gone when more civilized settlers planted themselves and their arts among the ruder natives. And
from those days our thoughts float on to those far later
days when the connexion of the Dorian city with the
lands beyond the Hadriatic was again renewed in so
strange a form, when the cities of Italy allied themselves alike with the Pontiff of the Old Rome and
with the Cæsar of the New, the better to shake off
their allegiance to the King and Emperor whom they

shared with the lands beyond the Alps. Fresh from
the painted forms of Justinian and Theodora at
Ravenna and of the triad of Heraclian Emperors at
Classis, we feel it less amazing to hear how the host
of Manuel Komnênos appeared on the same coast
among the many foes of his Swabian rival, how for
a moment it seemed possible that the Old Rome
and her Pontiff should again return to the allegiance
from which they had parted off at the election of the
Great Charles. We think of the great siege at the
hands of Archbishop Christian, of the long endurance
and hard privations so graphically set forth by a
writer of the next age; and we feel that, after all,
the place of Ancona in the world's history is one
not to be despised. And we may think too how
the long connexion of the city with the Eastern lands
went on in yet another form, how the prosperity of
Ancona in days nearer our own was largely due to
trade with the lands whence her first settlers had come
forth, and to the presence of fresh settlers from the
same land who found in her their harbour of refuge
from their Turkish oppressors.

The church which has supplanted the ancient temple
on the peninsular height is not wholly unworthy either
of the lordly position on which it stands, or of the long
train of associations which is called up by the prospect
on which it looks down so proudly. The Greek cross

perhaps makes us ask for the four subordinate cupolas gathering round the great centre, as in the three examples which form as it were the family tree of domical architecture, St. Sophia, St. Mark, and St. Front at Perigueux. Our first feeling perhaps is one of puzzledom at the seemingly amazing length of the transepts and shortness of the nave. The south transept indeed, furnished, as both of them are, with aisles and finished with apses, might for a moment pass for the eastern limb. In fact, the western limb is internally the shortest of the four. Each consists of three bays, and the eastern, northern, and southern were all originally furnished with apses. But the eastern apse has unluckily given way to a square-ended addition of a somewhat later time, which greatly mars the general proportion of the building. It is easy to see that, in more than one point, changes have taken place in the details of the ornamental pilasters and arcades; but, except the awkward addition at the east end, there is nothing to interfere with the general character of the building. It is a pure, but not very rich, specimen of the Italian Romanesque at its best point, when it had shaken itself quite free from classical trammels and was not yet corrupted by hopeless imitations of Northern forms. The chief ornamental feature outside, the only feature where there is any great degree of enrichment, is the magnificent western porch, with its many receding

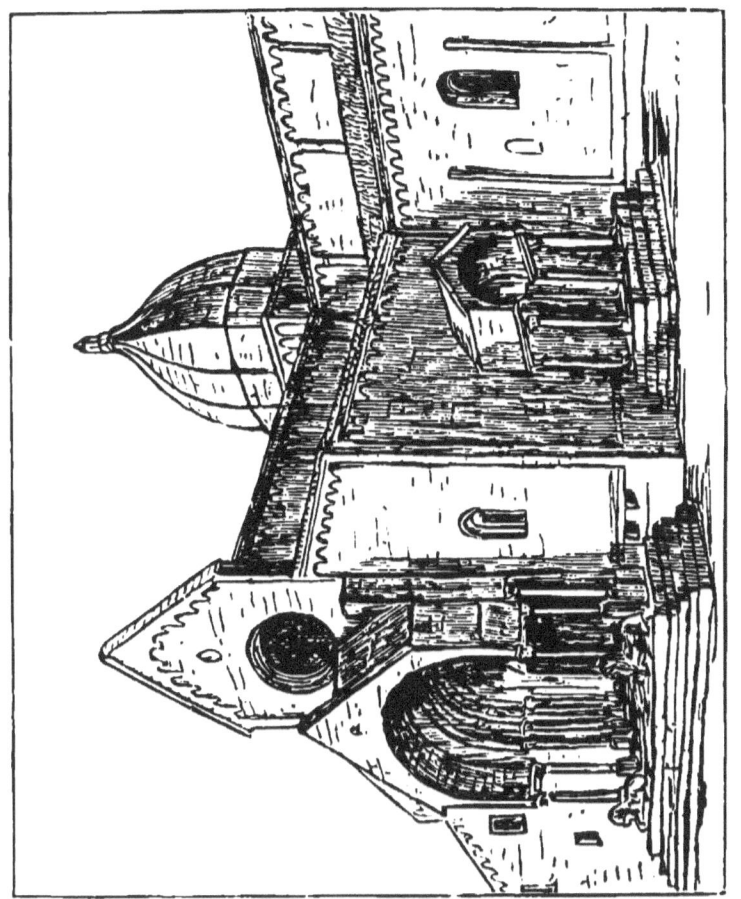

DUOMO, ANCONA, S.W.

To face page 152.

orders and its columns resting in true Italian fashion
on the backs of lions, lions among the most lifelike of
their kind. We fancy that in some of the orders the
beginnings of the pointed arch may be detected, but
they do not thrust themselves into such prominence as
seriously to interfere with the Romanesque purity of
the building. The rest of the front is plain; there is
no trace of the arcades of Pisa and Lucca, and St.
Zeno's wheel of fortune is, both here and in the transept, represented only by a single circle. But, when
we have once taken in the peculiar arrangements of
the church, the whole fits in well together, and the
octagonal cupola on its square base rises well over its
four supporting arms, far better than it could have
done if the nave had attempted anything of basilican
length. When we enter the church, we find the
cupola well supported by lantern arches, with an ingenious arrangement of pendentives, though we might
have wished that both the arches and the piers on which
they rest had been made more prominent objects in the
interior. The arches of the four limbs rest on monolith
columns, the spoils of the ancient temple, and they are
crowned by capitals of various forms, classical and *quasi-*
classical, some almost barbaric in their foliage, but still
all confining themselves to foliage, and not seeking for
richness in the shape of human or animal forms. Those
in the south transept are worthy of special study, as

showing some of the curious ways in which the volute
and the other classical details might be used in the
various attempts to avoid exposing the delicate work of
the capital to the full weight of the arch which it had
to bear. But in the *duomo* of Ancona the study of
the columns and capitals is a case of the pursuit of
knowledge under difficulties. Anconitan taste seemingly
looks on a marble shaft and a Corinthian capital as
less of a thing of beauty than certain fragments
of red rag with which the greater part of column
and capital are carefully covered. The first impression
is that the thing is a trick upon travellers, akin to
the swindle of covering up pictures in order to get
a franc by drawing back their curtains. But we suspect
that pilgrims to St. Cyriacus, and above all, students
of his capitals, do not come in such throngs that
a trade of this kind would be likely to be profitable.
The rags are meant as a permanent ornament; and they
are found, not only in the *duomo* but in a more thorough-
going shape in the lower church of St. Mary, where the
columns are so completely swathed that their material
and the form of their capitals cannot be made out at all.
In truth this wonderful notion of ornament is in no way
peculiar to Ancona nor to the western side of the Hadriatic. The rags flaunt in all their ugliness at Trieste
and at Zara; and to the shame of the Eternal City itself,
it may be seen on certain high days in the patriarchal

church of the world. And, after all, this display of
Anconitan taste is not more wonderful than that which
condemned the north transept and the crypt below it
to be mercilessly Jesuited. The crypt under the
southern transept has escaped; it keeps its natural
columns, and it is rich in tombs and inscriptions of
various dates and kinds, one of them in the Greek
tongue, recording the burial-place of the martyr Dakios.

The narrow and winding streets of this hill city,
many of which are actual stairs impassable for car-
riages, present many picturesque points, with peeps
here and there of the hills and of the harbour. But,
besides the arch and the *duomo*, the only building
worthy of special notice is the church which we have
already mentioned as having its pillars so utterly
shrouded from sight. Disfigured without mercy within,
hemmed in among mean buildings without, furnished
with an unworthy campanile, it still keeps its west
front of the very richest form of the more barbaric
variety of the Italian Romanesque, that which departs
most widely from classical, and approaches most nearly
to Northern forms. It is covered with arcades, with a
magnificent doorway in the centre, and almost every
arch of the design is living with figures, human, animal,
and vegetable. The doorway is utterly unlike its equally
splendid neighbour at St. Cyriacus. It has, in fact, not
only a Northern, but, one might almost say, an Irish or

North-Welsh character, in its utter rejection of the column in favour of a system of members, square and round, continued round both jamb and arch, the round members being repeatedly banded in a way which, to the few who have made their way to so wild a spot, will at once suggest the grand doorway of Strata Florida in Cardiganshire. Having thus come down to the lower town, we flit once more to the mole and the arch of Trajan. Tall, narrow, and simple, it stands with a dignity worthy of the prince whose name it bears, a contrast alike to the rudeness of some arches of the kind and to the overdone splendour of others. No greater contrast of proportion can be found than between the arch of Augustus at Rimini and the arch of Trajan at Ancona. Difference of position may perhaps account for it. One stands by itself as a monument; the other spans a street, and is practically a gateway. The arch at Ancona has the great advantage of omitting the sham pediment, the worst of all the features of the Greek masks with which the Roman architects faced their own constructions. The actual beauty of columns goes far to excuse their presence, even when constructively they are meaningless; but the sham pediment is a mere sham, and an ugly sham; it is a sign of advance in Trajan's architect at Ancona to have got rid of it.

ROME.

THE WALLS OF ROME.

THERE are some points in which Rome herself is less Roman than many of the cities which arose under the shadow of her dominion. It is a mere accident that the peculiar style of masonry which, in our own island and in a large part of Gaul, we are accustomed to look on as specially Roman, is hardly to be found in Rome itself. The small square stones alternating with courses of brick, such as we are used to at York, Lincoln, and Anderida, are not to be seen in Rome, because they belong to a stage of construction later than the walls either of Servius or of Aurelian. Nor are they universal even in Britain; in the Great Wall itself there is no sign of them. But it is no accident that the manner of laying out a city which we are accustomed to look for in our own Roman towns is quite unlike the ground-plan of Rome itself or of any other of the older Italian cities. As Tusculum and Capua are not Roman creations, so neither is Rome herself. The specially Roman character grew out of Rome; Rome was not called into being by it. But the Roman cities in

Britain, even more than in any other part of the Empire, were distinctly Roman creations, called into being after Rome had put on her distinctive character. Rome herself, like other cities of Italy, Gaul, and elsewhere, grew out of the primitive hill-fortresses; the distinction between Rome and other cities, the distinction which made Rome all that she became, was that Rome did not grow out of a single fortress of the kind, but out of several. But our own Roman towns rose for the most part out of Roman camps, and the form of the Roman camp has been impressed for ever on the main lines of their streets, even where, as at Gloucester and Chichester, all traces of actual Roman buildings will be looked for in vain. The provincial towns, in short, were the creations of Rome in the days of her greatness; Rome herself grew up to be their creator by the slow steps by which her littleness rose into her greatness.

It is in this way that the stamp of the Roman is in one sense less felt at Rome than it is at Chester or at Aosta. Nothing can be conceived more unlike the square outline of those cities than the irregular line both of the Servian and of the Aurelian walls. Rome ceased to be *Roma Quadrata* as soon as she spread herself beyond her first home on the Palatine. The two great fortifiers of Rome, separated by so many ages, followed much the same scheme of fortification. The early King—for a King he must have been—who is represented by the legendary name of Servius Tullius, seems, beyond all doubt, to have worked into his design such of the primitive defences of the separate hills as came in his way and suited his purpose. The story is none tho less clear because we cannot fix its date.

In matters before the beginning of trustworthy chronology, historical inquirers must be satisfied to follow the method of geological inquirers. The geologist tells us that a certain stratum is older than another stratum; he does not profess to tell us how many years, or thousands of years, it is older. So in dealing with the works of unchronicled ages, we must be satisfied with saying that a certain wall is older than a certain other wall, without trying to fix how much older it is. The defences of the earliest Rome on the Palatine are perfectly plain. And it is also perfectly plain that in various parts of Rome there are pieces of early wall which do not belong either to that line of defence or to the line of Servius. There is clearly an early wall which fenced in the Palatine settlement only, and there is clearly a still early but later wall which fenced in the Palatine settlement and something else. It is only when we are told that one was made in A.U.C. 1 and the other in A.U.C. 4, that it becomes so impossible to help laughing at the dates that we are tempted most unjustly to laugh at the facts also. A settlement on the Palatine only, and a settlement taking in the

M

Palatine, the Capitoline, and, we venture to add, part
at least of the Quirinal, belong to wholly different
states of things, and they must have been separated,
not by three years, but by generations, perhaps by
centuries. Where there is no chronology, we altogether
decline to do anything more than to fix the order of
things, without making any attempt to say how long
each state of things lasted. But that several hill-forts
were worked together at an early time into a single
city, with a continuous line of defence, no candid inquirer into the antiquities of Rome can doubt for a
moment.

Servius in short, or whoever was the real builder of
the Servian wall, acted exactly as Aurelian acted ages
after. That is to say, each of them acted like rational
men. Servius found several hills which had once been
distinct settlements, but which were now thoroughly
merged into a single city. He found them provided
with defences against one another which were no longer
needed, but not provided with those defences against the
common enemy which were needed. He provided such a
common line of defence by using the old walls of the
several settlements wherever any part of them took a
direction which suited his new object, and by connecting
them by new defences of earthwork or masonry wherever
such a bond of union was needed. The manner of his
work is still to be seen. The patching is as clear in the

earlier case as in the later. In the piece of masonry in the Servian wall which is still to be seen in the railway station, we can distinctly see a piece of early wall built up against a still earlier piece. The case is exactly the same as when, at a certain point of Aurelian's wall we see the wider-jointed brickwork of his age built up against a piece of fine brickwork of the time of Nero, the remains of some building which Aurelian pressed into the service of his new line of defence. So it is throughout; the visitor at first is puzzled at finding gateways in the wall of Aurelian which bear the names of Vespasian, of Claudius, of Augustus himself. A second glance shows that these gateways are simply arches of aqueducts, which, when they spanned a road, necessarily assumed something of the character of gateways, and which were worked into the new line of defence. Aurelian in short did exactly what Servius had done under circumstances which were practically the same He found the enlarged city in much the same case in which Servius had found the original. detached settlements. The city had so outgrown the Servian wall that it had no longer any defence. Aurelian made his new line of defence by taking such buildings as served his purpose—the walls of the prætorian camp, those of the *Amphitheatrum Castrense*, pieces of the line of aqueduct, in short any earlier building, any earlier earthwork, which could in any way be made use

of. These he kept as far as they served, and he joined
them by new works into a continuous line. That the
wall of Aurelian was built throughout on an earlier line
of defence, is a theory for which we see no evidence
whatever. It is distinctly contradicted by the description given by Dionysius of the state of Rome in his
own time, when he says that Rome was then practically
unfortified, because the Servian wall was so covered
with later buildings as to be no longer any defence.
This theory of an earlier fortification along the line of
Aurelian seems to us to rest on just as little ground as
the wild notion of some Italians that the wall of Aurelian stood miles out further in the Campagna, and that
the present walls date only from the time of Honorius.

The result of this system of fortification at the two
periods was that both the earlier and the later lines
of defence took a very irregular shape. The shape of
the Servian city was as unlike as possible to the
shape of the old *Roma Quadrata;* the shape of the
city of Aurelian was as unlike as possible to anything which Aurelian himself would have laid out if
he had been founding a new colony on the Caledonian
or the German frontier. In this way Rome is less
Roman than her own children. The ideal of a Roman
city must be looked for anywhere rather than in Rome
itself. That is to say, it must not be looked for in the
Rome either of Servius or of Aurelian. We might

indeed say that the later Rome is not strictly Rome at all, but Rome *plus* the neighbouring settlements which she incorporated. To this later composite, confederate, Rome, the Roman cities in other lands bear no likeness; but we may fairly say that the first *Roma Quadrata* on the Palatine was the parent of many another *Roma Quadrata* which our fathers found only to overthrow, on the Saxon shore or on the peninsula by the stream of Deva.

Nothing in an examination of Rome is more striking, nothing better brings home to us the history of the city, than to make the circuit of its walls. Of the walls of Servius the circuit can no longer be made, but the modern walls of Rome are essentially the walls of Aurelian. In a certain sense their preservation is wonderful. It is true that the walls, as they stand, are of all dates, from Aurelian, and those whose works Aurelian made use of, down to our own day. Every siege of Rome has involved the battering down and rebuilding of some part of their vast circuit. They contain therefore work—certainly they contain materials —of every date and style, from the days of the Kings of Rome to the days of the restored kingdom of Italy. But, with all this, the wall is still the same wall; it is the wall of Aurelian, not the wall of any one earlier or later. Save on the right bank of the Tiber, where the Leonine city follows wholly new lines, the course of the walls has not been interfered with in any of its endless repairs. All those repairs, from Honorius to Victor Emmanuel, have been repairs in the strictest sense; they have been a mere making good of something which the accidents of time and warfare had destroyed or weakened. The wall is still a boundary and a barrier, and it is kept on the whole singularly free from modern encroachments. And, when we think of all that this great line of defence has gone through, we shall be more inclined to wonder that so many of the ancient gates are left to us than that some of them have given way to modern successors. On each side of the wall, within and without the city, changes have swept away many an ancient feature. The Aventine and the Appian way are desolate; but the wall itself still abides, though standing sometimes almost as solitary as the wall in our own island which fenced in, not the Roman city, but the Roman Empire.

In truth, throughout the whole history of Rome, the walls of the city are its most living monuments. The primæval wall of the oldest Rome is the most speaking monument of the days when the first Latin settlers on the Palatine had to guard themselves against Sabine enemies on the Capitoline and the Quirinal. The wall of Servius is the wall of that Rome which, already the head of Latium, grew step by step to be the head of Italy. It is the bulwark of

Rome, first against the Etruscan and the Volscian, and in after times against the Gaul, the Epeirot, and the mightier Carthaginian. And there is one spot in its circuit around which the whole history of Rome seems to gather, and where the fate of Rome was decided in the last and most fearful of all her struggles with enemies within her own peninsula. Alike by Servius and by Aurelian the north-eastern corner of the city, its weakest point by nature, was made specially strong by art. Here on the eastern side, where there was no river to embank, no cliff to scarp, ran the mighty *Agger* of Servius. Near the angle where this artificial bulwark joined the natural bulwark of the Quirinal slope, within the line of the *Agger* and defended by a vast hornwork, stood the Colline gate. This was the great entrance to that side of Rome which lay on the *Colles*, the spurs of the high ground, as distinguished from the *Montes*, the isolated hills rising from what was once the swampy ground by the river. Here was the natural point of attack for every enemy. In the early days of Rome legends tell us of fights by the Colline gate with the Volscians and the men of Tibur. Through the Colline gate the revolted army came back to overthrow the tyranny of the Decemvirs. Over the Colline gate, so the tale ran, Hannibal hurled his spear—a tale wild enough, but one which still shows at what point men looked for Hannibal to have entered Rome, if he had entered her at all. And it was by the Colline gate that Rome fought her last battle for her being against Italian enemies. It was there that Sulla saved her on the day when the last Pontius came to root up the wood which sheltered the wolves that so long had ravaged Italy. On that day Rome fought, not for dominion, but for life; she had not to fight for life again till the Colline gate and the Servian *Agger* had passed away, and till Rome had found that she needed new ramparts to shield her against new enemies.

We pass from the inner circuit to the outer, from the walls reared to shield Rome against Italian enemies to the walls reared to shield her against enemies of our own blood. The building of the still existing walls of Rome was a sign that the Wandering of the Nations had begun, that the Teutonic race had begun to play its part in the drama of human history. Those walls were raised by Aurelian when the German was not only threatening on the Rhine and the Danube, but had to be overthrown in battle on the soil of Italy. They were strengthened by Stilicho when the Goth was marching at will through the lands on both sides of the Hadriatic. From the Colline gate it is but a short step to the Salarian. Modern barbarism has swept away the actual gate through which Alaric entered Rome, but some stones are there which still stand as they stood on the night when the slumbering city was "awakened by the tremendous sound of the Gothic trumpet." But the whole of the northern and eastern side of Rome is one monument of ‚Gothic warfare. We pass out of the city, if not by the Flaminian gate, yet by its modern representative; without the wall, above the modern Borghese gardens, rose the loftiest of the seven camps of Witiges; within the wall, high on the Pincian, stood the head-quarters of Belisarius. We walk, as it were, between the besiegers and the besieged; we pass by the leaning mass of the *muro torto*, with its strange legend as old as the days of that great struggle, the point of the rampart which the Apostle himself guarded, and which, weak as it seemed, Belisarius had no need to strengthen. We pass on by a long line of wall, now unbroken by a single gate, till we reach the Salarian again. A few yards more, and we have reached the history of our own times. Between the modern Salarian and the now closed Nomentane gate we see a piece of modern wall, pierced by the modern gate of *Porta Pia*, with its flaunting inscription in honour of the present bearer of that name. In that wall we see a few yards of brickwork newer still than the rest. Hard by it hangs a garland recording the names of men who died in our own times to undo the evil work of ages; where the new wall looks newest was wrought the last deliverance of Rome. Through that breach the army of united Italy entered her capital. In that quarter the history of Rome seems indeed crowded into a small space. The army of Alaric and the army of Victor Emmanuel entered Rome almost, as it were, abreast. One entry marked the beginning of the modern world, the world which grew out of the fusion of the two elements which were represented by the Roman and the Goth. The other entry marked the readmission of Rome within that world by her deliverance from the worn-out power which crumbled away as soon as it was no longer guarded by the bayonets of a foreign tyrant. From either point we soon make our way to the elder circuit. We are again by the Colline gate; we see that for the work of Victor Emmanuel the work of Sulla was needed. On the older day the hosts of united Italy marched on Rome as against a common enemy to be wiped out. On the later day, the hosts of united Italy marched on Rome as her deliverers from an alien yoke. In the one struggle Rome fought to win back Italy as her possession; in the other struggle Italy fought to win back Rome as her head. But both scenes were parts of the same drama. In each case, though by such different means, Rome became the head of Italy. The Roman Dictator had to force the yoke of Rome upon unwilling Italy in order that the Italian King might one day free willing Rome from the yoke of the priest and the stranger.

Here indeed is history pressed into a small compass.

With Sulla and Belisarius and the men of our own day before our eyes, we hardly care to dwell on the struggles of the days between them, on the raid of Robert Wiscard or on the sack by the host of the dead Bourbon. But these, and much beside, the walls of Rome have looked on. From the oldest stone in *Roma Quadrata* to the last course of bricks laid to repair the breach of 1870, they bear their witness that the history of Rome, and with it the history of the world, is one unbroken tale.

TUSCULUM.

———•◦•———

A CITY which has twice been the rival of Rome has of itself no mean place in history. But that the history of the world should run in such cycles that Rome could, at two stages of her being, find a rival within sight of the Palatine—that the city whose borders had 'once been on the Tigris and the Solway should come again to strive on equal terms with enemies on the Alban hills—this teaches us a more instructive lesson still. Rome was the victim of her own greatness. It was because Rome had first subdued, then incorporated, the whole civilized world—because all the Mediterranean lands had been merged in Rome and all their free inhabitants had become Romans—because, as Rome was everywhere, the sovereign of Rome was as much at home at York or at Antioch, at Byzantium or at Aachen, as he was on the Palatine or the Capitol—it was directly because of all this that a day came when Rome was again a single Latin city waging war with other Latin cities. Nay more, it was because of all this that a day came when Rome stooped to receive her Bishops at the bidding of the lords of the city whose earlier lords had fought to restore her Tarquins. On the same range of hills, within sight of Rome, lay two cities by whose side Rome was young. Both were kindred cities; one, so legend said, was Rome's own metropolis. Both were swept from the earth in local warfare with Rome. But a long time indeed passed between the earlier and the later deed of destruction. One perished before trustworthy history begins; the other perished as it were yesterday, in the twelfth century of our æra. Rome, in her infancy, deemed the ruin of Alba needful for her own safety. Then came a time in which the like plea called for the ruin of Corinth and Carthage and Jerusalem. Then came again a time when her enemies were once more at her gates, and Tusculum perished as Alba had perished eighteen hundred years before. And mark too that Rome's wrath in both ages was more abiding against the nearer victims. A day came when Roman Dictators and Emperors bade Corinth and Carthage and Jerusalem rise from their ruins. No such command ever went forth to Alba or to Tusculum. Tusculum is still a forsaken ruin on its hill-top; Alba has perished so utterly that scholars dispute about its site.

The site of Tusculum does not stand out in the general view of Latium as we might have expected either from the history of the city or from the real

height and strength of the place when we reach it.
The whole range of which it forms a part is over-
shadowed by the mighty peak of the Latian Jupiter,
the temple where Marcellus triumphed, and whose
remains were swept away by the fanatical barbarism of
the last Stewart. But besides this, the Tusculan height
does not stand out in any special way from the other
heights on its own level. In the general view it
forms part of the Alban range, and that is all. But a
visit to the spot itself shows what Tusculum really
was, and it shows also why Tusculum on its height was
outstripped by its younger rival by the Tiber. The
difference simply is that one was on the height and
that the other was by the Tiber. Tusculum belongs to
the oldest class of cities, to the days when defence was
all in all, when the main object was to find a spot
strong by nature and to make it yet stronger by art.
It was a step, and a great step, in civilization when
men came down from the heights and occupied sites by
the rivers, sites in which defence was no longer all in
all, but where commerce and general convenience were
thought of also. The change from Tusculum to Rome
is the change which Homer marks between Dardaniê on
Ida and holy Ilios in the plain. Tusculum on her
mountain top might well be the head of Latium; but
she could only be the head in the sense of dominion or
pre-eminence. Perched on her own height, she could

never incorporate the towns on the lower heights around her. They might be her enemies, her subjects, or her confederates; they could never become part of her own self. It was otherwise with the lower heights by the Tiber; there the process which in the end incorporated all the Mediterranean lands could begin with the incorporation of the Palatine and Capitoline hills into one city with a common Comitium. Tusculum might, in one state of things, be the head of a Latin confederacy; in another state of things it might be the seat of Counts powerful and dreaded by their neighbours. But it could never become the head of Italy; still less could it become the head of the Mediterranean world.

The true historic position of Tusculum is thus, if the phrase be not a bull, at least as much præ-historic as historic. To many minds the name of the city would rather call up associations belonging to a time between the days of its earlier and its later fame. As a favourite dwelling-place of Cicero, as having given its name to an important portion of his works, Tusculum suggests the thoughts of times widely different from those of either its earlier or its later rivalry with Rome. But this is what we may call an accidental interest. To have formed part of the Roman state is common to Tusculum with half Europe; to have been a favourite abode of the great men of Rome is common to

Tusculum with crowds of other spots in Italy. The distinctive history of the place lies in the earlier and the later times, and in the remarkable cycle by which the mediæval position of the place repeated its præhistoric position. On a visit to the spot itself, we see the traces of all other periods: but the traces of the last of all are conspicuous only by their absence. There is the Tusculum of the Latin Dictators and the Tusculum of the Roman Consular. For the Tusculum of the Counts, the Tusculum which fought for Cæsar when Cæsar was Rome's enemy, we look in vain. The remains of the Latin and of the Roman city are there in abundance. Of the mediæval city there is not a vestige. But the very absence of such vestiges is of itself the most speaking of all witnesses to the mediæval history of the city. In the first days of Henry the Sixth Rome avenged on Tusculum the overthrow which the Roman arms had suffered at Tusculan hands in the days of his father. And the vengeance of Rome was thorough. There was no motive to root up the scanty traces of days gone by, the traces of the citadel of Mamilius or of the villa of Cicero. But the Tusculum which Rome dreaded was utterly swept away. Of house, church, or castle, such as they must have stood in the twelfth century, not a sign is left. Mediæval Tusculum has vanished; in after days the insignificant Frascati lower down the hill arose as a poor substitute for the threatening rival of Rome.

The ascent to Tusculum really begins a long way off, on the road from Rome to Frascati; but it is at Frascati that the special climb to the ancient site begins. Frascati itself, in a Roman ruin which is pointed out as the tomb of Lucullus, gives a slight instalment of what is coming. As all roads lead to Rome, so many paths, from Frascati at least, lead to Rome's rival. A guide therefore is hardly needful, unless there are any in the company who shrink from the use of their own feet. Yet the guide's presence will throw some little light on an aspect of human nature which is always curious. The guide can hardly be persuaded that you do not want to stop and see some Villa Borghese or Buonaparte, or something of the kind—among the mushroom "princes" of Rome one is not always sure to which tyrant or Pope the particular one was nephew. And he is a little surprised that you do want to stop and see the first monument of the old city to which you come, the amphitheatre which he presently proclaims to be the School of Cicero. Yet the guide has his use; if asked, he does know the ancient remains, and he can show where some of them are which the traveller will often have some difficulty in finding. The guide, in short, adapts himself to those whom he guides; he himself knows better than most of them; but, as most of them think

N

more of a modern house and garden than of the remains
of the ancient city, he assumes that the villa and not
the amphitheatre is the point at which the traveller
will wish to stop. He himself, perhaps discreetly for
himself and his beasts, tarries at the highest level of
the Roman remains, and leaves the traveller to climb the
height of the oldest Tusculum for himself.

The existing ruins naturally fall into three parts, and
the traveller must necessarily reach them in an order
which is the reverse of chronological. First in date, last
to be reached, is the highest point of the hill, the
arx or acropolis, the old primæval fortress from which
Tusculum and its Dictators looked around on a crowd of
other heights crowned by confederate or hostile cities.
The Rome of those days, when there was as yet no
cupola on the Vatican, no lofty front on the Cœlian,
no soaring campanile on the Esquiline, faintly raised
its rival towers in the distance. The *fastigium* of
Jupiter on the Capitol may have dimly shown itself, as
a distant and lowlier rival to the prouder Jupiter of the
Alban Mount. We look over the lowlands of Latium
to the sea that wrought the civilization of the ancient
world; we think perhaps of Mamilius and his vest of
purple,

> Woven in the land of sunrise
>   By Syria's dark-browed daughters,
> And by the sails of Carthage brought
>   Far o'er the southern waters.

But we think too that the gifts of that sea were open to the city by the Tiber in a way in which they were not open to the city on the height; we remember that Tusculum could never have grappled with Carthage on her own element, or have reckoned the "land of sunrise" among her provinces beyond the sea. Yet we can believe that, in the eye of the men of earlier times, the *arx* of Tusculum on its mountain height may have seemed to have a right to look down with scorn on the fortresses on the Palatine and the Capitoline, mere molehills by the side of the river. The height was a citadel formed by nature, so steep and rocky that the greater part of its circuit needed no artificial defences. Its very gateway was already made; the men who first fortified the height had merely to hang their gate—the socket may still be seen—between two masses of rock which stood ready to receive it. On one side only, and that ominously the Rome-ward side, the hill is less steep and rugged, and there alone vestiges can be traced of a wall of massive square stones, like the earliest walls of Rome, and of a gate and approach made by the hand of man. The height of Tusculum was a point exactly fitted for the settlement of a primitive people in præ-historic times; it was no less fitted in after times to become the vulture's nest of a robber noble. But, small as are the traces of the wall of the Tusculan Dictators, some traces there still are, while

of the works of the Tusculan Counts not a stone is
left.

Within the *arx* the foundations of several buildings
can be traced, and the sides of the hill are honeycombed
with grottoes, chambers, whatever one chooses to call
them, in a way which reminds one of Nottingham
Castle. But the best preserved Roman remains, and
what is, after all, the most remarkable remnant of the
ante-Roman city, are found on the lower level. There
are the theatre, the reservoir, the odd little set of semi-
circular steps which some call a "children's theatre,"
and others, more reasonably, a lecture-room ; there is the
open space that was the forum, and a mass of sculpture
and architectural details may be seen built up into a
modern but forsaken house. All these things are plain
enough to be seen ; but the traveller might easily miss
something which is far more precious than any of them.
To the left of the theatre, as we go upwards, a little way
down the steep and rugged path up which Macaulay leads
the dark-grey charger of Mamilius, is a grand fragment
of the town-wall ; and, better than all, there is an undoubted monument of primitive times in a chamber
roofed, like the Tullianum at Rome, not with the real,
but with the apparent, arch. It is one of those examples of that striving after the arch, before its full
construction was reached, of which there are so many
examples in early works in Italy, Greece, and elsewhere.

And here, as in many other cases, the form which the apparent arch takes is not round but pointed ; the guide points to it as "arco Gotico." It is not beyond the bounds of possibility that some may believe that it is the work of Alaric or Totilas. It proves, like so many other examples, that the mere form of the pointed arch is at least as old as the round. But it was not till a good deal more than a millennium after the first days of Tusculum that the Saracen first learned to use it as the main constructive feature of great buildings, and it was not till some centuries later again that the architects of north-western Europe provided it with an appropriate form of moulding and ornament. We come up again to the level of the theatre, we pass along the ancient pavement, we mark the wheel-tracks which may have been made by the wheels of Cicero, we pass the ruins of what calls itself his villa, we come again to the amphitheatre, and our visit to Tusculum is done. We have seen the memorials of the Dictators, and we need not look for the memorials of the Counts. We see that mediæval Rome had at least not forgotten the art of Mummius, that she could still sweep with the besom of destruction, when vengeance or policy called for the utter rooting-up of a rival.

BASILICAN CHURCHES.

————◆◇◆————

THE shape and arrangements which, from the days
of Constantine onwards, have been usual in churches
throughout Western Christendom, are in themselves
the greatest of all triumphs of the new creed over
the old. We say creed, for the paganism which
Christianity had in the end to strive against and to over-
come really was a creed. Julian, Libanios, Zôsimos,
strove for a system which was to them, no mere poetic
fiction, no mere affair of state, but as truly a system of
faith and morals as the creed of their Christian adver-
saries. Christianity had to strive at once against the
superstition of the mere mob, against the political traditions of Romans of the old school, and against the
convictions of those with whom paganism was a real
religion. These last hated Christianity; but they
learned from it while hating it. The preaching of
Christianity reformed paganism, just as the preaching
of the Reformation reformed the Church of Rome.
Julian is to Caracalla and Gallienus what Sixtus the
Fifth is to the Borgias and the Medici. An ordinary

Roman Emperor or senator had doubtless no such deep faith in Jupiter Optimus Maximus as Julian had in his Hellenic deities. But Jupiter Optimus Maximus had so long formed a part of the very being of the Emperor, Senate, and People of Rome that it seemed to him that he who spoke against Jupiter could not be the friend of Cæsar. Christianity had to strive against both these forms of enmity, and it overcame both. Philosophic paganism died out; it was soon found that Christianity itself supplied room enough for both the higher and the lower parts of such a character as Julian's. Political paganism grew into political Christianity; the names of Christ and Cæsar became as inseparably bound together as the names of Jupiter and Cæsar once had been. It was indeed in the East rather than the West that this state of things attained its fullest developement; in the West the absence of the Emperors from Rome allowed the Popes to grow as their brethren of Constantinople never grew. Still the real Roman feeling must have been stronger in Rome, Italy, and the West generally than it ever could have been in the East. And, in the West as well as in the East, Christianity in the end triumphed over both forms of opposition. And no-where is the record of that triumph more legibly written than on the existing buildings of Rome herself.

The architectural monuments of earlier times which supplied the models and the materials for the early

Christian buildings fall mainly under two heads, which
answer to the two classes of enemies against which the
new faith had had to strive. These were the pagan
temples and the great secular buildings, the basilicas.
The new builders made free use of both, but they made use
of them in different ways. The temples were freely used
for materials; their columns were constantly set up
again in Christian churches; but the employment of an
existing temple without change as a Christian church
was always rare; and it was only an exceptional class
of temples which affected the arrangements of an
exceptional class of churches. Round temples, as
well as sepulchral monuments, had a share in the
parentage of that class of round and octagonal
churches which, though at all times comparatively
rare, have at all times gone on side by side with the
more usual forms. The Pantheon and the so-called
Temple of Minerva Medica, as well as the tomb of
Cæcilia Metella, doubtless had their effect on St. Vital
and Brescia, on Aachen and St. Gereon, on the Temple
Church and Little Maplestead, as well as on a long list
of baptisteries and sepulchral churches, including all
the churches of the Holy Sepulchre, whether at Jerusalem, Bologna, Cambridge, or Northampton. We see
the Pantheon itself consecrated as a Christian church,
as if to show how little suited for that purpose the
unaltered circular form was. We have the sepulchral

church which goes by the name of St. Constantia—the tomb which was the centre of its design and ornament has been stolen to stand as number this or that among the curiosities of a papal museum—where the inner range of coupled columns and arches brings us many degrees nearer to Aachen and the Sepulchre churches. And we have the wonderful church of St. Stephen on the Cœlian, with its three concentric circles—the outer one now shut out from the building—and the strange but bold triplet of arches built across the middle.

But buildings of this kind, though numerous enough to be ranked as a class by themselves, were still always a minority. Among all the churches in Rome, among all the remains of temples, the Pantheon is the only temple which was turned into a church in early times without change or mutilation. Such cases as the Temple of Faustina and the neighbouring temple which forms part of the church of St. Cosmas and St. Damian are after all mere cases of adaptation of fragments. The dedication of small temples like the two, round and oblong, called each by many conjectural names, which stand between the House of Crescentius and the church of St. Mary in Cosmedin was really little more than a pious freak of later times. Though many churches in Rome, like those just mentioned, have risen on the sites of temples and have preserved parts of temples in their structure, there is no case of a large oblong temple

in use as a church, as the Parthenon and the Temple of
Theseus were once used at Athens. The fact is that
the ordinary form of temple was not at all suited for
the purposes of Christian worship; the pagan temple
was all outside, the Christian church was all inside.
Temples were therefore freely destroyed to build
churches out of their remains; but the use of an actual
temple as a church was rare, and temple architecture
had no direct effect upon the arrangements of Christian
churches.

It was far different with the other class of buildings,
the buildings which symbolized, not the heathen creed
of the elder Rome, but the dominion of the Senate and
People and of their master. If the temple was unsuited
to Christian purposes, the basilica, the hall of justice,
was of all buildings the best suited. The basilica was
in fact the temple turned inside out. As the temple
consisted of a walled building surrounded by external
colonnades, so the basilica consisted of internal colonnades placed inside a walled building. Exactly as in
the temple, the colonnades in their various forms long
remained the only architectural feature, and it was a
standing difficulty to know what to do with either the
outside or the roof. Both at Rome and at Ravenna
we are constantly struck by the mean and shapeless
outsides of buildings which are of a truth all
glorious within. It is only in St. Apollinaris at Classis

that we meet with the first feeble approach to the later Romanesque forms of external ornament. But the temple thus turned inside out became, in the form of the basilica, exactly what was needed for Christian uses. There was the long nave ready to receive congregations which needed to assemble within and not without their houses of worship. There was the apse or tribune with its rows of official seats, ready to become the official seats of the bishop and his clergy; there were the *cancelli* ready made to part off the holier part of the building from the less holy. In those basilicas which had the *chalcidice* or transept, the symbolical form of the cross was already impressed on the buildings in heathen times. The basilica was in every point a ready-made church; it could at once be used as such, and it could become the model of new churches built after its likeness. And out of the basilica have grown all the forms of churches commonly used in Western Europe. The main internal features of all are the same; the chief difference is that Northern architects learned to give their buildings an external outline to which Italy even in its best days, in the days of Pisa and Lucca, always remained a stranger. The bell-tower, which in Italy stood apart, became part of the building, and was multiplied in number; the crossing, unmarked in the ancient basilica, was marked by the central cupola or tower. By these means the unadorned outside of the

old basilica grew into the varied outlines of Caen and
Ely and Lichfield, and into the outlines more varied
still of Worms and Bamberg and Gelnhausen.

To have thus turned the basilica to Christian uses
was almost a greater triumph than to have done the
like by pagan temples.   To destroy the temples and to
consecrate the basilicas was the most speaking expression of the facts that the pagan worship had come to
an end and that the Empire itself had become Christian.
When the seat whence the heathen judge had handed
over the martyr to the sword or to the lions became
the seat from which the Bishop arose to celebrate the
Christian mysteries, no more speaking embodiment could
be needed of the triumphant climax, "Christus vincit,
Christus regnat, Christus imperat."   It was a sign that
the Roman Empire was beginning to deserve its later
title of Holy, a sign that the Chief Pontiff of idols was
passing into the Advocate of the Universal Church.
Whether any building now exists which has served as
a basilica both in the heathen and the Christian sense
of the word may well be doubted; but that the
Christian church borrowed all its arrangements from
the heathen hall of judgement there can be no doubt.
They are as clearly marked, to the very *cancelli*, in the
small but most elegant *Basilica Jovis* on the Palatine
as in the most fully developed Christian building.   The
chief alteration which the basilican type received at the

hands of Christian builders was one purely architectural —the great invention of Diocletian, the discovery that the column might be used as the support of the arch.

The heathen basilicas followed two systems of construction; the division between the nave and its aisles might be made either by columns supporting an entablature, as in the *Basilica Jovis*, or by massive piers supporting arches, as in the Julian basilica and in that of Maxentius or Constantine, whichever it is to be called. The latter of these seems the natural prototype of the more massive Romanesque forms of Germany and Northern Italy; but we do not find it used in the basilican churches either of Rome or of Ravenna. Its great advantage was that it allowed the building to be vaulted—witness the mighty vaults of the basilica of Constantine—which could hardly be the case either when the building followed the Greek construction or when the arches rested on columns. This last, in its various shapes, became the received form; but it is wonderful how hard a fight the Greek construction made. Spalato first beheld the experiment. Diocletian or his architect boldly set the arch to rest at once on the capital of the column, and thereby planted the germ which was to grow into all arched architecture, Romanesque, Saracenic, and Gothic. The arcades of the peristyle at Spalato look like the arcades of a basilica standing out of doors, and asking to be taken inside the building. At

Rome and at Ravenna they find shelter. At Ravenna the entablature is nowhere used; the columns always support arches, though always with that intervening stilt which is the characteristic of the local style of that city. But at Rome, under the influence of the vast stores of heathen buildings, some of the greatest basilicas still kept the construction of the entablature. To mention, for the present, no other cases, it was so in the nave of the old St. Peter's, the Vatican Basilica, and it is so still in the great Liberian Basilica, better known as *Sta. Maria Maggiore*. But the arcade is clearly so far better suited for the uses of a church, or indeed for the internal uses of almost any building of any kind, that the other construction seems to have remained in use only in Rome, where the architects must have been, more than anywhere else, under the strongest influence of classical models. Elsewhere the arcade resting on columns became the universal use, and even in Rome it became more usual than its rival. Gradually, as the architects became more alive to the capacities of the form of construction which they had now worked out, the columns no longer gathered so timidly together as they do in the earlier examples, but began to stand further apart, and to support arches of greater span, as we see in the basilican churches of Lucca as compared with those of Ravenna. At Lucca also we have seen the column in certain positions supplanted by a square pier, which has nothing in common with the massive square piers of the German churches, being hardly thicker than the column itself. Still it is the column—if possible, the marble monolith column of classical type—which is the proper support of the arches in a basilican church. The column, which had been brought into artistic being as the support of the external entablature of the Grecian temple, had thus worked out for itself a use no less elegant, no less appropriate, when it became the support of the internal arcades of the Christian church.

But there was another step to be taken. As long as the arches rested on columns, so long the roof ever remained the great difficulty and the weakest point of the building. It had to keep its naked construction of tie-beams and rafters, which the architects of those days had not learned, like English architects of a far later day, to work into an ornamental form. The only other alternative was to hide the construction by a flat ceiling. The noblest form of roof, the stone vault, called for something more massive than the column as its support. The column and the vault could be used together only in cases like crypts, where a great number of columns support a vault and nothing more. In the main fabric of the church the vault and the column could not be used together, and, as the most perfect form of roof came more and more into use, the most graceful form of support for the arcades was necessarily laid aside.

We have said that all the later arrangements of
churches grew out of the basilica. As long as round-
arched architecture of any type remained in use, the
round apse was the direct successor of the tribune of the
basilica ; and in a great number of continental churches
the tradition of placing the seats of the clergy behind
the altar has lingered on in various corrupted forms.
It can keep its primitive effect only when the altar
is unencumbered by those monstrous excrescences of
later times with which most French and Italian altars
are disfigured. The change from the round to the polygonal apse was simply the necessary result of the
change from the round to the pointed arch. In Germany the single polygonal apse, as simple in its ground
plan as the round apse of the basilica, remained commonly in use. We see it on a gigantic scale at Aachen.
In France the habit of surrounding the great apse
with smaller apses, which began in Romanesque times,
and which was a natural result of the multiplication of
altars, grew into such east ends as Amiens, Rheims, and
St. Ouen's, as Köln, Westminster, and Tewkesbury
in other lands. We have now reached something
widely different indeed from the tribune of the *Basilica
Jovis*, and from the apses of St. Apollinaris and St.
Ambrose; but the steps by which one grew out of the
other are plain enough to see.

In the like sort, the constructive choir, which forms

so important a feature in most later churches, great and small, grew out of what in the ancient basilicas was a feature, not of construction, but of arrangement. While the Bishop and his priests occupied the seats behind the altar, the humbler ministers of the church had their places in the *chorus cantorum* in front of it. As has been pointed out over and over again, we see this arrangement in its perfection in St. Clement's at Rome, where the choir is fenced in by a low wall which does not stretch across the church. But it has not been so generally observed that a fashion set in very early of marking the extent of this part of the church by something in the architecture, by giving the columns or other piers at this point some character special to themselves, distinguishing them from those on either side of them. This we have marked at Lucca, and it may be seen in more than one church at Rome. The transition from this is very easy to churches like Westminster, Llandaff, Norwich, and St. Albans, and again to a vast number of our latest English parish churches, where nave and choir form one architectural whole, the distinction being made merely by screens and the like. And the more familiar form, in which the choir has a distinct architectural being, is again produced by a modification of another feature of the basilican type. The *chalcidice* or transept is always rather an awkward feature in a basilica : it is too distinctly at cross-purposes to the

O

nave and apse, and it is in no way fused into one whole with them. The Romanesque architects, by moving the tower or cupola to the centre of the church, at once gave the transept a meaning and made it part of one whole with the rest of the building. When the choir had once begun to be a marked feature in the building, it was a natural stage to make the transept and what the transept supports become the division between the nave and the choir. That is to say, the choir was placed east of the transept, as in most of our later cathedral and other great churches. The apse now became a mere finish to the choir, and in England it was commonly left out altogether. We have thus reached an arrangement yet further away from that of the basilica than the arrangement of the many-apsed churches of France. But here too the steps by which one grew out of the other are perfectly clear.

THE GREAT ROMAN BASILICAS.

WE spoke a little time back of the characteristic features of the ancient basilicas, and of the type of church which grew immediately out of them; and we showed also how all the arrangements of later churches, Romanesque and Gothic, even those which have gone furthest away from the original model, were developed, step by step, out of that one primitive pattern. We then dealt with the subject generally; but the churches of the city where the basilican forms were first applied to Christian uses, that is, the basilican churches of Rome itself, may fairly call for some special notice. At Rome the name "basilica" is commonly understood as the distinguishing title of certain churches of special dignity, without regard to their architecture or arrangements. And the name is often applied in the same way both by mediæval and modern writers to churches of special dignity or antiquity elsewhere. But the word is needed as a technical term, to express a particular type of church, that namely which follows the arrangements of the original basilica, a type of which in Italy,

Rome, Ravenna, and Lucca supply the best examples. It will therefore be convenient, even in dealing with Roman buildings, to extend the name to all churches of the basilican type, to all churches to which we should freely give the name elsewhere, whether it strictly belongs to them in Roman ecclesiastical topography or not.

The higher the dignity of a church in Rome the more unlucky has been its fate. The fury with which the Popes and Popes' nephews of the last four centuries have raged against the ancient buildings of their city, heathen and Christian alike, has reached its highest point in the case of the churches with which they have had most to do. In the smaller and more distant churches something has been spared. Some Pope or other has commonly destroyed the character of the outside; his infallible taste has also in most cases gone a long way to disfigure roofs and walls within; and a boastful inscription is sure to record the often very obscure name of the doer of the mischief. But in the smaller churches the columns and the mosaics of the apse have commonly had some mercy shown to them. Otherwise the works of early Emperors and' Bishops, works, some of them, which Alaric had spared and Theodoric restored, have perished, or worse than perished, at the hands of some Farnese, Borghese, or Barberino, or any other of the names which a visit to

Rome teaches us to loathe. At their own gates of course destruction has reached its height. In vulgar estimation, in Papal estimation, the Vatican Basilica, the church of St. Peter, has eclipsed the Mother Church of the City and of the World. The Bishops of Rome have forsaken their ancient church and home, and he who visits the lovely cloister of St. John Lateran may there see the patriarchal chair of Western Christendom cast forth as an useless thing, while he who should fill it sulks in a distant palace, refusing to be Bishop because he can no longer be King. But, precisely because the Bishops of Rome have forsaken their proper home by their own church, for that very reason the havoc at St. John Lateran has been one degree less destructive than the havoc at St. Peter's. The patriarchal church has been diligently and elaborately disfigured in detail; but it does keep something like its original shape and proportion; the apsidal mosaic and some of the smaller columns have been spared. There is therefore some kind of continuity between the church of Constantine and the building which we now see. But at St. Peter's all connexion with the past is lost; the crowning-place of Emperors has utterly vanished to make way for a pile devoted only to the glorification of Popes.

Of the modern St. Peter's a thousand critics have spoken, and we perceive that in the tourist mind

it is received as a kind of moral duty to look on the
Vatican Basilica as the noblest church in the world.
We saw a small book of travels the other day in which
the writer, after going through several cities of Italy,
is on the point of declaring St. Vital at Ravenna to be
the finest thing that he had seen on his journey. But
he checks himself, and puts in a proviso that of course
he only means after St. Peter's. This is not a bad
case of a man's natural sense revolting against the
dogmas of his guide or his guide-book. St. Peter's
and St. Vital have really so little in common that
any comparison between them would be unfair; but
the same limitation would most likely have been put
in as a matter of duty, if the rivalry had been between
St. Peter's and the basilica of the brother Apostle
beyond the walls. Now, assuming the modern St. Paul
as a fair representation of the pile which it succeeded,
such a comparison would be by no means unfair. Let
us premise that we are not going to maintain any such
paradox as to deny either the real majesty of the interior
of St. Peter's, the great triumph, both constructive and
æsthetic, of its cupola, or the external grandeur of
the cupola from without, wherever it can be seen—
that is, only when we have got a very long way off from it.
But we must be allowed to hold that it is no triumph
of art elaborately to hide such a structure when it is
once made, and we think that Brunelleschi's cupola

at Florence, rising boldly in the sight of all men above its supporting apses, is as far superior to St. Peter's without as it certainly is inferior within. The west —that is, the east—front of St. Peter's really might not be the front of a church at all. It would be unfair to compare an Italian church with Peterborough or York or Abbeville; but think of Verona, Lucca, and Pisa, and see what Italian art could come to under the patronage of a Borghese.

But the point on which we wish specially to insist at St. Peter's is one which concerns the inside. Everybody who goes into the church complains that at first sight it does not look so large as he expected to find it, or as it really is. Everybody, learned or unlearned, makes the same remark. Now the regulation answer is that it is the perfection of its proportions which makes the church look small. Such an answer is nonsense. Proportions which take off from the apparent size, and therefore from the dignity, of a building are in their own nature disproportions. It is certainly hard, on entering St. Peter's, to believe that we are in a church which is longer than St. Albans and higher than Amiens. The reason is that the architects of St. Albans and Amiens knew what to do with their length and their height, while the architects of St. Peter's did not know what to do with theirs. It is all the difference between the *magnifying* and the *multi-*

plying principle. At St. Peter's four arches of enormous height and enormous span occupy a length which in an ancient basilica would have been occupied by twenty arches. The necessary result is that, while both an ancient basilica and a mediæval church does full justice to its own length, St. Peter's looks a great deal shorter than it really is. So it is with the height; the space which a mediæval architect would have cut up into three or four stages makes only one stage at St. Peter's; therefore St. Peter's looks a great deal lower than it really is. Lofty pillars, with little or no triforium and a low clerestory, will often give a great effect of height, as at Milan Cathedral and in many of our Perpendicular churches. But at St. Peter's there are no lofty pillars, only enormous piers. There is nothing to carry the eye vertically; there is nothing to carry it horizontally. Nor is there anything for the eye to rest on as the expression of mere repose, as in the Norman and German Romanesque. The colossal statues again help to take off from the effect of size. So does the huge *baldacchino* of the misplaced high altar, while the apse, so glorious at Torcello, is thrown into insignificance. The main fault is indeed not peculiar to St. Peter's or to the style in which St. Peter's is built. This fashion of getting rid of the effect of vast spaces by dividing them among too small a number of members is one which the *Renaissance* inherited from the pseudo-Gothic of Italy. It is exactly the same in Arnolfo's nave at Florence; it is exactly the same in most of the famous pointed churches of Italy, save at Milan, where the German architect was able to produce so much nearer an approach to the true proportion and effect of a Gothic building. In the nave of Florence the effect of positively great height and length is wholly lost by making the nave of a few broad sprawling arches, instead of double the number of narrower ones. And the effect there is even worse than at St. Peter's, because there is nothing at St. Peter's which specially reminds us of anything better, while the pointed arches at Florence force on us the comparison with the true pointed buildings of England, Germany, and France. But both at Florence and at St. Peter's every pains has been taken to give a really vast church an appearance of far less size than it really has.

What has been done in the Vatican Basilica has been done also, though not quite in the same fulness, in the patriarchal church itself. No one would think that St. John Lateran is anything like so long as it really is. Papal barbarism has destroyed the long unbroken range of its mighty columns, and the length is further intruded on by the huge high altar and its accompaniments. The consequence is that St. John's too looks smaller than it is. Still here the lover of antiquity may comfort

himself with a few things in the retrochoir and the
cloister; at St. Peter's a man must go underground to
see the glorious objects which adorned the ancient
church, but which the destroying Pontiffs of modern
times thought worthy of nothing but to be stowed away
in the dark. There is the exquisite sarcophagus of
Junius Bassus, one of the loveliest specimens of early
Christian art. There is the one Imperial tomb which
Rome still shelters, the resting-place—we fear, the rifled
resting-place—of the second Otto, thrust down by
papal envy from his lawful place in front of his own
Imperial church. There are the tombs of a long line of
Pontiffs who had a history, but who seem to be deemed
less worthy of memory than their obscure successors
whose names flaunt on every ugly building of modern
Rome. It would seem that to no human creature is
beauty or antiquity so hateful as it is to a Pope or a
Pope's nephew.   .

At the same time we must make one exception in
favour even of the living author of the dogma of infal-
libility. One is disgusted at every corner in Rome
with fulsome inscriptions in honour of Pius the Ninth.
In some of them indeed, as in the case of many of his predecessors, the mind of the flatterers seems to have been
slightly confused between the Roman Jupiter and the
Roman Bishop, so that the simple "Præsul" or "Papa"
of earlier times grows into the somewhat heathenish-

sounding title of "Pontifex Optimus Maximus." Still
we must not forget that the present Pope has had
a hand in the great work of the restored basilica of
St. Paul. We have a vague notion that some part of
its vast length has been sacrificed, that the ancient
building was an arch or two longer than the present one.
Still, even if this be so, the reproduction is close enough
to make us understand, better than we can anywhere
else, what an arcaded basilica of the first class really
was, and how glorious a type of church it was that the
first Christian architects wrought out of their heathen
models. St. Paul's is the exact contrast to the basilica
of the brother Apostle. Here too something has been
done in the way of disfigurement in the shape of a
modern *baldacchino* overtopping the ancient one; but
we still have the endless rows of marble columns with
their arches, four or five of them answering to a single
arch of St. Peter's. What is the result? Simply that
not an inch of the length is lost; the building impresses
the eye with its full majesty; no one complains that
St. Paul's looks smaller than he expected to find it. Of
course St. Paul's lacks the cupola; but the cupola and
the basilican nave cannot be really fused together into
a harmonious whole. Pisa itself proves this; where
the cupola is, it should be all in all, as in the three
generations of St. Sophia, St. Mark, and St. Front.

But we can best call up the effect of the old St.

Peter's, the crowning-place of Charles and Otto, by looking at another of the great Roman churches, the Liberian Basilica or *Sta. Maria Maggiore*. Here, as in the central colonnades of the old St. Peter's, we find the purely Greek construction of the column and entablature applied to the inside of a church. To a Northern eye the arrangement is strange and unpleasing, and it can hardly be justified on any principle. The Greek entablature was meant simply to support its own pediment, not to carry a wall as high as the columns themselves. Yet the arrangement is not without striking effects. Nowhere does the effect of mere length come out as it does in the church of Liberius, in defiance of every barbarous interruption. Here an intercolumniation or two is blocked up to receive big images of Popes; here an arch is cut through the entablature because a Pope took a fancy to disfigure the building with a gaudy chapel; here the nave is defrauded of its proper proportion by the intrusive canopy of the great altar. Still the strong horizontal line asserts its supremacy, and gives the building that effect of vast unbroken length which is lacking alike in the new St. Peter's and in St. John Lateran in its present disfigured state. The Liberian Basilica is in fact the truest relic of the earliest type of church to be found among the great churches of Rome. St. Peter's is gone; St. Paul's exists only in a figure; the patriarchal church has been the victim of the barbarous sport of Popes and their architects; but the greater church of St. Mary is there to show what a Christian church looked like in the days of the first triumph of the faith. Of course we speak only of the inside. No building was ever more barbarously disfigured by papal abominations without. In short, for four hundred years, as an all but invariable rule, where a Pope has touched, he has destroyed. Why did the Popes not stay at Avignon, where there was less to spoil? Why did they ever come back to Rome on their errand of havoc and disfigurement?

THE LESSER CHURCHES OF ROME.

WE have spoken of the basilican type of church in general, and of some of those great churches in Rome to which the name of basilica is applied in a special sense. But, after the havoc which the greater buildings have undergone, almost more may be learned from those smaller buildings—including some which technically rank as basilicas and some which do not— on which the hand of papal devastation has on the whole fallen less heavily. In the case of the smaller churches the destroyers have commonly been contented with disfiguring the outside, sticking up some fulsome inscription to record the munificence of the disfigurer, and spoiling the inside as far as may be by incongruous attempts at ornament. But the main features, the columns with their arcades or entablatures, have, with a few exceptions, been spared, and the apse with its mosaics has very commonly been spared also. Hence many a church which looks most unpromising without will be found to contain rich stores of instruction within, and it may be laid down as a practical rule

at Rome, and indeed in Italy generally, to pass
nothing by simply because the outside is unattractive.

It is not easy to throw oneself into the position of
the disfigurers of the ancient Roman buildings. We
can understand how—especially at Rome—men may
have preferred classical to mediæval architecture, and
may have thought it a good work to make the one
give way to the other. We can understand a man
thinking a monolith column with a Corinthian capital
a fairer object than the richest cluster at Lincoln or
Ely. The truth of course is that each is equally
beautiful, equally fitting, in its proper place. But the
strange thing is that a man should think that he was
working an improvement by taking away or hiding the
columns of St. John Lateran to put masses of Jesuitical
ugliness in their room. And it is no less strange that
even a Pope should think it worth while to commemorate such an achievement as cutting through
the original round-headed windows of the famous
church of St. Clement to stick in hideous square things
instead. Yet a later Clement—we forget his number,
but we felt inclined to turn Clement into Inclement—
has thus barbarously dealt with the church of his
apostolic namesake. Still St. Clement has not suffered like the patriarchal church. The columns are
there ; the primitive arrangements are there ; nay
the earlier church is there below, and the temple, or

whatever it was, of Mithras is below that. Rome
contains so much that even a succession of *Renaissance*
Popes could not destroy everything; their wasting
fury has mainly spent itself on the greatest objects
of their city, and the smaller buildings, with their rich
stores of art and history, have thus escaped comparatively unhurt.

The Christian basilicas, as we have already set
forth, arose largely out of the spoils of heathen
buildings, and not uncommonly on the sites of heathen
temples. The columns of the churches were commonly
the columns of earlier buildings used up again. But
their architects seem seldom to have made use of the
columns of the temples on the site of which they were
building. The fact is that the columns of the temples
were seldom suited for that purpose. The columns of
the portico of a temple, columns which, with their
entablature, made up the full height of the wall, were
too lofty to be employed in the inside of any church
except one on the very greatest scale. Translated to
the inside of the basilica, the column had to bear its
arch, perhaps a stilt between its abacus and the arch,
to bear the clerestory range above, and the space
between arcade and clerestory devoted to mosaics or
other kinds of enrichment. Sometimes again, in the
Christian, as in the heathen, basilica there was one
arcade or colonnade above another. Smaller columns

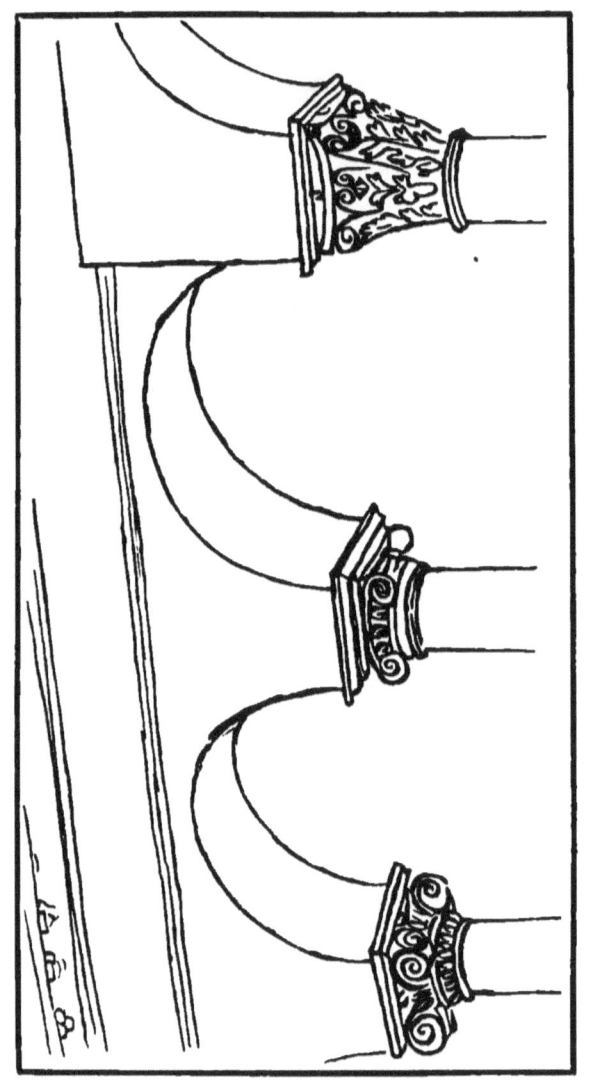

CAPITALS, ST. NICOLAS IN CARCERE, ROME.

To face page 209.

than those of the temples had therefore to be used for all but the very greatest churches. Of this comes the curious sight of churches built on the sites of ancient temples, out of the spoils of ancient temples, but where the columns of the temples on whose site they stand remain unused and embedded in the walls. This may be seen at St. Mary *in Cosmedin*, where five stately columns of the original temple are built up in the western and northern walls. It is almost more striking at St. Nicolas *in Carcere*, where the church—one of no great size—takes in parts of three neighbouring temples, with columns of different orders. In both churches the arcades rest on much smaller columns, doubtless brought from elsewhere. Had the columns of the original porticos been used for the churches, the churches must have been built on the scale of the Lateran or the Vatican basilica.

The different churches made up in this way out of heathen fragments show widely differing degrees of skill in the way in which the fragments are worked together. A range has to be made in which the arches must spring from the same level, while the columns which serve to support them are often of different sizes, very often of different orders, and therefore with shafts of different proportions and capitals of different forms. Add to this that at Rome, as at Ravenna, the need was often felt of putting in a new member, the

P

stilt or its equivalent, between the abacus of the capital
and the actual springing of the arch. Sometimes all
this is done in a very rude and inartistic way. Thus
at St. George *in Velabro* the arches hang in the most
awkward way over the capitals of various kinds, with
or without stilts; and some slender columns with
Corinthian capitals are cruelly set to support a wide
projecting mass, after the fashion of the market-place
at Verona. In other cases the work is done far more
skilfully. The arch, the stilt, if there be any, and the
capital itself, are all worked harmoniously together.
Any inequality in the height of the columns is often
got over by making a difference in the bases, where
it strikes the eye less than it does in the capitals.
This is done with one of the columns in the small
church of St. Bartholomew-in-the-Island, said to be
the work of the Emperor Otto the Third. It is but
a small building; but so much as has escaped the
disfiguring hands of Popes and Cardinals is worthy
to have been the work of the Wonder of the World.
Two fine arcades, with Composite columns well fitted
to their arches, form the main feature. In other cases
where columns and capitals of different kinds are
used, those opposite to one another are often made to
match. Ionic capitals are often set opposite Ionic,
Corinthian opposite Corinthian, plain shafts opposite
plain, and fluted opposite fluted. This nowhere comes

out better than in the beautiful basilica of St. Agnes-without-the-Walls, a building remarkable on many grounds. This church has a gallery round three sides, which follows the same arrangements of columns and arches as the higher stage below. Allowing for the difference between classical columns and massive square piers, the arrangement is exactly the same as that of the Great Minster at Zürich. In the upper range there is a great variety in the columns; but plain, fluted, twisted shafts carefully answer to one another. In this way the basilican architecture gets some share in that diversity in uniformity, or uniformity in diversity, which distinguishes mediæval from classical art.

But the pairs of columns at St. Agnes lead us to another way in which this same kind of diversity in uniformity is sought after with a practical object. Though the primitive choir did not, like the mediæval choir, stretch across the whole church from pillar to pillar, though it was not marked off by any great architectural feature like our chancel-arches—the successors of the arch of triumph moved westward — yet there clearly was a wish to mark, in the building itself, and not merely in the arrangement of the *cancelli*, the point to which the choir was meant to reach. This was often done by marking its extent by some difference in the architecture at that point, by breaking the continuous range of columns by a square pier, by using

P 2

a pair of columns at that point different from the
rest of the range, or by any other means which might
come into the architect's head. Thus at St. Agnes
the extent of the choir is marked by a fluted column
on each side, the only pair of that form in the lower
range. The breaking of the continuous range by a square
pier at this point has been already noticed at Lucca, and
it comes out very conspicuously in the famous upper
church of St. Clement. This is the building where
the primitive arrangement of the *chorus cantorum* in
front of the altar is better preserved than anywhere
else. And in St. Mary *in Cosmedin*, though the actual
arrangement of the choir is less perfectly preserved
than in St. Clement, its effect on the arrangements of
the structure is yet more marked. Instead of a continuous arcade, we have in this church a range in
which three groups of arches are divided by two
massive pieces of wall. The altar stands in its proper
place on the chord of the apse; its steps are marked
by a group of three arches on each side; the *ambones*
stand against a massive pier; four arches again mark
the extent of the choir; then another massive pier
and four more arches to the west. In the centre
of the eastern group of four arches a pair of fluted
columns, with plain ones on each side of them, stand
opposite to each other. In the centre of the western
group two capitals wrought with figures stand opposite

to each other, while all the other capitals in the church are Corinthian of different degrees of goodness and badness. From this there is only one step to the spanning arches which at St. Praxedes cut through the line of the entablature, the forerunners of the glories of St. Zeno.

St. Agnes is in every way one of the most pleasing of the Roman churches, and it is still more important as supplying the key to the original state of a far more wonderful building, the great church of St. Lawrence-without-the-Walls. Here, on passing from the portico into the present nave, we are staggered to find the purely Greek construction with the column and entablature applied to the inside of a church so late as the days of Honorius the Fourth, the adversary of Frederick the Second. We are hardly less staggered to find the altar standing, without any apse or triumphal arch, against a flat east end—we use the word " east " conventionally — with a gallery like that at the west end of St. Agnes. Nor is it much less wonderful in a Roman church to find that altar at the end of a long raised choir, parted off from the nave by an arch after the manner of churches north of the Alps. The key to all this is to be found in one of the strangest transformations that any church ever went through. The present choir is in truth the original church, a church which in its first estate must have had much in common with St. Agnes. As at St. Agnes, there was a gallery round three sides, including the conventional west or end of entrance, while the altar was approached as usual by an arch of triumph. But in the thirteenth century, the church was, so to speak, turned round, like St. Frediano at Lucca; the apse was pulled down; a nave was built where it had stood, and the original church was turned into the choir. The arch of triumph thus becomes a chancel-arch in the English sense, leading into what is now the choir. The altar, with the Bishop's throne behind it, is necessarily moved to the (conventional) west end of the original church, now become the (conventional) east. In this choir the gallery takes the form of an arcade, resting on a lower stage which consists of noble fluted Corinthian columns. These support an entablature, one pair alone having capitals introducing human figures. The greater part of the height of the columns is hidden by the arrangements of the choir, and their full proportion can be seen only by looking down into what were the aisles. The entablature is made up of scraps of friezes from different places. Yet they fit together better than might have been looked for, and the whole effect is striking and not wholly unsatis-factory. The entablature does not seem out of place when it merely supports the light gallery above; and it forms a marked contrast to the effect of the same

ST. PETER IN VINCULIS, ROME.

To face page 215.

construction in the nave, where the columns have, as in the Liberian Basilica, to support a heavy wall, answering to the triforium and clerestory range.

The capitals of these churches are of course commonly classical capitals used up again. Among them we get every variety of Ionic, Corinthian, and Composite forms; the Doric is rare. It is wonderful that it should be so; the more massive Doric is really more in its place as a support for the arch than the slender Corinthian. There are no nobler ranges in the world than the Doric columns of St. Peter *in Vinculis*, which hardly any one looks at, their fame is so utterly sacrificed to that of the image of Moses in a corner. Yet a more stately and solemn interior cannot be imagined; the Doric columns forestall, with greater elegance of workmanship, something of the majesty of the Northern Romanesque. The Ionic is far more common, and sometimes, as in a side chapel of St. Praxedes, we find later imitations of its forms, such Ionic, for instance, as could be made in the time of Pope Paschal the First. We have already mentioned a few cases of capitals which introduce human forms. These belong to a class whose history needs minutely working out. The trophy capital, as we may call it, made up of armour without any actual human figure, is found in the Temple of the Twelve Gods. Capitals with the actual human figure, capitals of the most splendid workmanship, may be seen lying about, seemingly uncared for, in the Baths of Caracalla. Among the fragments found in the lower chambers of the Tabularium or Senatorial Palace are capitals no less well wrought, in which volutes are made of animal forms. These varieties are most important in the true history of architecture. Here, in classical Rome, we find ourselves on the high road to the rams of St. Ambrose, to the eagles of Lucca, Wetzlar, and Gelnhausen. To one who recognizes the continuity of history, and therein the continuity of architecture, to one who does not dream that there was any time when the building art perished from the earth, the works of classic Rome are in all things only a transition to the more perfect works of Pisa and Durham. The age of Diocletian, the age which reared the court of Spalato, though its bricks may be wider apart than bricks were in the golden age of Nero, is seen to be the age of the greatest architectural developement that the world ever saw.

MONS SACER.

We know not whether we are right in assuming, or whether so to assume is only a judgement of charity, that every visitor to Rome makes a point of going at least as far out of the city as the church of St. Agnes-without-the-Walls. Of that church in its character as a basilica we have already spoken. And we have also raised our moan over the neighbour of St. Agnes, St. Constantia, and the tomb stolen thence by the barbarous whim of a destroying Pope of modern times. Papal caprice glorifies Agnes and robs Constantia; the lover of Christian antiquity can only wish that Popes would keep their hands alike from glorifying and from robbing. But just now we have to deal with both buildings simply as a landmark; they are to us for the nonce no more than the villa of some mushroom "prince" on the same road, who has amused himself by setting up sham ruins, and sometimes, it is whispered, stealing real columns to eke them out. We set out along the *Via Nomentana :* we pass by the gimcrack Colosseum of the prince;

we pass by the two churches which have fared in such
opposite ways at infallible hands; we ask ourselves the
purpose of the ruin which stands in their close neighbourhood, and which, like so many others, bears the
name of Maxentius. But this time we do not turn back
when we have reached the basilica; we go on further
along the somewhat dreary road. We are seeking a spot
which tells us of days when Rome had as yet no prince
but her *Princeps Senatûs*, no Pontiff but the head of
the religion of Jupiter and Minerva. But before we
altogether cast the modern world behind us, we are
forcibly reminded of its presence as we cross the
modern substitute for Appian and Flaminian ways,
the network of railways which carry out the saying
that all roads lead to Rome. Nor is the reminder
out of place; the great works of ancient and modern
engineering skill have much in common. There is
a likeness, sometimes even in their actual appearance,
always in the mighty spirit of enterprise, the boundless
command of physical resources, which is common to both
and unknown to intermediate ages. We cross the
iron road and go down into the valley of the Anio; we
pass over a bridge, of which more anon, and we find
the other side of the stream guarded by a group of low
hills whose place in history is no mean one. There
is more than one among the neighbouring mounds
which claims to itself the honour of being the spot

where the Sacred Laws were passed, where the tribuneship was ordained, and where Agrippa Menenius spoke
his famous parable of the Belly and the Members.
About the exact spot it is idle to dispute. Gibbon
says that people often forget that a battle is not fought
on one particular spot, because two armies in action
cover a good deal of ground. And so the place to
which the Roman Commons seceded with the object
of founding a new city must have been something
more than any one of the little knolls more than one of
which is marked in different maps as the exact spot.
The contemplated city, the actual encampment, must
have taken up a good deal of ground. It is enough
that it was on these low hills beyond the Anio that
the Commons designed to found their city of refuge
from patrician oppression, and that some one of them,
likely enough the small, but marked, knoll just beyond
the river with two ancient tombs at its foot, was the
actual spot which kept to after ages the honoured name
of the Sacred Hill.

The legend of the secession of the Commons is one
of those stories which come before the time of trustworthy history, but whose general truth there is no
reason to doubt. It gives an account of the origin
of an important part of the Roman constitution, of
the Sacred Laws and of that memorable office of the
tribuneship which those laws so specially hallowed.

Stories which give the origin of laws and offices are very often among the silliest of legends, because they are in truth no legends at all, but mere guesses to explain something whose meaning was forgotten. But the story of the secession to the Sacred Hill is not one of this kind. It will stand the test of the comparative method. It is in every way probable, according to what analogy teaches us must have been the real state of things; but it is not a story which a later age would be likely to invent. It takes for granted the real origin of the Roman Commons. Had the Commons been simply the poor or ignoble class in Rome, like the poor or ignoble class in a modern state—had they been, as Livy conceived them, a class artificially divided from the patricians by the first founder of the city—we can hardly fancy them forming the plan of leaving Rome, and setting up a new town of their own in the immediate neighbourhood. In a modern state, or in such a state as Livy conceived Rome to have been, the poor and ignoble, even though they may be wholly shut out from the government of the state, are still as much members of the state as the rich and noble. But, when we take in what the Roman Commons really were, we shall see that it is only in a very imperfect sense that they were members of the state at all. The patricians were the old citizens; the Commons were the new. The patricians were the

men of the old settlements on the Palatine and the
Capitoline, strengthened probably by the Luceres of
the Coelian. The Commons were the later settlers on
the Aventine, dwelling indeed physically within the
city wall, but not admitted within the sacred shelter of
the *pomoerium*. Many among them might be rich,
many might have been noble in earlier homes; but
neither riches nor nobility could win for them political equality with the elder citizens. It is not very
wonderful if on such men the tie of local allegiance
sat very loosely; they were only half Romans, and
it seemed to them no strange thing to leave Rome
and plant a new town somewhere else. In such a
town they would be the old citizens, and a day might
come when they might have the pleasure of themselves
acting as patricians towards fresh bodies of new settlers.
There they might have their own gods; they might take
their own auspices; they might do what they would
as an independent commonwealth, perhaps as a thirty-
first Latin city. All this they could easily do; they
were not mere units, like those members of a modern
state whom poverty or any other cause shuts out from
a share in its government; they were an organized
community, with their own assemblies and magistrates
and with the full habit of united action. Debt was one
great cause of the wretchedness of the poorer plebeians
yet the Sacred Hill was not an Adullam where every

one took refuge who was discontented or in debt.
It was a spot to which a community which at Rome
was dependent proposed to move in order to become independent. The whole thing is perfectly in harmony
with all that we know of the way in which early com-
munities grew up. Till all the elements of the state
were fully welded together, secession was a natural
resource, more than once resorted to by the element
whose citizenship was imperfect. As the old distinc-
tions die out, secessions cease to be heard of. When,
in the later days of the commonwealth, we come to
dissensions of quite another kind, we do not hear of
secession as a remedy. The idea is as wholly foreign
to the later state of things at Rome as it is natural
in the earlier. The whole story bears about it the
stamp of being genuine tradition, not an invention
or a guess of later times.

In all the disputes between the patricians and the
Commons, we naturally take the side of the Commons,
as the cause of freedom and equal right against an
exclusive oligarchy. But this story, like many others,
shows that the patricians were the truer Romans. No
wonder; they were the old settlers; they came of the
pure blood of the founders of the city ; theirs were the
Gods of the city, whose will no man of the stranger
Commons knew how to interpret. Their love for
Rome herself, as a spot, as a city, as a commonwealth,.

might be narrow and selfish, but it was strong and real. Their love for Rome involved the dominion of Rome over other commonwealths, and their own dominion in Rome herself; but they had at least no object apart from Rome; they sought no greatness for themselves in any character but that of Romans. To secede from Rome, to divide Rome, were thoughts which to them were worse than death. The time came when all barriers were broken down, when Roman feeling was as strong in the plebeian as in the patrician; but it was not so as yet. The patrician was already rooted to the soil of Rome; the plebeian could still endure the thought of ceasing to be a Roman. The patricians were not ready to grant equal rights to the Commons; but they saw that a secession of the Commons would be the ruin of the Roman commonwealth; they saw that a purely patrician Rome could no longer stand. To hinder the division of the commonwealth, they were therefore ready to make large concessions to the inferior community; but they were concessions which marked out the Commons as a separate community almost more distinctly than before. By so doing, as afterwards by hindering the proposed migration to Veii, the patricians undoubtedly saved the Roman state. The greatness of Rome was so closely bound up with the site and with the associations of Rome that we may be sure that a new city by the Anio, or a Roman commonwealth transferred to Veii, could never have become what the true Rome by the Tiber did become.

It is a point to be noticed that, whichever of the hills we may pitch on as the actual *Mons Sacer,* the new town by the Anio would have been out of sight of Rome. From the hill just above the river, and from the hill a little way further on, the eye catches some of the loftiest towers and cupolas of mediæval and modern Rome; but that is all. Of the city, as it stood in the days of the secession and for many ages after the secession, nothing could be seen from the Sacred Hill. In this there is no doubt a moral. Tusculum might look down upon a hated rival. We may doubt whether the city of the *Plebs* was meant to be a rival or an enemy of Rome. We may fancy that a wish to forget Rome was mingled with a sort of half attachment to the old spot, which forbade the discontented community to migrate to any great distance. But what would have followed if the parable of Agrippa Menenius had had no effect? No one can dream that the town on the Anio could have grown ever to be the head of Latium. But the division, the secession, the probable border-wars between the old and the new city, might have hindered the town on the Tiber from becoming the head of the world.

That the secession really was made, according to Livy's account, to a point, like the Sacred Hill, beyond

the walls of the city, there can be no reasonable doubt.
Livy quotes from Piso another version, according to
which the secession was made to the Aventine. This
he wisely rejects. But Piso's story is valuable, as
showing the way in which legends were arbitrarily
patched up. Piso, or those whom he followed, knew
that there was a special connexion between the
Commons and the Aventine: so he thrust in the name
of the Aventine into a story about the Commons in
which it was quite out of place.

One point more. It is not unlikely that here, as in
so many other places, we are brought face to face with
some of the strange contrasts of history. The hill
nearest to the river looks down on one of the most
picturesque of covered and fortified bridges, clearly
of more dates than one. Some hold that part of the
structure is the work of Narses. This bridge on the
Via Nomentana must not be confounded with the
more famous bridge of Narses on the *Via Salaria*,
which once bore the boastful inscription commented
on by Gregorovius. But it is in no way unlikely that
he built both. And as we look down from the Sacred
Hill, we feel inclined to hope that this bridge may
be the work of the first Exarch. If so, two ends of
Roman history are here brought together. We stand
on the scene of an event which seemed likely to tear
Rome asunder before the elements out of which she

Q

grew were yet fully welded together. We stand, three
miles from the elder gates of Rome, on a spot where
a part of the Roman people dreamed of founding a new
city out of sight of the old one. We look down on the
work of an age when a Roman Augustus still ruled
alike in Spain and in Syria, but when a secession of
another kind from that which led men to the Sacred
Hill had moved his throne from the Tiber to the
Bosporos, and when another secession stranger still
had for a while cut off Rome herself from the Roman
Empire. As the voice of Menenius had won back the
severed Commons, so the arms of Belisarius had won
back the severed capital. In the one case the new
Rome, if a new Rome it was to be, was, before its
birth, again incorporated with the Old. In the other
case the Old Rome was not indeed incorporated, but it
was brought into subjection to the New. Menenius might
well boast that he had given Rome peace and freedom.
Justinian too boasted that he had given Rome peace
and freedom ; but it was such peace and freedom as
was consistent with the position of an outlying province,
and with the rule of a Byzantine Exarch. But the
very degradation of Rome took a form which was the
direct result of her greatness; she became the slave
of her own name and her own shadow. Had the
Roman people parted asunder at the Sacred Hill, the
Roman name could never have won the magic power

which it did win, a magic which could live, not only
through the transfer of Rome's name and place to her
own colony, but through the actual subjection of the
parent to the child. There is a cycle in all things.
Rome, as the legend goes, destroyed her own metropolis. If so, the wrongs of Alba were strangely and
tardily avenged when Rome became a dependent
outpost of Byzantium.

SOUTHERN ITALY.

GREECE IN ITALY.

THE shores of the Bay of Naples, and of the two bays which stretch north-west and south-east on either side of it, have their attractions for all. There is the mere natural aspect, the land and the sea, the coast, the mountains, and the islands—the heights of Capreæ and of Ischia, anchored as it were like guard-ships before the peaceful bay—Vesuvius, with its pillar of cloud, reminder of fearful days when the pillar of cloud has been changed into a pillar of fire. There are the long associations of the history of that memorable coast, Oscan, Roman, Byzantine, Norman. We look on a land which formed one of the fairest spots in the fairest realm of the Wonder of the World, a land which in our day was wrested from the oppressor by exploits more wonderful than any of which its own long history had to tell. We look on the city stretching along the shore, the city for which so many lords and so many nations have striven; we look back from the struggles of Bourbon and Habsburg, of Anjou and Aragon, to the days when the Norman added to his realm the first and last possession of the Eastern Cæsar in the Western seas, when the city which had been won by Belisarius yielded to the arms of Roger. We cast our eye along the coast, and every inch of ground seems to have its special association for the student of the early Imperial days of Rome. Here almost every famous man of the late Republic and the early Empire had his retreat from the honours and the cares of the city. On one side of the great bay we are shown the villa of Cæsar and the villa of Lucullus; we see too the scene of the wildest freak of Caius and of the blackest crime of Nero. On the other side is the seaside home of Cicero, a contrast indeed to his airy Tusculum; and there is the spot where Pliny, father of a long line of scientific admirals, gave his life as the price of the knowledge which he loved. And, in the midst, to remind us of the greatest of all changes, we see the spot where Paul of Tarsus looked on the now ruined temples and amphitheatre of Puteoli. And, as if purposely to embody that remembrance, there is the height crowned by the *duomo*, worthless in itself, but which becomes a speaking memory indeed when we see built into its wall the columns of the temple which looked down on the Apostle as he landed. It was the temple of the deified founder of the Empire, that Empire whose chiefs were, under the teaching of the faith which Paul brought with him, to change from

heathen Pontiffs into God's temporal Vicars upon earth.
It is well that, in a region made so fair by the hand of
nature, so foul by the deeds of man, there should be this
one link to bind our thoughts to other and higher things
than the crimes of the early Cæsars. And yet there
is a relief of another kind; here is the region to which
poetic fancy has transferred so many of the thoughts
and names and legends of the older Hellenic days.
We are here in the land of Virgil; here is Misenum;
there is Avernus, a lake at least of higher memories
than its Lucrine neighbour. And thus we are carried
back by the wand of the Mantuan magician to
thoughts of the earliest times of which that land
awakens memories. We begin to remember that
the living Neapolis, the buried Hêrakleia, were not, in
their first days, cities of the Roman or of the Oscan.
Here again, as in other lands, a cycle has been played
out. When Belisarius entered Naples, he entered it
as a Roman general victorious over the Goth. What
in truth he did was to win back for the new Greek
world a city which had been part of the Greek world
of elder times. If Naples so long remained a distant
outpost of Byzantium, we have but to double the Cape
of Misenum, to pass along the coast which parts the grave
of Æneas' trumpeter from the grave of his nurse, and we
light on a spot more truly memorable in the history of
the world than any of the spots renowned for the crimes

or the victories of Kings and Cæsars. The Apostle himself, citizen of a Greek city, putting forth his teaching in the Greek tongue and enriching it with Greek associations, must have found some other form for the Gospel which he preached, had not the Greek of earlier days spread his tongue and his philosophy through all lands. We may for a moment forget all that has happened from the first alliance between Rome and Capua to the modern deliverance of Capua and Rome, as we look on the first outposts of Hellas in the West. As we stand on the akropolis of Cumæ, what we elsewhere look on as ancient seems to belong to the old age of the world. From that desolate height we can drink in the fulness of the fresh breezes of the youth of Europe and of European man.

It is a feeling which indeed carries us out of the common world and of the common range of history, when we can say for the first time that the soil on which we tread is Hellas. We need not say that, wherever Hellênes dwelled, there was Hellas, and that the furthest outpost in the Iberian or the Tauric peninsula was as truly Hellas as Sparta or Athens. So, in this sense, Neapolis and Massalia were Hellas also, but from them the fatal gift of long-continued prosperity has wiped away the Hellenic character. Cumæ—let us rather cast aside the barbaric form, and give back her true name to the Chalkidic Kymê—has had the luck to perish, and in perishing she has kept all the old associations of her name. True, the traces of her Hellenic days are of the very scantiest; but there are no traces of other days to interfere with them. We pass by the shore of Avernus and through the vast tunnel of Agrippa, or we trace the Roman pavement under the bold span of *Arco Felice*, and, when the other side of the hill is reached, we leave Rome and the younger world behind us. Straight before our eyes, rising above vineyards and scattered cottages, soars the hill of the akropolis, the first point, as tradition told, of Italy and the Western world in which Hellenic settlers found themselves a home. If the tale be true, Sicily and Korkyra, the sites of Sybaris and Taras, were still barbaric ground, untrodden by an Hellenic foot, when the first colonists from the Æolic Kymê lighted their fires and raised their first defences on that solitary hill. A coast, already Hellenic in its natural character, a coast of bays and islands and promontories, stretched far on either side; but all on either side was strange, all was barbarian. It was for them to win for the Hellenic name a land on which nature seemed to have set her seal as a destined dwelling-place of Hellenic man.

And, be the tale true or false which makes Kymê absolutely the first Greek settlement in the western seas, there can be no doubt that it was a settlement of high antiquity, a settlement made in days when the earliest type of city was still the rule. Kymê is a hill-fort; its akropolis overhangs the sea, but the sea is not immediately at its foot. Such was the kind of site chosen for the most ancient cities in Greece itself, and a wide gap parts a city of this kind from Naples on her bay and Syracuse on her island. Kymê was a part of Hellas; but, when Kymê first arose, it was indeed a small and isolated fragment of Hellas that she formed. The first object of her settlers was defence against barbarian neighbours, and they found their defence in such a site as their barbarian neighbours loved. The akropolis of Kymê suggests the *arx* of Tusculum, and a strange companionship unites the two. Even here, on the oldest site of Italian Hellas, we cannot wholly shut out the memory of Rome. Tusculum and Kymê alike, so the story goes, gave shelter to the King whom Rome had driven out. When the arms of the Thirty Cities had failed to restore the banished Tarquin, Kymê, or at least her tyrant Aristodêmos, welcomed him to a refuge beyond the reach of the new-born common-wealth. The last shelter of the fallen King, the Greek akropolis, less lofty than the Latin *arx*, was hardly less strong. And on the side of it away from the friendly sea, the side most open to the inroads of barbarians, the hill was scarped away and strengthened by mighty stones worthy to have found a place in the oldest wall of the city from which Tarquinius had been driven.

The thought of this strange episode in the history of the Greek city may perhaps present itself to the mind; but there is nothing left on the height of Kymê specially to call up the memory of Aristodêmos and his guest. It is one of the charms of the scene that so little is left of any kind, that the desolation of Kymê is almost as complete as the desolation of the spot could have been before Kymê was. There is nothing to interfere with our musings. Some slight traces of the great temple of the patron-god Apollo may be made out on the highest point. But the columns of his portico are gone; they have been stolen by some of the bandit princes, prelates, and potentates who have wrought their wicked will on the monuments of Italy; they have been carried off to adorn some villa or palace or museum, and they are no doubt duly ticketed to record the " munificence " of the robber. We have forgotten the name of the savage and the whereabouts of his lair, and we care not to search them out again. Kymê is desolate, save the mighty stones of her wall and the small traces of her temple; a few remains too of Roman brick-work, to be seen as we pass from the wall to the temple, survive from the days when Kymê had paid the penalty of sheltering Rome's banished tyrant. Here and there too, in the vineyard or by the pathway, we see some scrap of wall,

some fragment of carved work, to show that a city has
been there. But we read the history of Kymê, as we
stand on her height, and look out on the hills, the
flats, the lake, and that great and wide sea which made
Europe to differ from Africa and Asia, which gave
the Hellenic man power to spread Hellas, and all that
is implied in her name, over every coast where his one
worthy barbarian rival had not forestalled him.

We change the scene to another spot on the same
coast, on the other side of the central city, where we
are still on Hellenic ground, and where the men of
Hellas have left signs of their presence which have
outlived all the works of successive waves of conquerors.
We set forth from Naples; we pass along the

> Vicina Vesevo
> Arva jugo;—

"jugum" no longer, since the cities at its base were
preserved for posterity by their overthrow. We pass
by spots famous in the history of after-days. We
pass by Angri; hard by is the mountain-slope where
the great struggle of Italian history was ended; there is
the scene of the last fight of Teias and Narses, where the
last Gothic King sank beneath the arms of the mighty
eunuch, and where it was fixed for ever that Italy
should not become a national kingdom under a Teutonic King. We pass on by Nocera and Pagani, names

which speak of the great house under whom Italy had
again a chance of union; we call up Frederick and
Manfred, and those faithful Saracens who died around
their King at Benevento when his Christian warriors
had forsaken him. And, if Nocera speaks to us of the
most renowned of Emperors, Salerno on its bay speaks
to us no less of the most renowned of Pontiffs. There,
lik Scipio at Liternum, Gregory died, as he deemed,
in exile, though there were those around him who
deemed that the Vicar of Christ could be an exile in
no spot of the earth whose utmost parts were given him
for his possession. Through spots like these, where
the great events of man's history press upon us at every
step, we fly away, as it were, from the modern world,
the world of Rome and all that sprang from her, to see
another spot where all that is left speaks to us of the
days of the world's youth, and speaks to us with a
clearer voice than the desolate hill of Kymê. If the
Gods of Hellas were Gods of the hills, they were Gods
no less of the plain and of the shore; and here we
again find ourselves on true Hellenic ground, but on
ground utterly unlike the forsaken akropolis of the
Chalkidic city. On that akropolis the monuments of
Hellas were eloquent by their absence; we have now
reached a spot where they are no less eloquent by their
everlasting presence.

Kymê bore the name of one of its joint parent cities;

the city of the sea-god, Pæstum on Latin lips, bore in its own tongue the name of its divine patron. On no hill-top, but on a dreary flat between the sea and the mountains, the temples of Poseidônia still stand, a wreck indeed of what they once were, but a wreck which seems perfect beside the far more utter wreck of the works of so many later ages. Yet we feel that, ancient as Poseidônia seems, it is young beside Kymê. There is again before us the same difference as that which divides Dardaniê from Ilios and Tusculum from Rome. Things must have greatly changed since the foundation of Kymê before Greek settlers on Italian soil could have fixed themselves on such a spot as Poseidônia. Here was no akropolis, no inaccessible height; the colonists trusted to their walls, to the sea, to the natural superiority of the Greek over the barbarian. The change involves all the difference between the first solitary Greek settlement in the West, the colony which came straight from the Eastern and Asiatic shores, and the colony whose metropolis was itself on Italian ground, the city planted by Sybaris in the days of her power, when southern Italy had won the name of the Greater Hellas. Kymê is primarily a fortress; Poseidônia is essentially a city. Like other cities, it needed defence; but defence was not the one object present to the mind of its founders. There was no rock to scarp, or, trusting in its natural strength, to leave unscarped. There was simply such a space as was needed to be fenced in by the mighty Hellenic walls, which, broken down and overgrown as they are, may still be traced and walked on through nearly the whole of their pentagonal range. Within those walls a crowd of later buildings have risen and fallen; the theatre, the amphitheatre—the sanctuary of Roman cruelty thrusting itself within the Hellenic city—the temple of Roman date, may all be traced, and it would be a good deed to set the spade to work to dig them out more thoroughly. Yet it is with a certain pleasure that we see the amphitheatre and the Roman temple level with the ground, while the Hellenic temples still raise their massive columns above the fallen works of the barbarian conqueror.

Few buildings are more familiar than the temples of Pæstum; yet the moment when the traveller first comes in sight of works of untouched Hellenic skill is one which is simply overwhelming. Suddenly, by the side of a dreary road, in a spot backed indeed by noble mountains, but having no charm of its own, we come on these works, unrivalled on our side of the Hadriatic and the Messenian strait, standing in all their solitary grandeur, shattered indeed, but far more perfect than the mass of ruined buildings of later days. The feeling of being brought near to Hellenic days and Hellenic men, of standing face to face with the fathers of the

world's civilization, is one which can never pass away.
Descriptions, pictures, models, all fail; they give us
the outward form; they cannot give us the true life.
The thought comes upon us that we have passed
away from that Roman world out of which our own
world has sprung into that earlier and fresher and
brighter world by which Rome and ourselves have
been so deeply influenced, but out of which neither the
Roman nor the modern world can be said to spring.
There is the true Doric in its earliest form, in all its
unmixed and simple majesty. The ground is strewed
with shells and covered with acanthus-leaves; but no
shell had suggested the Ionic volute, no acanthus-leaf
had suggested the Corinthian foliage. The vast columns,
with the sudden tapering, the overhanging capitals,
the stern square abacus, all betoken the infancy of art.
But it is an infancy like that of their own Hêraklês;
the strength which clutched the serpent in his cradle
is there in every stone. Later improvements, the
improvements of Attic skill, may have added grace;
the perfection of art may be found in the city which
the vote of the divine Assembly decreed to Athênê;
but for the sense of power, of simplicity without rudeness, the city of Poseidôn holds her own. Unlike in
every detail, there is in these wonderful works of early
Greek art a spirit akin to some of the great churches of
Romanesque date, simple, massive, unadorned, like the

Poseidônian Doric. And they show too how far the ancient architects were from any slavish bondage to those minute rules which moderns have invented for them. In each of the three temples of Pæstum differences both of detail and of arrangement may be marked, differences partly of age, but also partly of taste. And some other thoughts are brought forcibly upon the mind. Here indeed we feel that the wonders of Hellenic architecture are things to kindle our admiration, even our reverence; but that, as the expression of a state of things which has wholly passed away, nothing can be less fit for reproduction in modern times. And again, we may be sure that the admiration and reverence which they may awaken in the mind of the mere classical purist is cold beside that which they kindle in the mind which can give them their true place in the history of art. The temples of Pæstum are great and noble from any point of view. But they become greater and nobler, as we run over the successive steps in the long series by which their massive columns and entablatures grew into the tall clusters and soaring arches of Westminster and Amiens.

LOMBARDY.

ROMANESQUE ARCHITECTURE IN LOMBARDY.

WE have gone far to the south, into that elder Italy which, in some aspects of its mediæval history, is hardly Italy at all. We will now pass back again to the land which in an intermediate stage of geography was the borderland of Italy and Cisalpine Gaul. And then from Ravenna, Lucca, and Pisa we will pass yet again into that old Gaulish land which in mediæval times became the truest Italy. From Tuscany we will again turn ourselves northward, and trace the forms assumed by Romanesque art in a district which, in the fluctuations of Italian geographical nomenclature, we may perhaps be allowed to speak of as specially Lombardy. This is a Lombardy which stretches on both sides of the Po, but which does not take in the most eastern province of the Lombard Kingdom, the land known in earlier and later times as Venetia, and in an intermediate day by the startling, but perfectly harmless, name of the Lombard *Austria*. Our present district lies mainly within the Lombard

Neustria, but we will venture to take in some more southern cities, lying all of them within the Lombardy of the Hohenstaufen, most of them within the dominion of the Dukes of Milan of the House of Visconti. We purpose, in short, to take an architectural glance at the cities of Modena, Parma, Piacenza, and the once rival capitals of Pavia and Milan. The last-named city indeed might, from other points of view, claim as full a notice as Pisa and Ravenna. But as a contribution to the history of Romanesque architecture, the buildings of Milan, though of very high importance, are still of a kind which will be best treated in a group along with several others.

The student of Romanesque who transports himself suddenly from the Arno and the Apennines to the river-basin of the Po will find himself spirited away into a new architectural world. Let him flit from Pisa to Modena. Pistoia, a city of high interest on other grounds, will not long detain him. A single noble campanile is attached to a basilican *duomo* which would hold a third or fourth-rate place at Lucca, and which at Pisa no one would think of mentioning at all. But at Modena his halt must be longer. The church of Pisa and the church of Modena are contemporary buildings, and the Great Countess is honoured as a benefactress by both; but they are as unlike one another as any two buildings of the same

DUOMO, MODENA, S.E.

To face page 249.

date and general style well can be. At Modena we get our first glimpse of the genuine Lombard form of the Italian Romanesque, a form wholly unlike either the domical or the basilican type, and which makes a far nearer approach to the Romanesque of the lands beyond the Alps. The approach is indeed only an approach; the *duomo* of Modena is Italian, and not English, French, or German; still it is a form of Italian far less widely removed from English, French, or German work than the style of Pisa or St. Vital. As at Pisa, the architect seems to have halted between two opinions. The church is cruciform, but the transepts have no projection on the ground-plan; there are real lantern-arches, not obscured as they are at Pisa, but they do not bear up any central dome or tower. The lantern-arches are pointed; but here, as at Pisa, the pointed form is more likely to be Saracenic than Gothic. Without, three eastern apses, rising from between pinnacles of quite Northern character, group boldly with one of the noblest campaniles in Italy, which is certainly not improved by the later addition of a spire. The great doorways rest on lions; the west front has a noble wheel window; the greater part of the outside is lavishly arcaded, but the arcading is of a different type from the long rows of single arcades at Lucca and Pisa; the favourite form at Modena is that of several small arches grouped under a containing arch.

With such an outside, we are not surprised to find, on entering the church, an elevation more nearly after the Northern type than anything which we have yet seen in Italy. At Pisa we saw an arcade, triforium, and clerestory; but the triforium was not so much the Northern type itself as the Northern type translated into Italian language. But at Modena we find as genuine a triforium as in any minster of England or Normandy. Its form indeed seems somewhat rude and awkward, as if the containing arch had been crushed by the lofty clerestory above. And eyes familiar with Norman detail may possibly be amazed at the sight of mid-wall shafts, and those of a somewhat rough type, showing themselves in such a position. But the mid-wall shaft is constructively as much in its place in a triforium as it is in a belfry window, and in the whole elevation there is nothing lacking. There is pier-arch, triforium, and clerestory, and the deep splay of the highest range hinders the presence of any continuous blank spaces such as we have seen in the basilican churches. The capitals are a strange mixture of classical and barbaric forms, and in the alternate piers, supporting the arches which span the nave, we find huge half-columns, which form a marked contrast to the tall slender shafts commonly used in like positions in Northern churches. Altogether the cathedral of Modena is strictly an Italian church, yet the approaches

INTERIOR OF DUOMO, MODENA.

To face page 250.

to Northern forms are very marked, and they are of a kind which suggests the direct imitation of Northern forms or the employment of Northern architects.

At our next stopping place, if we venture to discern traces of the same influence, it is to a much smaller extent, and the church in which we discern it is one of far more distinctly Italian character than that of Modena. At Parma attention may easily be drawn away from the church itself to the noble baptistery, one of the grandest in Italy, and in which most of the details show the widest departure from anything to which we are used north of the Alps. Here, in most of the stages within and without, the ornamental arcade has been cast aside for the ornamental colonnade. Instead of a range of arches, the small decorative shafts support a true entablature. Yet even here, in the strange capitals of some of the lower columns, and in the vast doorways with their many receding arches, we may see a certain approach to Northern forms which contrasts strangely with the ultra-classical survival in the other details. In the *duomo* itself it is not always easy to say how much is genuine Romanesque work, and how much is that later reproduction or adaptation of Romanesque work of which we see so many examples in Italy. The west front is thoroughly Italian; nothing can be less like a Norman church; but at the same time few

architectural objects can be nobler than the present
effect of the apsidal east end and apsidal transepts
joining to support the octagon cupola. But inside
we have, as at Modena, the genuine pier-arch, triforium, and clerestory, just as we might see them in
England or Normandy, except that the triforium consists
of a range of four arches in each bay, not grouped
together under a containing arch as at Modena. Yet
this arrangement may possibly remind the spectator of
Queen Matilda's church at Caen, and the vaulting shafts
at Parma approach far more nearly to Northern forms
than those of Modena. Still at Parma the departures
from the more purely Italian type are of a kind which
do not force themselves upon the eye so strongly as
they do at Modena.

The *duomo* of Piacenza, though much altered,
contains some fine Romanesque portions, but there is
nothing in them which especially connects itself with
the Romanesque of the North. We pass on to two
churches of the highest interest, both architectural and
historical, an examination of which may perhaps throw
some light on the questions which we have already
started. These are the two great Romanesque churches
which still survive in the once rival cities of Northern
Italy, in Guelfic Milan and in Imperial Pavia. We
pass by the crowds of other objects presented by those
two noble cities, and we fix our attention on the two

ST. AMBROSE, MILAN.

To face page 253.

buildings which will teach us most for our immediate purpose, the churches of St. Ambrose at Milan and St. Michael at Pavia. At Milan we will turn away from the dazzling exterior, the really solemn interior, of the comparatively modern *duomo*, and fix our thoughts on a more venerable temple. The church of St. Ambrose covers the dust of the patron saint of Milan and the dust of the most truly Italian Emperor, and it boasts, truly or falsely, of containing the resting-place of the one worthy antagonist whom Rome sent forth to withstand the Gothic invader. A flash of the old magic of Ravenna passes over us as we look on the tomb of Ambrose, on the tomb of Lewis the Second, and on what at least professes to be the tomb of Stilicho. The mosaics of the spreading apse might hold their own in Pisa, in Ravenna, or in Venice, and one small portion of the pile lays claim to a date going back to the days of the saint whom it commemorates. But for our purpose we must pass on from the days of the saint to the days of the Cæsar, the Cæsar who was the champion of Italy against the Saracen, the truest Emperor that she had seen since Majorian, the truest King that she has seen from Theodoric to our own day. It was under the worthiest of the Karlings, Lewis, King and Emperor, that the pile arose in which he lies buried, and of which we would fain believe that the main portion still exists.

The date of the building has been stoutly disputed, but it seems impossible to withstand the direct evidence which assigns, not only the glorious goldsmith's work of the high altar and the soaring *baldacchino* above it, but the main part of the building itself, to Archbishop Ansbert in 868. The building has received large changes and additions; the vault with pointed arches over the nave, the octagonal dome, the advanced upper story of the west front, must all belong to a renovation which began in the twelfth century, most likely after the overthrow of the city by Frederick Barbarossa. But everything leads us to believe that, in the main arcades of the nave, and in the most distinctive feature of the whole building, the *cortile* or western cloister, the pillars of the ninth century still survive. All are of the genuine Lombard style, something utterly unlike the classical forms of Ravenna, Lucca, and Pisa. Nay more, they supplanted a church of a more classical type; at the bases of more than one we can see traces of basilican columns, the work most likely of Ambrose himself. But the architecture of the existing church comes far nearer to our Northern Romanesque in its Norman variety, though it has throughout an earlier and ruder air. The general look of the building is dark and cavernous; the proportions are low and broad; the arcades support a large open triforium, like Norwich or Waltham, but without a clerestory—in that

CAPITALS.

To face page 255.

resembling the great minster of St. Sernin at Toulouse. As at Pisa, the arcade is continued across the transept arches, and here also the triforium assumes the form of coupled arches under a containing arch. The compound pier is used throughout, both in the church and the *cortile*, to the exclusion alike of the classical column, of the square piers of the German Romanesque, and of the vast cylindrical piers of the English form of Norman. But there is a heavy squareness and flatness throughout which surpasses anything in Norman work. If the whole building is really of the days of Bayeux and Rochester, Normandy and England had greatly outstripped Italy in art of this particular form.

But whatever may be the date of the arcades, the capitals are a special study. They are famous for the lavish use of animal forms ; nowhere in Italy is there less imitation of classical models. The Ionic volute alone seems here, as everywhere, to have lived on in the mind of the artist, and, both here and elsewhere, many strange forms occur which show that that favourite form of ornament was never forgotten. A bunch of leaves, a head, human or animal, may easily be so disposed as to keep the general effect of the volute ; and when the beast represented happens to be a ram, one of those cycles which play their part in art as well as in everything else has brought back the architectural form to its first legendary origin. Some of the double-headed beasts at Milan can hardly fail to remind us of some of the

double-headed beasts at Persepolis; but the likeness
is doubtless as purely accidental as the likeness which
has been often remarked between the columns in the
Treasury at Mykênê and those of many a Romanesque building among ourselves. The subjects of some
of the capitals should be noticed, as well as those
in other parts where animal forms are used. Some
are mere plays of fancy; others seem to represent
hunting scenes; but there is a more remarkable one in
the west front, representing a human figure between
two lions. The reference to the sports of the amphitheatre is obvious, but its special purport may be
doubted. It may of course refer to some legend of
martyrdom; but it should not be forgotten that the
combats with wild beasts went on at least as late as the
reign of Theodoric, though they were looked on with
no favouring eye by the Gothic King and his great
minister. Altogether, if we can really believe this
church to be in its main features the genuine work of
Ansbert, we have in it one of the most instructive
buildings in all Christendom. And to our mind the
evidence seems directly in favour of such a belief.

From St. Ambrose we naturally turn to St. Michael
at Pavia, and there, as at St. Ambrose, we find, among
many later changes, the main portions of a church of
the same character, but most likely somewhat later
in date. The general effect of the interior is less dark
and cavernous, but the arrangement of arcade and

triforium without any clerestory is essentially the same, and the same flatness and squareness reigns in the compound piers and their capitals. But one feature is prominent at Pavia which is not to be seen at Milan. The mid-wall shaft has thrust itself into places where we should least have looked for it, into the transept front and into a range of coupled windows running across the whole western façade itself. In both these two remarkable churches it is far from easy to distinguish the earliest work from later changes which follow the same general forms. But we have little doubt that in the main arcades of both we have work of an age of which in Northern countries we have nothing but a few uncertain fragments.

It is indeed hard to believe, even if we bear in mind the wide differences which probably existed between Lombardy and Tuscany, that these buildings can be of later date than the columnar churches of Pisa and Lucca, with their elaborate and highly classical detail. Tuscany may either have uninterruptedly retained classical forms, or it may have deliberately fallen back upon them; but it is hardly possible that Milan and Pavia should have so far lagged behind as to have produced such work as we see in St. Ambrose and St. Michael in the twelfth century, after such work as we have seen at both Lucca and Pisa in the eleventh. And if the ruder parts of St. Ambrose do not date from

s

the reparation in the twelfth century, they can hardly fail to date from the rebuilding by Ansbert in the ninth. We have then in these examples a genuine Romanesque style, which had worked itself remarkably free from classical detail, while preserving the main constructive features of Roman architecture. It is probably the earliest form of pure Romanesque which was worked out, a form distinct alike from German and Norman, but from which both German and Norman architects borrowed ideas in after times.

If this be allowed, this more distinctly Lombard, this half Northern style, gave way to the great architectural movement of the eleventh and twelfth centuries, which, in different ways, so greatly modified the Romanesque of all Western Europe. In Italy it chiefly took the form of a *Renaissance*, a falling back on classical forms, as at Pisa and Lucca, at Murano and Torcello. In other cases, as at Parma and more strongly at Modena, the style took a direction which distinctly assimilated it to Northern forms, whichever side of the Alps we may hold to have borrowed from the other. In a third class, as at St. Zeno, we get a type which makes some approach to the classical forms of Tuscany and Venice, but which may be looked on as an improved and refined variety of the Lombard style of Milan and Pavia. The Italian Romanesque thus offers many types, varying considerably, partly according to date, partly according to district. But all are Italian; all agree in those points of difference from Northern buildings which are caused partly by difference of climate, partly by difference of national traditions. However nearly an Italian church may approach to a Northern one in its internal arcades, the external effect is always utterly different. No really Italian church shows the varied outlines, the ever-shifting groupings, of the great churches of Germany. Even the less elaborate outline of a Norman or English church with its three towers finds only a feeble approach to it at St. Ambrose. The high roof is unknown, and the absence alike of the high roof and of any towers thoroughly worked into the building gives an utterly different form to the main fronts. The style, in all its various forms, is thoroughly national. It is a style which has largely attracted the attention of architectural students, but it may still be studied with advantage according to a more strictly historical and comparative method than has hitherto been brought to bear on it. It should especially be compared with the contemporary forms of other Southern countries, of Provence and Aquitaine. For our own part we have done nothing more than throw out a few hints suggested by a few particular buildings. Of some specially historical cities, of some buildings which form special lessons in themselves, we have still somewhat to say.

s 2

MONZA.

———◦◦———

THE Kingdom of Italy is at this moment a fact, but it is hard, even in Italy itself, to take in the truth that it was a fact in ages long past as well as in our own. The world in general finds it hard to understand that Victor Emmanuel is not the first King of Italy, or at all events that Napoleon Buonaparte was not the first and Victor Emmanuel the second. And, as usual, the popular notion has some truth in it; like most popular notions, it is a half truth. It is certain that there never was till now a Kingdom of Italy with exactly the same titles and exactly the same boundaries as the present one. By an odd chance, Victor Emmanuel really is the first King of Italy who, as King of Italy, has reigned over the land which first bore the name of Italy. That name, as every scholar knows, first belonged to a small part of the late Kingdom of Naples or Sicily; and though several Kings of Italy—Henry the Sixth, for instance, and Charles the Fifth—have also been Kings of one or both Sicilies, yet Victor Emmanuel is the first King of Italy who has held either of the Sicilies as an integral part of the Italian Kingdom. On the other hand, a land which was not counted part of Italy till a comparatively late time, a land which was not yet Italy when Cæsar marched to Ariminum, became in another stage the specially Italian land, the seat of the Italian Kingdom, the theatre of the earliest life of the Italian commonwealths. For some centuries Lombardy was the truest Italy; and, oddly enough, ages afterwards it was one part of the old Lombardy which formed the groundwork of the sham Italian Kingdom of Buonaparte, as another part has been the groundwork of the real Italian Kingdom of Victor Emmanuel. Whenever there has been a King of Italy, he has been specially King of Lombardy; the Italian Kingdom in short has been a continuation of that Lombard kingdom from which Charles the Great did not disdain to take a separate title. Between the memories of Imperial and Papal Rome, between the glory of the Italian commonwealths and the shame of the later Italian principalities, the memory of the true Italian Kingdom has almost died out. Being in truth little more than a name for several ages, it had few associations to set against those of the rival phases of Italian history. It is therefore perhaps in some sort not unfit that the home and seat of this almost shadowy kingdom, the "head of Lombardy," the "first place of the Crown of the Italian Kingdom," should be found on a spot which has but small claims to fame except on the ground of its being the home of the symbol of Italian kingship. The King of Italy, as King of Italy, had his special seat in a place which hardly claims the rank of a city, which can show no remains of classical antiquity, whose name is not mentioned in classical history, and which, on the other hand, plays no part of the least importance ' either in the communal, the ecclesiastical, or the dynastic history of later times. Modoetia, Monza, *Terra de Modoetia*, is the seat of the old Italian kingship, and it is nothing else.

The kingdom of Italy, at least in any reign before the present century, must be looked on as a Teutonic kingdom. The idea of such a kingdom could not arise till the old notions of the Empire had been greatly enfeebled by the Teutonic invasions. The Italian kingdom was first Lombard, then Frankish, then claimed of right by the prince who was chosen to the German crown. It was only during the first half of the tenth century that the crown of Italy was worn by princes who, though doubtless of Lombard or other Teutonic descent, could in any way claim to pass as native Italians. For such a kingdom as this Monza was a most fitting seat. The very existence of the place in earlier times may be doubted. At all events it could have been a place of no moment whatever till its site attracted the discerning eye of the great Goth. Theodoric, not indeed a King of Italy, but a King reigning in Italy, was the fitting founder of the future home of the Italian crown. The Lombard Paul tells us how he built himself a palace at *Modicia*—seemingly the eldest of the endless spellings of the name—on account of the healthiness of the air in a spot so near to the Alps. We can bear our own witness to the wisdom of the great King's choice from personal experience. When it is cold and foggy at Milan, so foggy that the great cupola of *Santa Maria della Grazia* cannot be seen by one standing just below it, the half-hour's run which carries the traveller to Monza carries him to a spot where all is clear and warm and sunny. One almost wonders that the spot was not lighted on in the age when Milan was the dwelling-place of Emperors; but, as far as we know, Theodoric was, if not the first to make the spot a dwelling-place of man, at least the first to make it a dwelling-place of Kings. If Ravenna can show his church and his tomb, if Verona can boast of having inseparably yoked together her name with his, lowlier Monza in one way surpasses both of them as being his own creation.

The earliest certain notice of Monza is an incidental mention in a letter by the contemporary Ennodius Bishop of Pavia, who complains that " Martinus, conductor de Moditia," was doing wrong to a blind woman,

and who speaks of the offender's "rustica temeritas."
This looks as if the house of Theodoric was not a city
palace, but a country seat. Monza then was the work
of the Goth; but the glory of the Goth shone only for
a moment; the continuous history of Monza begins with
the more lasting dominion of the Lombard. At Monza,
as elsewhere, the name of the Arian was wiped out, and
local devotion gathers round the second foundress, the
famous Queen Theodolinda. The local chronicle itself
records indeed the earlier work of Theodoric; but the
legend which that chronicle preserves, a legend which
represents the Queen as converting her husband Agilulf
from the worship of idols, evidently looked upon Monza
as· a site which before her time stood desolate. She
vows to build a church, an *oraculum,* to St. John the
Baptist, and a miraculous voice causes her to build it
on a spot where before there was only a great tree.
And as the voice said "Modo," and the Queen
answered "Etiam," the name of the place was called
Modoetia. And when we remember how Theodoric is
dealt with by the sculptor's art in the great minster of
his own Verona, we can hardly wonder that he should
be forgotten in his own Monza. Theodolinda stands by
herself. When we read of the Bavarian princess as
"filia Garibaldi," the name seems to carry us from the
earliest age of strictly Italian history to the latest.
And her two romantic marriages, allowed as she was to

carry the Lombard kingdom as her dower, her missionary zeal for the Orthodox faith, her friendship with the
great Gregory—if these things do not really put her on
a level with her Gothic predecessor, they may at least
have easily made her more dazzling in local eyes.

Of the buildings of Theodolinda, we have to judge
only by the description of those who had seen them.
She built the palace of whose painted ornaments the
Deacon Paul gives so vivid a picture; in his day it
could still be seen what manner of men the Lombards
were in her day, and how, among other points of costumes
and manners, they wore inner garments, loose and of
various colours, " qualia Angli Saxones habere solent."
She too founded the great church of Monza, the basilica
or *oraculum* of St. John, which we would gladly see in
such sort as the famous queen left it. The fame of its
foundress and the riches of its treasury put her church
almost on a level with churches of higher rank. It
was not an episcopal church, but only a chapter of
secular canons; but the chief of its canons, the Archpresbyter, bore, like our mitred abbots, the episcopal
insignia, and asserted, at least in theory, his right to
perform the most dazzling of episcopal functions. The
treasury, as every visitor knows, contains, among its
other wealth, the comb of Theodolinda, her gilt hen and
chickens, and the manuscript which an Englishman looks
on with reverence, and feels in no mood to doubt or

criticize when he is told that it is the very handwriting
of the apostle of his nation. The church itself, rebuilt
in honour of certain miracles which are recorded in the
year 1300, will probably draw to itself less attention
than its contents. Yet a glance may well be given, if
to nothing else, to the capitals made up of strange
groups of human and animal forms, among which, as
becomes the close connexion of the church with a line
of Kings who were also Emperors, the bird of Cæsar
holds one of the chief places.

The local history of the church of Monza consists
largely of the taking away and bringing back of its
precious treasures, a process which happened more than
once. The last taking away and bringing back of its
most precious treasure has happened in our own day.
The greatest possession of which Monza boasts itself,
after an Austrian captivity happily not long enough to
be called Babylonish, has come safe back to its own
place, and is still kept with all reverence in the church
of Theodolinda. Since the freeing of Venice and Verona, Italy has again got back the crown of her Kings,
the famous Iron Crown of Monza. We almost tremble
as we speak of this venerable relic, lest we should anyhow get wrong between the Iron Crown and the crowns
of Agilulf and Theodolinda, all of which are engraved
together by Muratori, in illustration of the text of Paul
the Deacon. Then too it is somewhat fearful to find

the great Italian scholar casting to the winds the legend
on which Monza has for ages dwelled with delight.
Nothing is more certain than that the Iron Crown is so
called, not because it is made of iron, but because a
rim of iron is wrought in the inside of the circle of
gold and jewels. This rim of iron the local legend
asserts to have been made out of one of the nails of
the Crucifixion. Against this belief Muratori argues
with great force. If the story were really of early date,
the local historian of the fourteenth century, Bonincontro Morigia, would surely have said something about
it. Bonincontro has wise reasons to give us why the
crown should be of iron; iron is the strongest and
hardest of metals, and rules over all other metals; so
an iron crown rightly expresses the strong justice of
the Emperor who reigns over all things earthly. It
expresses too the greatness of the church of Monza,
the noblest spot in all Lombardy, as Lombardy is the
noblest land in all Italy. Surely, Muratori argues,
if this writer had ever heard that the crown contained
so holy a relic, he would never have been driven to
such arguments as these. He argues further against a
certain Archbishop who was shocked at his disbelief, and
who defended the genuineness of the relic on the ground
that Matthew Villani spoke of the crown of Monza as
a " holy crown." Muratori argues, first, that any crown,
as being used in a religious ceremony, may be called holy ;

and secondly, that there was a mistake in the text; the abbreviation which Matthew meant for *Seconda* had been mistaken for *Santa.* "Secunda Corona" is a regular name of the Iron Crown of Monza; for, when things were done in due order, it was taken after the Silver Crown of Aachen, and before the Golden Crown of Rome. But, as usual, the arguments of outsiders have not much weight when the honour of a local relic is concerned, and Monza believes in the sanctity of the Iron Crown as if Muratori had never written. The crown is shown to the stranger for the proper fee, but it is shown only with much of religious ceremony, with bending of knees and burning of incense. And, setting the religious legend aside, the heretic visitor is not disinclined to shew some reverence to a crown which had rested on so many illustrious heads, dashed perhaps a little by the thought of the sham coronations of the elder Buonaparte and of an Austrian Archduke of our own day. We seem to come nearer to a past world as we look on the badge of dominion, not only of Charles and Otto and Henry and Frederick, but of Kings older still, Kings of the nation which first established a lasting Teutonic dominion on Italian soil.

That the Iron Crown is at home at Monza, as the *Bambino* is at home in the church of Araceli, no man has ventured to doubt. The question is, whether the

Iron Crown ought ever, like the *Bambino*, to go out to meet its votaries, or whether its votaries should not always come to it. On the walls of the church of Monza may be seen the names of the four honourable men who carried the crown to Bologna for the crowning of the last Roman Emperor and King of Italy. But that journey at all events is no precedent. Charles the Fifth took his degrees in an irregular way by accumulation. He did everything in the wrong place; if Bologna is not Monza, neither is it Rome. But how stands the case between Monza and the neighbouring metropolis? That is a point on which Monza and Milan, the Archpresbyter and the Archbishop, have always held different views. Milan holds that the King should be crowned by the Archbishop in the church of St. Ambrose; Monza holds that King and Archbishop are bound to come to Monza for the ceremony, and that, if the Archbishop will not come, the Archpresbyter has a full right to crown the King without him. There are undoubted precedents both ways. It is certain that several Kings have been crowned at Monza and several at Milan. Frederick Barbarossa, for instance, was undoubtedly crowned at Monza. But when the men of Monza earnestly prayed Henry the Seventh to come to be crowned in the right place, Milan got the better of them. Monza, we must think, somewhat weakens its argument by asserting a distinct

Modoetian coronation, which sounds to us not a little legendary, for several Kings who certainly were crowned at Milan as well. On the other hand, we think that Mr. Tylor would argue that, if Milan were the right crowning-place, the crown would always have lived at Milan and not at Monza. Little Monza could never encroach on the rights of great Milan, while great Milan could easily encroach on the rights of little Monza. This ground is, we think, enough to make us decide for Monza as his crowning-place, whenever the King of Italy chooses to take his crown.

Besides the *Oraculum* there is, perhaps not unfittingly, but little to see at Monza. There is a town-house called the *Broletto*, a rather striking building of the thirteenth century. We might almost think that the town was unwalled till the fourteenth century, as we find that between the years 1334 and 1336 the "Terra de Modoetia" was strongly fortified by Azzo Visconti. It had stood a siege about ten years before; but then it was defended only by a ditch and a "palangatum," which we take to mean a palisade. Of course the "Terra" had its ancient and noble families, some Guelf and some Ghibelline, but as a whole, the municipal history of the place does not go for much. It is the crowning-place of the Italian Kingdom, or at least the dwelling-place of its crown, and it is nothing more. We may add that one some-

what irregular coronation, that of Conrad the Third
as opposition King to the Emperor Lothar, was done in
a somewhat irregular place—not in the *Oraculum* of
St. John, but in the lesser church of St. Michael. He
heard mass however at St. John's, and was presently
crowned afresh, or at least wore his crown, at Milan.

Why the crown of Monza should be said to be, as it
is by the local historian, " super Italiam, Normandiam,
et Saxoniam," we do not at all understand. We must
decline all allegiance on behalf of all the lands which
have at any time borne either of the two latter names.

COMO.

————◦◦◦————

IT was by the side of the Lake of Como that Dr.
Stanhope, according to Mr. Anthony Trollope, had his
villa and made his collection of butterflies. One can
fancy that it was in some points pleasanter living there
than either at Barchester or at Eiderdown. If one
wished to dream away life, one could hardly desire a
place better suited for the purpose than the shores of
one of those Italian lakes; and yet they suggest a great
deal besides matter for dreaming. The professed
climber would most likely despise the heights immediately above the Larian Lake; yet there is a good
deal of snow within sight from more than one point of
it. The geographer will be relieved from all difficulties
on that one of the greater lakes which is wholly Italian,
and no part of whose shores is either Austrian or Swiss.
The Swiss frontier indeed comes amazingly near to the
city of Como; but from the lake itself it seems, as it
were, studiously to keep away, as if to make up for the
large share of the lake of Lugano which the Confederation
has taken to itself. Then the sides of this lake, as of

its fellows, are so thickly inhabited, there is such an endless succession of houses, villages, and churches, dotted up and down over the mountains, that there are few places where the general effect of the Italian style of building, as applied to something other than great cities, can be better taken in. And almost our first thought is the extreme unpicturesqueness of most of the buildings which find themselves in such picturesque sites. It is so throughout Italy. A small Italian town perched on a hill-side or a hill-top ought to add to the effect; but it seldom does so. In some of the most striking points of Tuscany and Umbria one cannot help wishing to exchange the little towns and villages on the heights for some of the picturesque little towns of Franconia, with their gates, towers, spires, an outline of some kind about everything. The ruined castle, so common along the Rhine, is rare, though not absolutely unknown, among the Italian lakes. When it is to be seen, the picturesque element at once comes in; otherwise an Italian village has everything so white and flat as not to be an addition to the landscape, as a little German town would be, but rather the opposite. The flatness is relieved only by the campaniles of the churches, churches with which the hill-sides are thick set. These supply many good specimens of the true type, tall, square, hard, with the coupled windows and mid-wall shafts, which all Western Europe once borrowed

T

from Italy. And these smaller towers in the villages by the lake lead well up to the two nobler ones which form the chief architectural ornament of the city from which the lake takes its modern name, Imperialist Como itself.

To the architectural student the lake-side city is certainly most attractive on account of a building which is not strictly part of the city itself, the minster of St. Abbondio without its walls. Yet Como has a good deal to say for itself on other grounds. It is the city of the Plinies, as modern Como has not forgotten; for she carefully keeps, built into the wall of her cathedral church, a stone with an inscription preserving the name of her most renowned heathen inhabitant. We began with a reference to one novelist, and chance supplies us, at Como itself, with a reference to another. From a passage in *My Novel* it seems that Lord Lytton —we will not say thought, but allowed himself for a moment to write—that the elder Pliny died in the crater of Ætna. The confusion is amusing; still, as things go, when two sages died of two volcanoes, it is perhaps a light matter to couple the wrong sage and the wrong volcano.

> Deus immortalis haberi
> Dum cupit Empedocles, ardentem frigidus Ætnam
> Insiluit.

No such motive, we are sure, was present to the mind of the diligent compiler of the Natural History and loyal admiral of Vespasian's fleet. Deity was not for him, but only for the master who, when he began to sicken as a man, said merrily that he felt himself beginning to be a god. Anyhow Como may well be proud both of the uncle who died among the ashes of Vesuvius, and of the nephew, somewhat of a prig as he was, to whom we owe the account of the Bithynian Christians and the first and most decent of the Panegyrics.

But it was hardly by producing either the elder or the younger Pliny that Como had its chief share ·in influencing the destinies of mankind. For such a share it has had, though not in so direct a way as greater and more renowned cities. Twice in the history of Europe have the wrongs of Como or its citizens been counted among the causes or occasions of events which have turned the world upside down. One of the alleged grounds for the rebellion of the first Cæsar was the scourging of a citizen of Como in despite of the patron who had bestowed on him exemption from such treatment. And, twelve hundred years afterwards, not the stripes of a single man of Como, but the general wrongs which the whole commonwealth had suffered at the hands of Milan, were among the alleged grounds for the first great Italian expedition of a later Cæsar. In those days

Civitas Ambrosii velut Troja stabat;

T 2

not in the new form in which she again rose by the
help of Cremona and Brescia, but in the stateliness
handed down from the old days when Milan was a seat
of Empire. In the eyes of the men of Como, Milan, the
centre of Lombard independence, was simply the local
tyrant under whose yoke they were writhing; the
German conqueror was to them their lawful sovereign
and deliverer, the "dulcissimus Imperator," as yet more
fortunate than Augustus, better than their own Pliny's
own Trajan. And, as if expressly to make the parallel
between Julius and Frederick yet more speaking, the
fellow-sufferer of Como, who prayed, like her, for deliverance by the hand of Frederick from the power of
Milan, was the city which bore the name of the rival of
Julius, Lodi, once *Laus Pompeii*. The city which rejoiced
in the patronage of Cæsar and the city which rejoiced
in the patronage of Pompeius joined to crave the help of
the Emperor who, when in his later days he set forth on
his last crusade, did not forget to proclaim himself as the
avenger of Crassus and Antonius on the Parthian.

Como then, without having any great direct place in
history, has a considerable indirect place. The existing
city itself has a character which is somewhat analogous
to its historical position. It has no particular interest
as a whole; there is nothing specially characteristic in
its plan or its architecture; but it stands on a beautiful
site, and it contains two or three buildings of some

importance. Standing on the edge of its lake, encircled by mountains, with the castle-crowned peak of Baradello looking down on it—like a vaster St. Michael's Tor on Avalon, when Avalon was an island—the general aspect of Como is altogether a taking one. But, if we walk through its streets, we shall find few Italian cities which have so little to show in the way of arcades or street architecture of any kind. Without comparing Como in this way to Bologna or Padua or Verona, there is really more of characteristic Italian domestic architecture hidden in the narrow streets of its small neighbour Lugano. But some particular buildings deserve notice. At Como Church and State must have been on friendly terms. The home of the commonwealth joins hard to the synagogue; the *duomo* and the *broletto* make up a single range. The secular building is the more pleasing of the two. The tower is plain, one might say rude; but the body of the building belongs to that momentary stage, early in the thirteenth century, when the use of the pointed arch was just beginning to creep into the Italian Romanesque, but when the distinguishing faults of the Italian Gothic had not yet begun to show themselves. The massive piers support slightly pointed arches; but there is no other departure from the true national forms of Italy; the grouped windows above are round. In the west front of the cathedral all the faults of the sham Gothic of

Italy come out. The front itself is a sham; there are
doors and windows because doors and windows are
things which no building can do without; but, as usual
in the Italian Gothic, they are simply cut through
the wall, not worked into the design, as either in the
Italian Romanesque or in the Northern Gothic. The
lover of genuine mediæval art will at Como be most
likely to say that the *Renaissance* choir, transepts, and
cupola are really better in their own way than the
Gothic nave. Yet, after all, the Italian Gothic, as it is
seen at Como, is not of the worst kind. The church
seems to have caught a little of the spirit of the great
duomo of Milan. The arches at least do not sprawl
over the same frightful width as those at Florence and
elsewhere. And we feel kindly towards the fourteenth
or fifteenth century architect for preserving the two
lions which now do duty for another purpose within,
but which must have served in an earlier church to
bear up, as at Ancona and St. Zeno, the columns of a
mighty doorway in the true native style of Italy.

But, as everywhere in Italy, the true glory of Como
is to be found in one of the earlier buildings reared
in the genuine national style of the country, the style
which all Western countries learned of her. The
church of St. Fidelis within the city, though sadly
spoiled, keeps some good Romanesque portions, especially its apse. But this is a small matter compared

ST. ABBONDIO, COMO.

To face page 279.

with the great minster without the walls; for Como
has no lack of walls and gates, though they cannot be
called specially attractive. The St. Augustine's or
St. Ouen's of Como is the church of St. Abbondio.
The eye is at once caught by the admirable grouping
of its east end, a grouping German rather than Italian,
an apse of extraordinary height and richness rising
between two tall campaniles of the type which Germany borrowed from Italy. It shows the real identity
of the older German and Italian styles that the
grouping of the towers at once suggests thoughts
of Germany. Had one of them stood detached, it would
have simply passed as a fine example of the usual Italian
type. But the great height of all this part of the church,
quite unlike the wide, spreading apse, so common both
in Germany and Italy, and without the open gallery
usual in both countries, gives St. Abbondio a character
of its own. This part contrasts a good deal with
the rest of the building, where, in the outside view,
width is the prevailing dimension. Double aisles, un-
masked in any way, with a double clerestory, form a
body as stately in its own way as the eastern part, and
inside height strongly predominates. Of the four ranges
of piers, the two central ranges are tall columnar piers
of masonry, something like those of our own Gloucester
and Tewkesbury, but with a more distinct cushion
capital. The southern range are tall monolith columns

lofty beyond any classical proportion, also with cushion capitals; but those which answer to them on the north side seem to be classical columns lengthened to the proportion that was needed, and fitted with various capitals. An English eye of course misses the triforium, or its equivalent of some kind, between the arcade and the clerestory; but the whole interior is of singular dignity. The western gallery within, the signs of a western portico, destroyed or never added, without, are points to be noticed; indeed the church would well deserve a monograph. As to its present state, it has either been singularly fortunate in having escaped the destroying hands of Popes and Jesuits, or else it has been restored in a singularly conservative fashion. Something has plainly been done; but, to judge from the building itself, no mischief. Yet a pile of broken columns and fragments of sculpture of all kinds and dates lying about close to the church suggests natural suspicions. Some pieces seem actually of Roman date, and indeed the lower part of the walls of the church itself appear to be made out of the massive stones of a Roman building. Be all this as it may, the minster of St. Abbondio is indeed a thing to see, an example of a kind of Italian Romanesque, not untouched by Northern influences, but quite free from the strange forms of St. Ambrose at Milan and St. Michael at Pavia.

On the whole, Como, though not at all a city of the first antiquarian rank, is one far from lacking in interest. And the slight Northern tinge to be seen in the architecture of its chief monument does not seem out of place in a city where men must have so often sent up the strains of the loyal hymn—

> Princeps terræ principum, Cæsar noster, ave,
> Cujus jugum omnibus bonis est süave ;
> Et si quis recalcitrat, putans illud grave,
> Obstinati cordis est et cervicis pravæ.

BRESCIA.

FROM Como, a roundabout, but highly attractive, journey by lake and railway will lead, without passing through mightier Milan, to another city with whose place in Italian and general history that of Como may be compared and contrasted. As a city, Brescia ranks far higher than Como; it does so even now; much more so did it in the days when Brescia was looked on as a rival to Milan. And the direct part which Brescia has played in history has been incomparably more important than that which has been played by Como. If its wrongs were never made the pretext of such mighty movements as those which sprang out of the earlier and the later wrongs of Como, the doings and the sufferings of the city itself are far more prominent and important. Brescia played her part as an important member of the Lombard League, and her name and the effigies of her citizens were set up by grateful Milan over the gate which recorded her rebuilding, partly by Brescian hands, after her overthrow by the later patron of Como. Prominent as

Brescia thus was in opposition to the claims of Frederick, she appears as no less prominent in withstanding the last of his successors whose Imperial claims were other than a mockery. The city stood a siege at the hands of Henry of Lüzelburg; and if her own chief Tebaldo Brusati died by what some called the cruelty and some the justice of the Emperor, his loss was avenged by the death of Henry's own brother Waleran, in the struggle beneath her walls. In later times, when Brescia, like so many of her sister cities, had passed under the dominion of St. Mark, we find her the centre of the strongest resistance to the Kings who leagued together to wipe out the wise aristocracy from among the ruling cities of the world. The name of Brescia may be familiar to many who have but vague ideas of Frederick of Swabia and Henry of Lüzelburg, because there the knight " without fear and without reproach " gained himself the praise of superhuman virtue by not playing what among honest men would be called the part of a superhuman scoundrel. That Brescia fell from her old place was largely due to the havoc and massacre wrought by her French conquerors in a warfare as unprovoked and inexcusable as any in which French conquerors ever engaged. The blood of Avogaro, shed at the bidding of Gaston of Foix, could more rightly. cry for vengeance than the blood of Brusati shed at the bidding of Henry the Seventh.

What was, from his own point of view, a deed of stern justice at the hands of the lawful King of Italy sinks into simple murder when it was done merely to glut the pride of an unprovoked invader.

Brescia then is a city which has lived a life in the very thick of Italian history, while Como has, so to speak, lived only on its outskirts. The contrast is marked in the position of the two cities. Both lie on the northern frontier of Italy, at the foot of her great mountain bulwark. But they look different ways. Como, in her valley, by her lake, looks northward, as if opening her arms to welcome the Teutonic King who comes to her relief. Brescia, not lying in an Alpine valley, but with her citadel perched on a spur of the Alps themselves, instead of turning away her eyes from Italy to the north, looks down upon nothing short of Italy herself. The view from the castle of Brescia is indeed a noble one. And it is not a mere noble view; it is a view on which the characteristic history of Italy is legibly written. It may remind us of the famous letter of Sulpicius to Cicero. With a single glance of the eye we look down on a crowd of cities, each of which once was an independent commonwealth, with its name and place in history. On one side are the spurs of the Alps on which we are standing, reminding us that there is a land beyond, from which Emperors came down to demand the crowns of Italy and of Rome. To the far

east we get a glimpse of smaller hills on the extreme
horizon, suggesting that the natural ramparts of Verona
are not beyond our sight. But to the south the eye
ranges over the boundless plain of Lombardy, spreading
like a sea, with a tall tower here and there, like the
mast of a solitary vessel. Each of those towers marks
a city, a city which once ranked alongside of princes,
cities which made war and peace, and which contained
within their walls the full life of a nation. The map
shows that one of them is the mighty tower of Piacenza,
and that another is the yet mightier tower of Cremona,
the fellow-worker of Brescia in the great work of
restoring Milan. But we look out on even more than
this. We have vividly brought home to us how near
the great cities of Northern Italy lie to the Alpine
barrier, the barrier which was so often found helpless to
shelter them against the Northern invader. We think
of all the conquerors who have crossed the mountains
from Hannibal to our own day. And we go back to
times earlier still, when the land which became the truest
Italy was not yet Italy at all, when the Po was as truly
a Gaulish river as the Seine. If the Alps themselves
proved so feeble a barrier for the shelter of Italy, how
far more feeble was the barrier which sheltered Etruria
and Rome, when what is now Northern Italy was still
Gaul within the Alps. From such a point we may well
run over the shifting fates of the land before us from

Brennus to either Buonaparte. And, as our thoughts
flit on beyond Po and Macra and Arno to the seven hills
by the Tiber, we may feel thankful that the dominion
of the last invader has become as much a thing of the
past as the dominion of the earliest.

Yet, though the great historic view of Brescia lies to
the south, it may be well for him who stands on that
height to turn his eyes to the north also. There is one
period in the history, if not of Brescia, yet of the most
renowned man of Brescia, which makes us look alike
northward and southward, which makes us span the
space which lies between the Tiber and the Limmat.
If Como looks beyond the Alps for her own deliverer,
Brescia too looks beyond the Alps, not for a deliverer
for herself, but for a place of shelter for the citizen
whom she sent forth to deliver others. In the life of
the Brescian Arnold his native city seems like a halting-
place between his city of refuge at Zürich and his city
of glory and martyrdom at Rome. We need not be
harsh either on Frederick or on Hadrian. In the eyes
of a Pope and an Emperor, a republican reformer could
hardly fail to bear the guise of a heretic and a traitor.
On the heights of Brescia we feel, as we look Rome-ward,
a regret that it was at Swabian and English hands that
he met his doom. But, as we look northward, we may
feel comfort that it was a Teutonic and Imperial city
which sheltered him. And for his own city it is no

small part of her fame to have reared the man who, if he took his memories for hopes, could yet call back for a moment the days when Rome had not to seek her master either in a German King or in an English Pontiff.

The view of the city itself on which we look down from the castle is hardly worthy of the general landscape of which it forms a part. Its look is indeed striking ; but it is hardly more so than that of any city of decent antiquity must be when it is looked down on in such a way. But the view of Brescia does not send up any object on which the eye at once seizes as something specially to dwell on. There are towers and cupolas ; but there is no tower or cupola which kindles any very strong desire for a further acquaintance. And, as we walk the streets, there are fewer attractive buildings, whether ecclesiastical or domestic, than in most Italian cities. Yet Brescia by no means lacks objects deserving study. But the chief antiquities of the city lie somewhat hid, and have to be looked for. The most striking when we come near to it, though it necessarily makes no show in the general· view, is the *duomo vecchio,* the old cathedral, the famous round church of Brescia. The new cathedral by its side is a building of no importance; but it is at least to the credit of its builders that they left the old one standing. Had the same discretion been shown in some other places, we should have many more monuments of early times than we have. But if the round church has not been destroyed, a vast deal of labour has been spent on the characteristic work of spoiling it. The upper round, the clerestory, has not been seriously meddled with. It still keeps the majesty of its circular outline, with a far greater effect of spreading massiveness— the proper effect of a round building—than any of the round churches of England. But the lower range has been sadly tampered with. The round rests on massive square piers, and the whole has been, like St. Vital at Ravenna, bedaubed to imitate *Renaissance* architecture. This makes the general look of the inside sadly disappointing. But the disappointment begins to vanish as soon as we make our way underground and see the spacious crypt, with the endless variety of its columns and capitals of all manner of forms, some of them clearly classical ones used up again. This crypt proves that the round church of Brescia had, as all the round churches of England have at present, a choir projecting to the east, but the choir to which the crypt belonged has made way to a late building on a much larger scale.

Besides the round church, there is also in Brescia a Romanesque church of the basilican plan to match it; but this has emphatically to be looked for. Within the range of the extensive buildings which go by the

common name of St. Julia—a suppressed monastery,
now put to various military and municipal uses—are
three churches. One of these, St. Mary *in Solario*, a
square Romanesque building with an octagon top, shows
itself in the street; but, unlike the usual rule of Brescia,
the inside, except the crypt, hardly fulfils the promise
of the outside. In truth, a small building of this kind,
where there can hardly be any columns, allows of
but little scope for display within, unless, like the
buildings of its class at Ravenna, it is covered with
mosaics. Far more important than this is another
of the same group, St. Saviour, attached at a lower
level to the worthless church of St. Julia proper.
Here, when we have made our way to it, we find a
genuine church of the basilican type, which to some
travellers may chance to be their first specimen of that
type. Two ranges of columns above and a crypt below
exhibit the usual features of buildings of this class,
columns with capitals of various kinds, classical and
otherwise, ranged as happened to be convenient. Every
building of this kind has its interest, and to some it
may happen to be the first foreshadowing of its more
stately fellows at Ravenna, at Lucca, and at Rome.

But the chief attraction of Brescia is hardly to be
found in its churches. Had it been left uninjured, the
great *Broletto*, in much the same style as the smaller
one at Como, and like that, joining hard to the *duomo*,

U

though not actually touching it, would doubtless have claimed the first place. And its historic interest is not small; it was round this spot that the fight raged most fiercely when Brescia had thrown off the heavy bondage of the Gaul to return to the lighter yoke of the Serene Republic. But the building is sadly disfigured; its blocked windows merely peep through to show what they were. On the whole, the first place among the antiquities of Brescia must be given to the museum, formed out of an excavated temple. The remains of the building itself, the stately columns of its portico which still survive, are striking in themselves, and they supply one piece of detail which is interesting in the history of architectural forms. The columns do not form a continuous range, but the portico has projections in front. The angles have thus to be provided for, and they are provided for by forestalling, in the architecture of the days of Vespasian, the section of the mediæval clustered pillar. Within, in the restored triple *cella*, is a whole store of antiquities, classical and mediæval. The gem of the collection in an artistic point of view is doubtless the figure of Victory, of Greek workmanship; but more light is thrown on Brescian history by the long series of inscriptions ranging from the first Imperial days to Gratian and Theodosius, and by the other long series of architectural details, classical and Romanesque, from the destroyed buildings of the city.

The library too is rich in treasures, precious manu-
scripts of various dates, jewelled crosses, carvings, and
an object which, if we were right in our reading of it,
is of surpassing interest. This is a consular diptych,
bearing the name of Boetius. This is a relic indeed,
though it would have had a more melancholy interest
still, if it had been found at Pavia instead of at Brescia.
At Ravenna we would fain not be reminded of the one
crime of the reign of the prince under whom Rome
and Italy were happy.

Such are a traveller's impressions of Brescia. It is a
witness to the amazing historical wealth of the Italian
cities that a place like this, which has so many memories
and so much to show for them, can hardly, in an antiquarian point of view, claim a place above the third
rank.

THE BURGUNDIAN MARCH.

VERCELLI.

GEOGRAPHY is now and then so fluctuating, one is tempted to say so accommodating, that the great fight of the Raudian Fields, where Marius and Catulus —Sulla would have us believe that it was Catulus only—overthrew the Northern invader, is sometimes said to have been fought near Verona and sometimes near Vercellæ. The distance is certainly considerable, all the more so as no less a city than Milan lies between. We believe that we can honestly say that the evidence is strongly in favour of the neighbourhood of Vercellæ. But possibly some caviller may hint that our judgement is not wholly disinterested. For a far better moral may be pointed, if we place the battle near Vercellæ than if we place it near Verona. A moral might be pointed at Verona also; but it could not be carried out in such curious detail as the moral which is supplied at Vercellæ. We could not at Verona bring it home so nearly to ourselves as Englishmen. No one will venture for a moment to compare the two cities. Verona is as it were many cities; it has played so great a part in history at so many different times; its monuments are of so many kinds and are spread over so many ages. Vercellæ, as a city of Roman days, has nothing to show but the memory of the great fight which we are determined to place not far from its walls. And when we turn to modern Vercelli, instead of the varied interests and monuments of Verona, we find only a respectable Italian city, whose attractions are almost wholly ecclesiastical, and whose ecclesiastical attractions gather almost wholly round one great building. Yet, in a strange way, the ecclesiastical interest of the city takes forms which may be looked on as, in some sort, the exact reverse of the event which gave Vercellæ its fame in earlier days. And yet the later history of Vercelli is not wholly a revival of its earliest history; from one point of view it may even pass as its continuation. The fame of Vercellæ of old was as the place where the final and overwhelming check was given to the greatest inroad upon Italy which had as yet been made by the nations beyond the Alps. In this light the ethnological question matters but little. Celt and Teuton might, in the days of Marius, be looked on as parts of one whole in opposition to the common enemy, the common teacher, at Rome. And so, in the later aspect of Vercelli, we feel that, in later times also, all the nations beyond the

Alps, all the Barbarians of Pope Julius' hatred, have something in common as contrasted with later Italy. The place which saw the overthrow of the Northern invaders became in a singular way the seat of more than one form of close connexion between Italy and the lands beyond the Alps. It became, in a way in which no other Italian city ever did, the special seat of the influence of Northern art on the Italian side of the Alps.

This may sound like a paradox; yet to the Englishman the name of Vercelli suggests, or should suggest, a manuscript and a church, in both of which England is in a manner transplanted to Italian soil. To the student of the earliest forms of our tongue Vercelli is as familiar, as dear, as Exeter or Peterborough; perhaps it is even dearer and more familiar. That a book at Vercelli and a cross in old Northumberland should have preserved two different copies of the same ancient English poem is what no one would have looked for beforehand. Yet so it is. The book of Vercelli, like the book of Exeter, is among the most precious storehouses of our ancient speech. How came it hither? That question we are not prepared to answer; but thither by some means it did come. Here is direct connexion with the North, its special connexion with England. But this is not all. There is at Vercelli direct influence, direct artistic influence, from Northern lands, and from our own land among them. The building which now gives Vercelli its chief attraction is far less Italian than it is Northern. But with that general word we must be satisfied. It is Northern opposed to Italian : but it is not distinctively English or French or German. It has elements drawn from all three sources, but it does not belong exclusively to any one.' Thus far the northern nations may seem to have repaid at Vercelli in the way of art the overthrow which ages before they suffered there in the way of warfare. But there is another side to the picture. We see at Vercelli Northern influence ; we see even distinctly English influences. But how came they thither ? The work of Marius might still seem to be going on in the thirteenth century, when Vercelli was enriched not merely by the arts of the North, but by its plundered treasures. We feel half conquerors, half conquered, when we look at a pile built on Italian soil in direct imitation of buildings of our own country, but which we at the same time cannot forget was built by an enemy of England, out of the spoils of England.

Now if we had placed the battle of the Raudian Fields hard by Verona, we could have pointed our moral in one way only. We might have said that the blow dealt by the Roman to the Northern invader, was repaid when the Goth ruled by the Adige, and when Verona became *Dietrichsbern*. Verona has nothing which connects it with the English tongue, with English

art, with English money. There is no book of Verona dear
to the Old-English scholar. St. Zeno has no English
features in its architecture, nor had the men who
reared it enriched themselves at the cost of England.
St. Andrew at Vercelli has another tale to tell. In
the later days of John and the earlier days of Henry
the Third, the Legate Walo or Gualo fills a prominent
place in English history. After the King of the
English had stooped to become the man of the Bishop
of Rome, Walo appears everywhere as the champion
of his master's vassal and the denouncer of all who
opposed him and his son. Things were so changed by
the death of John that our English feelings almost
go round to the side of the Roman Legate, when we
find him encouraging the troops of Henry at the Fair
of Lincoln. Yet Walo appears throughout as one of
those papal emissaries who went so far towards becoming the actual rulers of England during the minority
of Henry. And, as became a papal emissary, he appears
also as a merciless plunderer of the clergy and nation
of England. The fruits of his plunder we see in one of
the stateliest piles in Italy, the only one which would
not seem out of place on Northern ground. Out of
the spoils of England Walo reared the half English-
looking, hardly at all Italian-looking, minster of St.
Andrew.

But the general effect of Walo's church, as we see it

from the outside, is neither English nor Italian, but distinctly German. When we first come in sight of Vercelli, the wonderful grouping of its towers at once strikes us with amazement. There is nothing like it in Italy; we seem to be suddenly carried off into the Teutonic land. We have seen a slight approach to a German effect even in St. Ambrose at Milan, and something much nearer to it in St. Abbondio at Como. But here we seem to have come to the thing itself; here is an outline as varied as Bamberg or Gelnhausen. A little further examination will show that, though its varied grouping is thoroughly German in its general effect, St. Andrew's does not exactly follow any of the received types of German churches. There is no approach to the most truly German pattern of all, the apse at each end, each with its pair of towers, often each with its central lantern. The east end has no apse, no towers; it is flat, like an English east end, though we may doubt whether an English architect, left to himself, would have put a wheel-window immediately over his three great lancets. At the west end the spirit of the North prevailed so far as to plant two towers, but the influence of Italian soil and atmosphere cut them down into mere slender turrets, with a wide west front, under a single low gable, between them. Over three splendid doorways is a wheel; over that two rows of arcading. The central lantern is a massive octagon bearing a

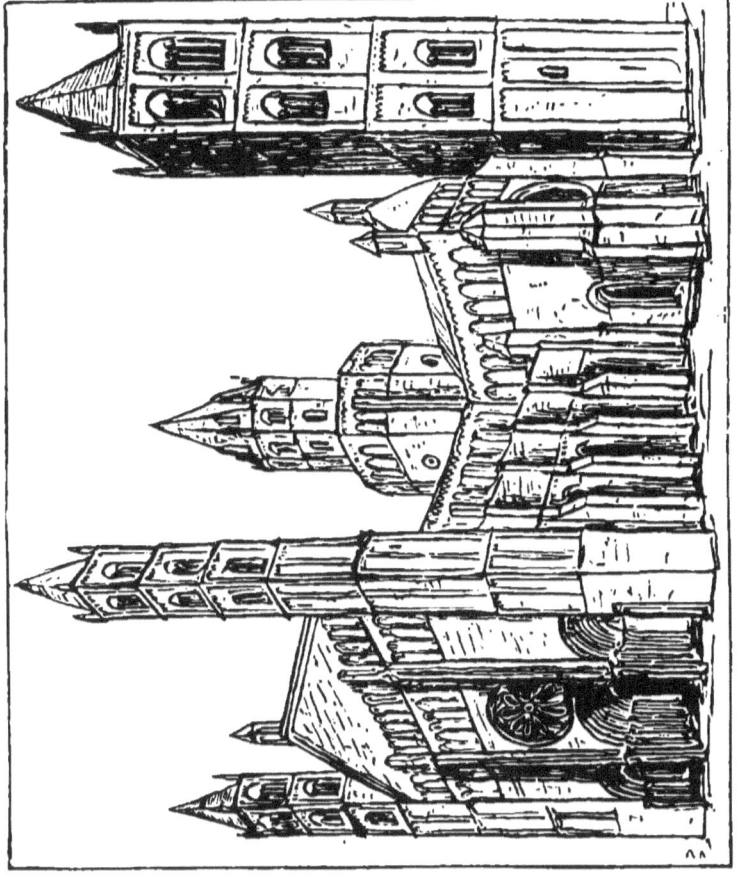

ST. ANDREW, VERCELLI.

To face page 300.

lighter one; and the grouping of this with the western turret, was the whole amount of grouping which the church had as it came from the hands of Walo. But a great addition of later times completed the work, and completed it in a way quite worthy of its beginning. Walo, with his lantern and his slender western turrets, had supplied no fitting bell-tower. But an Italian church, even though so little Italian in its character as St. Andrew's, could not go without its campanile. A tower accordingly arose which forms one of the most important elements in the general grouping, and without which Vercelli would hardly seem itself. The ingenuity with which it is adapted to the church is admirable. St. Andrew's was no basilica to be mated with the traditional detached tower; the spirit of the building called for something which should be more thoroughly part of itself. A huge square tower of the best Italian type accordingly arose, neither wholly attached to, nor wholly detached from, the church. It just joins on the corner of the south transept, and is set on so as not to stand parallel with any part of the building, an arrangement which is no small element in this wonderful piece of grouping. The architect who could thus adapt an addition to what he already found existing must have had a genius higher than that of the original designer.

The style of the whole exterior is that later form of Romanesque which we may say was common to

Germany and Italy, and which, even in Germany, lived on some way into the thirteenth century. The round arch is used throughout, except in the *quasi*-English lancets at the east end, and in the transepts. It is when he gets inside that the Englishman feels more at home. It might indeed be argued that the inside of St. Andrew's is, after all, not so much English as French. It is of course neither purely English nor purely French; but the style which it exhibits is that form of the early Gothic, or, more strictly, the last stage of the Transition from Romanesque to Gothic, which is common to France with a part of England. It will not remind any one of Ely or Salisbury or Beverley; but it ought to remind any one who has seen them of Wells and Glastonbury and Llandaff. And yet, in the mere shape of the clustered columns, Vercelli really comes nearer to Ely than to Wells, while the mouldings are—here the Italian element comes out—less advanced than they would be in any English, or even French, church of the date. But the capitals would seem quite in place in the great churches of the West of England, and in many French churches too. The proportions are quite Northern; there are no broad sprawling Italian pier-arches here. That the clerestory windows are round-headed is not wonderful, but the blank triforium space is an eye-sore In this point Modena, a hundred and fifty years earlier, had got ahead of Vercelli.

On the whole perhaps the inside of St. Andrew's is less satisfactory than the outside. Yet its slender columns, its vaults, its noble octagonal lantern, make a grand interior in itself, while the interest of seeing forms of this kind where one would so little have looked for them is something beyond words. Walo helped to rob us of our money and our freedom; but he certainly learned a good deal in the way of art, most likely in our own island, certainly on our side of the Alps. By this time the seed sown at Spalato and Ravenna had grown in northern lands into something which Italy might well try to transplant, but which she never succeeded in reproducing.

The rest of the city of Vercelli is quite worth going carefully through; but the rest of its churches and other buildings are dwarfed beside so wonderful a pile as St. Andrew's. There is more than one good tower, including one attached to the *duomo*, a building of the *Renaissance*. But, as Walo's minster is the first thing which catches the traveller's eye in drawing near Vercelli, he will be well pleased to come back to it before he bids the city farewell. He will feel that here is indeed a spot where if the North suffered one signal overthrow, she has had her revenge in other ways. To see the Roman Legate going home to imitate the arts of Germany, France, and England on Italian soil, is a sight which is unique in the world.

We may well use Vercelli as a step from Italy to the lands on our side of the mountains. We may well make it our path to the last city on our list, a city which modern geography places within the bounds of Italy, but in which we shall find that Northern forms are not, as at Vercelli, exotics brought in at the will of a single man, but are the genuine growth of the soil. As we entered Italy by the borderland of Trent, we will leave it by the borderland of Aosta.

AOSTA.

THE cities named after the first Augustus rival in their number those named after the Macedonian Alexander. Some indeed of the many cities which bore the name of Augusta were actually named in honour of later Emperors; still the title and tradition of him who was Augustus before and above all others is in a manner carried on even in those later Augustæ of which he was not the immediate founder. But from most of the cities which bore the Imperial name that name has utterly vanished, or has survived in some strange and corrupted form. It needs some effort to believe that there was, as Ammianus bears witness, a time when the name of London was remembered only as the former name of the Augusta on the Thames. In Augsburg we can still see the traces of the Imperial name; but it is only the Italian tongue which still allows its full measure of syllables to Augusta Vindelicorum. In Augustodunum the title itself was but an element in the name; and it has left traces, though but feeble traces, in the name of Autun. It is still less obvious at first sight that two Imperial

x

titles lie hidden in the name of one of the most renowned of Spanish cities, and that Zaragoza in all its
spellings is only a corruption of *Cæsar-Augusta*. But
some of the Augustæ have not kept even such signs of
their origin as this. From Augusta Taurinorum and
the more renowned Augusta Treverorum all traces of
the name have vanished; indeed Augusta must have
been from the beginning little more than an official
name of the city of the Treveri. But there is another
Augusta, perhaps of less renown in history, certainly
of less account in the present state of things, to which
the Imperial name still cleaves with only a slight
phonetic change. Deep in its Alpine valley, by the
side of its rushing rivers, still girded by its Roman
walls, still entered by its Roman gate, the fortress by
which the first Augustus sought to secure Rome and
Italy from the untameable barbarians of its north-
western corner still stands, and, as it has good right
to do, it still keeps its Imperial title. Augusta Prætoria, Augusta Salassorum, has hardly changed its
name by passing into Aosta, birthplace of Anselm.

The Salassian, like the Treveran, Augusta has a
mythical founder, at whose bidding the city arose in an
age long before Romulus had scarped down the sides
of the Palatine hill. But the legend which sprang up
by the Dora is hardly so well conceived as the legend
which sprang up by the Mosel. There is something

bold, at any rate, in the notion of Trier being founded
by Trebetas the son of Ninus; but we do not exactly
see why an unknown Cordelus should have founded an
unknown Cordelia on or near the site of Aosta. The
only question which such a story awakens is whether
the name anyhow comes from the same mint, whatever
that mint may be, as the famous daughter of Lear.
But, leaving fables of this kind, the true history of the
valley of Aosta is one of those pieces of history of out-
of-the-way parts of the world which sometimes show
how a lasting historical character may cleave to a
particular district through all ages. One of the first
things which catch the eye of the traveller is the fact
that in Aosta and the coasts thereof notices are no
longer written up in Italian, but in French. French, in
short, is the received tongue of the district. No doubt,
if one came to examine the real speech of the people,
it would prove to be, not French but Provençal, not
the tongue of *oïl*, but the tongue of *oc;* but at any rate
it is not the tongue of *si*. French is the speech of
literature and society at Aosta, so far as literature and
society can be said to exist there. Now this use of French
—at least of *Gal*-Welsh, as distinguished from *Rum*—in
the city and vale of Aosta is no mere accident; it is
the very essence of their history. The district is, and
always has been, a piece of Gaul on the Italian side of
the Alps. That it was so in the days of Augustus is

the cause that the vale was ever honoured by the
presence of an Augusta. After Cisalpine Gaul was
held to have become Italy, after Transalpine Gaul had
become a province of Rome, the unconquerable inhabitants of this Alpine corner still maintained a practical
independence. The Salassi had, like other people,
received defeats from the Roman arms; but they had
also inflicted defeats in their turn, and their final
conquest was looked on as one of the most memorable
events of the reign of the second Cæsar. The tribe
was held to have been utterly rooted out by the arms
of his general Varro; those who escaped the sword
were sold as slaves; the land was parted out among
Roman soldiers, and the camp of Varro grew into the
city of Augusta Prætoria, Augusta Salassorum. Still,
though its old defenders were swept away, the land
did not lose its character as an outpost of Gaul within
the bounds of Italy. When lands were shifting to and
fro at the time of the Wandering of the Nations, and
again when they were doing the like after the break-up
of the Carolingian Empire, the vale of Aosta often
changed masters. But it always showed a tendency to
attach itself to the master of Burgundy rather than to
the master of Italy. It formed a part of several of the
many Burgundian kingdoms, and, whenever it was
separated for a while, it seems always to have found
its way back to the Burgundian connexion. It belongs

in fact to the same group of lands as Maurienne, Vaud, Bresse, the Lower Wallis, and the other dominions of the House of Savoy. Under the rulers of that house Aosta was raised to the rank of an Imperial duchy, and it still gives the ducal title to one of its princes. Since the first rise of the Savoyard power in the eleventh century, Aosta has always been a cherished possession of the dynasty, and it still remains the last fragment of their once great Burgundian dominion on both sides of the Alps, on both sides of the Leman Lake. Perhaps it was only ignorance of its peculiar history which saved the vale of Aosta from the fate of Savoy and Nizza.

We thus see why the speech of the vale of Aosta is not an Italian, but a Gaulish tongue. The old allegiance of the land was due, not to the crown of Monza, but to the crown of Arles. Augusta Salassorum came within the archchancellorship of the Primate of Augusta Treverorum. And what is true of language is equally true of architecture. There is not a trace of Italian work in the buildings of Aosta, save only the towers with open arcades at the top which are seen in some of the greater houses. Otherwise every feature is Burgundian. The doors and windows of houses and churches are such as are nowhere seen in Italy, but such as may be found anywhere from Dijon to Constanz. Indeed to an eye long accustomed to Italian forms it is a relief to see real mullions and mouldings.

The traveller who knows not, or who has forgotten, the special history of the district says at once, This is Burgundy and not Italy. And he finds that the witness of history and language only confirms the witness which he draws at the first glance from the buildings of the unsavoury suburb which lies between the arch of Augustus and the Prætorian gate.

At Aosta it is the Roman remains which have the first claim on our attention. Their extent and the importance of some of them are wonderful. The Prætorian Gate of Aosta cannot compare—it never can have compared—with the Black Gate of Trier; but its wide arches, with a smaller one on each side, are still grand in their half-ruined state, and the remains of the marble casing and ornaments show that it was a work rich in detail as well as stately in composition. But at Aosta, before we reach the gate, we pass under the triumphal arch of the founder, reminding one somewhat of Rimini, though at Rimini there are real columns, while at Aosta there are only half-columns clinging to the wall. Oddly enough, these half-columns of the Corinthian order support Doric triglyphs. There is no reason in the eternal fitness of things why they should not, and there is nothing at all displeasing to the eye in the arrangement; but we fancy that the sight would put a classical architect into the same state of mind as a herald who should see colour put

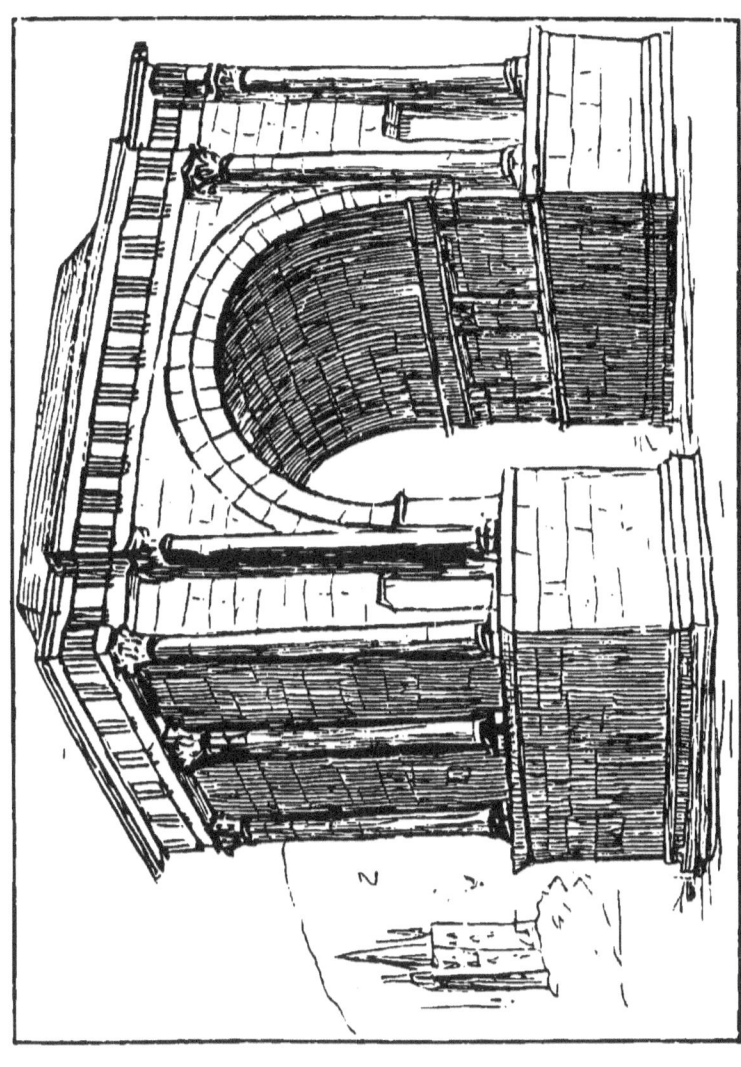

ARCH AT AOSTA.

To face page 310.

upon colour. The street between the arch and the gate partly bears the name of St. Anselm, and partly the evidently ancient name of *La Cité*. But why is the city outside the gate? The cathedral church too is within the Roman walls, though the collegiate church of St. Urse stands without them. The walls themselves, enclosing, as usual, a square space, remain throughout their whole extent, and they have had the great good luck to keep several of the square Roman towers nearly untouched. But some of them have been seized on by mediæval builders, and turned into fortresses of their own pattern. And the walls have suffered greatly in another way through the very excellence of their workmanship. Brick, such as we see at Rome and at Trier, is unknown in the Roman buildings of Aosta; and that form of Roman masonry to which we are most accustomed in Britain, the alternate courses of brick and stone, was not known till long after what at Aosta is doubly the Augustan age. The walls of Aosta were cased throughout with squared stones, and, as always happens, these have for the most part been picked away. Besides the arch, the gate, the walls, and their towers, there is also a noble fragment, forming the straight side of a theatre, and more diligent search among the gardens will find some traces of the amphitheatre. There are also some vaults under one of the canons' gardens, and,

out of the town and beyond the arch, is a Roman
bridge of a single arch of massive stones. Altogether
the city of the Salassi is, as far as the remains of
Imperial days go, no unworthy rival to the city of the
Treveri. Aosta has no one object of such surpassing
grandeur; the arch of Augustus cannot dare to match
itself with *Porta Nigra;* but, as a whole, as an example
of the fortification of a Roman town, it is far better
preserved than Trier.

The mediæval antiquities of Aosta consist chiefly of
the churches and their contents. We have said that
the domestic work is of strictly Burgundian character ;
but there is nothing that can be called street architecture. And the military works of mediæval times
consist only of the round towers added to the Roman
walls, picturesque, but nothing more. The churches
are chiefly remarkable for their towers of the Primitive
Romanesque pattern, a pattern which is Italian in
the sense in which all Primitive Romanesque is Italian,
but which is not more Italian at Aosta than it is at
Cambridge, at St. Aventin, or at St. Maurice. It is
said that in the tenth century the effects of war and
pestilence had made Aosta almost forsaken, and that
the city began to revive early in the eleventh. One
can have little doubt in assigning to this date
the twin towers of the cathedral church of Aosta, the
minster of St. Gratus and St. Jocundus. They must

have been new when Anselm was born beneath their shadow. The northern tower is untouched, a magnificent example of the stern grandeur of this early style, which in England we see only in smaller and ruder examples. Of the southern tower the upper part must have been rebuilt at the end of the twelfth or beginning of the thirteenth century, but with a certain adaptation to the earlier work, the mid-wall shaft being still used. The towers flank the apse; but so great is the width of the church between them that they hardly seem to belong to the same building. The church itself is plain and much disfigured, but its massive square piers are most likely original. On its north side is an apsidal chapel of the fourteenth century which would look quite in place either in Germany or in England, and a cloister, bearing date 1636, of debased style certainly, but which might well have passed for a century older. The choir has a splendid mosaic pavement of about the fourteenth century and a noble set of stalls; below it is a Romanesque crypt in which classical capitals have been used up again. The treasury has also shrines and vestments to show, and a consular diptych of the time of Honorius.

The other great church of St. Urse beyond the walls has a detached tower of the same class as those of St. Gratus; but it is at once plainer and more artistically designed, and is probably a little later in date. The smaller churches of the city, not remarkable for much else, supply several towers of the same general type. But St. Urse has also, like the cathedral, a fine set of stalls, and it has moreover a Romanesque cloister of singular beauty and curiosity. The whole history of Jacob and Esau, with other Scriptural and legendary scenes, is carved on the capitals. The sculpture is of course rude, but it is not lacking in spirit, and the artist's attempts to represent camels are curious enough.

We need hardly say that the mountain views in the valley of Aosta, the valley of the rushing Dora and of its no less fast rushing tributary the Buthier, are glorious beyond words. And the city itself, with its towers—their low spires showing in the distance— is no contemptible addition to the general landscape. And we may stop to think how that valley, which nature might seem to have made so inaccessible, has been in all ages a highway of armies. We will not take on ourselves to settle where Hannibal did cross the Alps; it is the fixed belief of Aosta that he passed by the place where Aosta was to be. It is more certain that a crowd of later warriors, down to the elder Buonaparte, have marched along the same track. His career might have ended hard by Aosta, had an Austrian officer, whose prisoner he was for a moment, only been a little quicker. The remembrance of so famous a visitor is preserved in the name of the

Rue du Premier Consul, which name no one at Aosta has been silly enough to change into anything else. And, while we think of conquerors, we may think also of holier names, of Bernard of Menthon, of our own Anselm. We are apt to look on Anselm as an Italian, and to be puzzled at the statement of his biographer, that to him, a stranger in Italy, the heat of that land was oppressive. When we have seen his birthplace, we better understand the words of Eadmer; and we grasp the fact that Anselm was in no sense a countryman of Lanfranc, but that he was, in a wide sense, a countryman of St. Hugh. It was the Imperial Burgundy which gave us alike the saint of Canterbury and the saint of Lincoln.

Such is Aosta: its only drawback is the filth of the place and the wretched look of the dwarfed, diseased, and cretinized inhabitants—strange descendants, whether of Salassi, Prætorians, or Burgundians. But fresh air and more of real comfort than is found in many grander places may be had at the little *Hôtel du Mont Blanc* just outside the town. Nine hours and more of diligence from Ivrea—a distance which an English coach would have done in four—is really no heavy price for a visit to such a place.

THE END.

LONDON:
PRINTED BY WILLIAM CLOWES AND SONS,
STAMFORD STREET AND CHARING CROSS.

MACMILLAN & Co.'s CATALOGUE of Works in the Departments of History, Biography, Travels, Critical and Literary Essays, Politics, Political and Social Economy, Law, etc.; and Works connected with Language.

HISTORY, BIOGRAPHY, TRAVELS, &c.

Arnold.—ESSAYS IN CRITICISM. By MATTHEW ARNOLD, New Edition, with Additions. Extra fcap. 8vo. 6s.

CONTENTS :—"*The Function of Criticism at the Present Time;*" "*The Literary Influence of Academies;*" "*Maurice de Guerin;*" "*Eugenie de Guerin;*" "*Heinrich Heine;*" "*Pagan and Mediæval;*" "*Religious Sentiment;*" "*Joubert;*" "*Spinoza and the Bible;*" "*Marcus Aurelius.*"

Atkinson.—AN ART TOUR TO NORTHERN CAPITALS OF EUROPE, including Descriptions of the Towns, the Museums, and other Art Treasures of Copenhagen, Christiana, Stockholm, Abo, Helsingfors, Wiborg, St. Petersburg, Moscow, and Kief. By J. BEAVINGTON ATKINSON. 8vo. 12s.

"*Although the main purpose of the book is strictly kept in view, and we never forget for long that we are travelling with a student and connoisseur, Mr. Atkinson gives variety to his narrative by glimpses of scenery and brief allusions to history and manners which are always welcome when they occur, and are never wordy or overdone. We have seldom met with a book in which what is principal and what is accessory have been kept in better proportion to each other.*"—SATURDAY REVIEW.

Baker (Sir Samuel W.)—Works by Sir SAMUEL BAKER, Pacha, M.A., F.R.G.S. :—

ISMAILIA : A Narrative of the Expedition to Central Africa for the Suppression of the Slave Trade, organised by Ismail, Khedive of Egypt. With Portraits, Maps, and fifty full-page Illustrations by ZWECKER and DURAND. 2 vols. 8vo. 36s.

"*A book which will be read with very great interest.*"—TIMES. "*Well*

Baker (Sir Samuel) (*continued*)—

written and full of remarkable adventures."—PALL MALL GAZETTE. "*These two splendid volumes add another thrilling chapter to the history of African adventure.*"—DAILY NEWS. "*Reads more like a romance .... incomparably more entertaining than books of African travel usually are.*"—MORNING POST.

THE ALBERT N'YANZA Great Basin of the Nile, and Exploration of the Nile Sources. Fourth Edition. Maps and Illustrations. Crown 8vo. 6s.

"*Charmingly written;*" says the SPECTATOR, "*full, as might be expected, of incident, and free from that wearisome reiteration of useless facts which is the drawback to almost all books of African travel.*"

THE NILE TRIBUTARIES OF ABYSSINIA, and the Sword Hunters of the Hamran Arabs. With Maps and Illustrations. Fifth Edition. Crown 8vo. 6s.

The TIMES says: "*It adds much to our information respecting Egyptian Abyssinia and the different races that spread over it. It contains, moreover, some notable instances of English daring and enterprising skill; it abounds in animated tales of exploits dear to the heart of the British sportsman; and it will attract even the least studious reader, as the author tells a story well, and can describe nature with uncommon power.*"

Baring-Gould (Rev. S., M.A.)—LEGENDS OF OLD TESTAMENT CHARACTERS, from the Talmud and other sources. By the Rev. S. BARING-GOULD, M.A., Author of "Curious Myths of the Middle Ages," "The Origin and Development of Religious Belief," "In Exitu Israel," &c. In Two Vols. Crown 8vo. 16s. Vol. I. Adam to Abraham. Vol. II. Melchizedek to Zechariah.

"*These volumes contain much that is very strange, and, to the ordinary English reader, very novel.*"—DAILY NEWS.

Barker (Lady).—STATION LIFE IN NEW ZEALAND. By LADY BARKER. Third Edition. Globe 8vo. 3s. 6d.

"*We have never read a more truthful or a pleasanter little book.*"—ATHENÆUM.

Bathgate.—COLONIAL EXPERIENCES; or, Sketches of People and Places in the Province of Otago, New Zealand. By ALEXANDER BATHGATE. Crown 8vo. 7s. 6d.

Blackburne.—BIOGRAPHY OF THE RIGHT HON. FRANCIS BLACKBURNE, Late Lord Chancellor of Ireland. Chiefly in connexion with his Public and Political Career. By his Son, EDWARD BLACKBURNE, Q.C. With Portrait Engraved by JEENS. 8vo. 12s.

Blanford (W. T.)—GEOLOGY AND ZOOLOGY OF ABYSSINIA. By W. T. BLANFORD. 8vo. 21*s.*
This work contains an account of the Geological and Zoological Observations made by the author in Abyssinia, when accompanying the British Army on its march to Magdala and back in 1868, and during a short journey in Northern Abyssinia, after the departure of the troops. With Coloured Illustrations and Geological Map.

Brimley.—ESSAYS BY THE LATE GEORGE BRIMLEY, M.A. Edited by the Rev. W. G. CLARK, M.A. With Portrait. Cheaper Edition. Fcap. 8vo. 2*s.* 6*d.*

Bryce.—THE HOLY ROMAN EMPIRE. By JAMES BRYCE, D.C.L., Regius Professor of Civil Law, Oxford. Fourth Edition Revised and Enlarged. Crown 8vo. 7*s.* 6*d.*
*This edition contains a supplementary chapter giving a brief sketch of the rise of Prussia, and of the state of Germany under the Confederation which expired in 1866, and of the steps whereby the German nation has regained its political unity in the new Empire. "It exactly supplies a want: it affords a key to much which men read of in their books as isolated facts, but of which they have hitherto had no connected exposition set before them."—*SATURDAY REVIEW.

Burke.—EDMUND BURKE, a Historical Study. By JOHN MORLEY, B.A., Oxon. Crown 8vo. 7*s.* 6*d.*
*" The style is terse and incisive, and brilliant with epigram and point. Its sustained power of reasoning, its wide sweep of observation and reflection, its elevated ethical and social tone, stamp it as a work of high excellence."—*SATURDAY REVIEW.

Burrows.—WORTHIES OF ALL SOULS; Four Centuries of English History. Illustrated from the College Archives. By MONTAGU BURROWS, Chichele Professor of Modern History at Oxford, Fellow of All Souls. 8vo. 14*s.*
*"A most amusing as well as a most instructive book.—*GUARDIAN.

Carstares.—WILLIAM CARSTARES : a Character and Career of the Revolutionary Epoch (1649—1715). By ROBERT STORY, Minister of Rosneath. 8vo. 12*s.*
" William had, however, one Scottish adviser who deserved and possessed more influence than any of the ostensible ministers. This was Carstares, one of the most remarkable men of that age. He united great scholastic attainments with great aptitude for civil business, and the firm faith and ardent zeal of a martyr, with the shrewdness and suppleness of a consummate politician. In courage and fidelity he resembled Burnet; but he had what Burnet wanted, judgment, self-command, and a singular power of keeping secrets. There was no post to which he might not have aspired if he had been a layman, or a priest of the Church of England."
—MACAULAY'S HISTORY OF ENGLAND.

Chatterton : A BIOGRAPHICAL STUDY. By DANIEL WILSON, LL.D., Professor of History and English Literature in University College, Toronto. Crown 8vo. 6s. 6d.

The EXAMINER *thinks this "the most complete and the purest biography of the poet which has yet appeared."*

Chatterton : A STORY OF THE YEAR 1770. By Professor MASSON, LL.D. Crown 8vo. 5s.

Cooper.—ATHENÆ CANTABRIGIENSES. By CHARLES HENRY COOPER, F.S.A., and THOMPSON COOPER, F.S.A. Vol. I. 8vo., 1500—85, 18s. ; Vol. II., 1586—1609, 18s.

Cox (G. V., M.A.)—RECOLLECTIONS OF OXFORD. By G. V. Cox, M.A., New College, late Esquire Bedel and Coroner in the University of Oxford. *Cheaper Edition.* Crown 8vo. 6s.

"An amusing farrago of anecdote, and will pleasantly recall in many a country parsonage the memory of youthful days."—TIMES.

"Daily News."—THE DAILY NEWS CORRESPONDENCE of the War between Germany and France, 1870—1. Edited with Notes and Comments. New Edition. Complete in One Volume. With Maps and Plans. Crown 8vo. 6s.

Dilke.—GREATER BRITAIN. A Record of Travel in English-speaking Countries during 1866-7. (America, Australia, India.) By Sir CHARLES WENTWORTH DILKE, M.P. Sixth Edition. Crown 8vo. 6s.

"Many of the subjects discussed in these pages," says the DAILY NEWS, *"are of the widest interest, and such as no man who cares for the future of his race and of the world can afford to treat with indifference."*

Drummond of Hawthornden : THE STORY OF HIS LIFE AND WRITINGS. By PROFESSOR MASSON. With Portrait and Vignette engraved by C. H. JEENS. Crown 8vo. 10s. 6d.

"Around his hero, Professor Masson groups national and individual episodes and sketches of character, which are of the greatest interest, and which add to the value of a biographical work which we warmly recommend to the lovers of thoroughly healthy books."—NOTES AND QUERIES.

Dürer (Albrecht).—HISTORY OF THE LIFE OF ALBRECHT DÜRER, of Nürnberg. With a Translation of his Letters and Journal, and some account of his Works. By Mrs. CHARLES HEATON. Royal 8vo. extra gilt. 31s. 6d.

Elliott.—LIFE OF HENRY VENN ELLIOTT, of Brighton. By JOSIAH BATEMAN, M.A., Author of "Life of Daniel Wilson, Bishop of Calcutta," &c. With Portrait, engraved by JEENS. Extra fcap. 8vo. Third and Cheaper Edition, with Appendix. 6s.
"*A very charming piece of religious biography; no one can read it without both pleasure and profit.*"—BRITISH QUARTERLY REVIEW.

Elze.—ESSAYS ON SHAKESPEARE. By Dr. KARL ELZE. Translated with the Author's sanction by L. DORA SCHMITZ. 8vo. 12s.
"*A more desirable contribution to criticism has not recently been made.*" —ATHENÆUM.

European History, Narrated in a Series of Historical Selections from the best Authorities. Edited and arranged by E. M. SEWELL and C. M. YONGE. First Series, crown 8vo. 6s. ; Second Series, 1088-1228, crown 8vo. 6s. Third Edition.
"*We know of scarcely anything,*" says the GUARDIAN, *of this volume,* "*which is so likely to raise to a higher level the average standard of English education.*"

Faraday.—MICHAEL FARADAY. By J. H. GLADSTONE Ph.D., F.R.S. Second Edition, with Portrait engraved by JEENS from a photograph by J. WATKINS. Crown 8vo. 4s. 6d. PORTRAIT. Artist's Proof. 5s.
CONTENTS :—*I. The Story of his Life. II. Study of his Character. III. Fruits of his Experience. IV. His Method of Writing. V. The Value of his Discoveries.*—*Supplementary Portraits. Appendices :—List of Honorary Fellowships, etc.*

Forbes.—LIFE AND LETTERS OF JAMES DAVID FORBES, F.R.S., late Principal of the United College in the University of St. Andrews. By J. C. SHAIRP, LL.D., Principal of the United College in the University of St. Andrews ; P. G. TAIT, M.A., Professor of Natural Philosophy in the University of Edinburgh ; and A. ADAMS-REILLY, F.R.G.S. 8vo. with Portraits, Map, and Illustrations, 16s.
"*Not only a biography that all should read, but a scientific treatise, without which the shelves of no physicist's library can be deemed complete.*"—STANDARD.

Freeman.—Works by EDWARD A. FREEMAN, M.A., D.C.L. :—
HISTORICAL ESSAYS. By EDWARD FREEMAN, M.A., Hon. D.C.L., late Fellow of Trinity College, Oxford. Second Edition. 8vo. 10s. 6d.
CONTENTS :—*I. "The Mythical and Romantic Elements in Early English History;" II. "The Continuity of English History;" III. "The Relations between the Crowns of England and Scotland;" IV.*

Freeman (E. A.)—*continued.*

" *St. Thomas of Canterbury and his Biographers;*" V. " *The Reign of Edward the Third;*" VI. " *The Holy Roman Empire;*" VII. " *The Franks and the Gauls;*" VIII. " *The Early Sieges of Paris;*" IX. " *Frederick the First, King of Italy;*" X. " *The Emperor Frederick the Second;*" XI. " *Charles the Bold;*" XII. " *Presidential Government.*" —" *All of them are well worth reading, and very agreeable to read. He never touches a question without adding to our comprehension of it, without leaving the impression of an ample knowledge, a righteous purpose, a clear and powerful understanding.*"—SATURDAY REVIEW.

A SECOND SERIES OF HISTORICAL ESSAYS. 8vo. 10s. 6d.

The principal Essays are:—" *Ancient Greece and Mediæval Italy:*" " *Mr. Gladstone's Homer and the Homeric Ages:*" " *The Historians of Athens:*" " *The Athenian Democracy:*" " *Alexander the Great:*" " *Greece during the Macedonian Period:*" " *Mommsen's History of Rome:*" " *Lucius Cornelius Sulla:*" " *The Flavian Cæsars.*"

HISTORY OF FEDERAL GOVERNMENT, from the Foundation of the Achaian League to the Disruption of the United States. Vol. I. General Introduction. History of the Greek Federations. 8vo. 21s.

OLD ENGLISH HISTORY. With *Five Coloured Maps.* Third Edition. Extra fcap. 8vo., half-bound. 6s.

" *The book indeed is full of instruction and interest to students of all ages, and he must be a well-informed man indeed who will not rise from its perusal with clearer and more accurate ideas of a too much neglected portion of English history.*"—SPECTATOR.

HISTORY OF THE CATHEDRAL CHURCH OF WELLS, as illustrating the History of the Cathedral Churches of the Old Foundation. Crown 8vo. 3s. 6d.

" *The history assumes in Mr. Freeman's hands a significance, and, we may add, a practical value as suggestive of what a cathedral ought to be, which make it well worthy of mention.*"—SPECTATOR.

THE GROWTH OF THE ENGLISH CONSTITUTION FROM THE EARLIEST TIMES. Crown 8vo. 5s. Second Edition, revised.

THE UNITY OF HISTORY. The "REDE" LECTURE delivered in the Senate House, before the University of Cambridge, on Friday, May 24th, 1872. Crown 8vo. 2s.

GENERAL SKETCH OF EUROPEAN HISTORY. Being Vol. I. of a Historical Course for Schools edited by E. A. FREEMAN. 18mo. 3s. 6d. Fourth Edition.

" *It supplies the great want of a good foundation for historical teaching. The scheme is an excellent one, and this instalment has been executed in a way that promises much for the volumes that are yet to appear.*"—EDUCATIONAL TIMES.

Galileo.—THE PRIVATE LIFE OF GALILEO. Compiled principally from his Correspondence and that of his eldest daughter, Sister Maria Celeste, Nun in the Franciscan Convent of S. Matthew in Arcetri. With Portrait. Crown 8vo. 7s. 6d.

Gladstone (Right Hon. W. E., M.P.)—JUVENTUS MUNDI. The Gods and Men of the Heroic Age. Crown 8vo. cloth. With Map. 10s. 6d. Second Edition.

"*Seldom,*" *says the* ATHENÆUM, "*out of the great poems themselves, have these Divinities looked so majestic and respectable. To read these brilliant details is like standing on the Olympian threshold and gazing at the ineffable brightness within.*"

Goethe and Mendelssohn (1821—1831). Translated from the German of Dr. KARL MENDELSSOHN, Son of the Composer, by M. E. VON GLEHN. From the Private Diaries and Home-Letters of Mendelssohn, with Poems and Letters of Goethe never before printed. Also with two New and Original. Portraits, Fac-similes, and Appendix of Twenty Letters hitherto unpublished. Crown 8vo. 5s. Second Edition, enlarged.

" *The volume is most welcome, giving us, as it does, vivid though brief glimpses of the famous musician as a boy, a youth, and a man. But above all, it gives us a glowing picture of the boy Mendelssohn at Weimar in its golden days. . . . Every page is full of interest, not merely to the musician, but to the general reader. The book is a very charming one, on a topic of deep and lasting interest.*"—STANDARD.

Goldsmid.—TELEGRAPH AND TRAVEL. A Narrative of the Formation and Development of Telegraphic Communication between England and India, under the orders of Her Majesty's Government, with incidental Notices of the Countries traversed by the Lines. By Colonel Sir FREDERIC GOLDSMID, C.B. K.C.S.I., late Director of the Government Indo-European Telegraph. With numerous Illustrations and Maps. 8vo. 21s.

" *The second portion of the work, less historical, but more likely to attract the general reader, is composed of bright sketches from Persia, Russia, the Crimea, Tartary, and the Indian Peninsula; both sketches being illuminated by a profusion of delicate woodcuts, admirably drawn, and as admirably engraved. . . . The merit of the work is a total absence of exaggeration, which does not, however, preclude a vividness and vigour of style not always characteristic of similar narratives.*"—STANDARD.

Green.—A SHORT HISTORY OF THE ENGLISH PEOPLE. By J. R. GREEN, M.A., Examiner in the School of Modern History, Oxford. With Coloured Maps and Genealogical Tables. Crown 8vo. 8s. 6d.

"*To say that Mr. Green's book is better than those which have pre-*

celed it, would be to convey a very inadequate impression of its merits. It stands alone as the one general history of the country, for the sake of which all others, if young and old are wise, will be speedily and surely set aside. It is perhaps the highest praise that can be given to it, that it is impossible to discover whether it was intended for the young or for the old. The size and general look of the book, its vividness of narration, and its avoidance of abstruse argument, would place it among schoolbooks; but its fresh and original views, and its general historical power, are only to be appreciated by those who have tried their own hand at writing history, and who know the enormous difficulties of the task."—MR. SAMUEL R. GARDINER in the ACADEMY.

Hamerton.—Works by P. G. HAMERTON:—

THE INTELLECTUAL LIFE. With a Portrait of Leonardo da Vinci, etched by LEOPOLD FLAMENG. Crown 8vo. 10s. 6d.

"We have read the whole book with great pleasure, and we can recommend it strongly to all who can appreciate grave reflections on a very important subject, excellently illustrated from the resources of a mind stored with much reading and much keen observation of real life."— SATURDAY REVIEW.

THOUGHTS ABOUT ART. New Edition, revised, with an Introduction. Crown 8vo. 8s. 6d.

"A manual of sound and thorough criticism on art."—STANDARD. "The book is full of thought, and worthy of attentive consideration."— DAILY NEWS.

Hole.—A GENEALOGICAL STEMMA OF THE KINGS OF ENGLAND AND FRANCE. By the Rev. C. HOLE, M.A., Trinity College, Cambridge. On Sheet, 1s.

Hozier (H. M.)—Works by CAPTAIN HENRY M. HOZIER, late Assistant Military Secretary to Lord Napier of Magdala.

THE SEVEN WEEKS' WAR; Its Antecedents and Incidents. *New and Cheaper Edition.* With New Preface, Maps, and Plans. Crown 8vo. 6s.

"All that Mr. Hozier saw of the great events of the war—and he saw a large share of them—he describes in clear and vivid language."— SATURDAY REVIEW.

THE BRITISH EXPEDITION TO ABYSSINIA. Compiled from Authentic Documents. 8vo. 9s.

"This," says the SPECTATOR, "will be the account of the Abyssinian Expedition for professional reference, if not for professional reading. Its literary merits are really very great."

Hübner.—A RAMBLE ROUND THE WORLD IN 1871. By M. LE BARON HÜBNER, formerly Ambassador and Minister. Translated by LADY HERBERT. 2 vols. 8vo. 25s.

"It is difficult to do ample justice to this pleasant narrative of travel .... it does not contain a single dull paragraph."—MORNING POST.

Hughes.—MEMOIR OF A BROTHER. By THOMAS HUGHES, M.P., Author of "Tom Brown's School Days." With Portrait of GEORGE HUGHES, after WATTS. Engraved by JEENS. Crown 8vo. 5*s.* Sixth Edition.

"*The boy who can read this book without deriving from it some additional impulse towards honourable, manly, and independent conduct, has no good stuff in him.*"—DAILY NEWS. "*We have read it with the deepest gratification and with real admiration.*"—STANDARD. "*The biography throughout is replete with interest.*"—MORNING POST.

Hunt.—HISTORY OF ITALY. By the Rev. W. HUNT, M.A. Being the Fourth Volume of the Historical Course for Schools. Edited by EDWARD A. FREEMAN, D.C.L. 18mo. 3*s.*

"*Mr. Hunt gives us a most compact but very readable little book, containing in small compass a very complete outline of a complicated and perplexing subject. It is a book which may be safely recommended to others besides schoolboys.*"—JOHN BULL.

Huyshe (Captain G. L.)—THE RED RIVER EXPEDITION. By Captain G. L. HUYSHE, Rifle Brigade, late on the Staff of Colonel Sir GARNET WOLSELEY. With Maps. Cheaper Edition. Crown 8vo. 6*s.*

The ATHENÆUM *calls it "an enduring authentic record of one of the most creditable achievements ever accomplished by the British Army."*

Irving.—THE ANNALS OF OUR TIME. A Diurnal of Events, Social and Political, Home and Foreign, from the Accession of Queen Victoria to the Peace of Versailles. By JOSEPH IRVING. *Third Edition.* 8vo. half-bound. 16*s.*

"*We have before us a trusty and ready guide to the events of the past thirty years, available equally for the statesman, the politician, the public writer, and the general reader.*"—TIMES.

Jebb.—THE CHARACTERS OF THEOPHRASTUS. An English Translation from a Revised Text. With Introduction and Notes. By R. C. JEBB, M.A., Fellow and Assistant Tutor of Trinity College, Cambridge, and Public Orator of the University. Extra fcap. 8vo. 6*s.* 6*d.*

Kingsley (Charles).—Works by the Rev. CHARLES KINGSLEY, M.A., Rector of Eversley and Canon of Westminster. (For other Works by the same Author, *see* THEOLOGICAL and BELLES LETTRES Catalogues.)

ON THE ANCIEN RÉGIME as it existed on the Continent before the FRENCH REVOLUTION. Three Lectures delivered at the Royal Institution. Crown 8vo. 6*s.*

Kingsley, Charles—*continued.*

AT LAST: A CHRISTMAS in the WEST INDIES. With nearly
Fifty Illustrations. Third and Cheaper Edition. Crown 8vo. 6s.

*Mr. Kingsley's dream of forty years was at last fulfilled, when he
started on a Christmas expedition to the West Indies, for the purpose of
becoming personally acquainted with the scenes which he has so vividly
described in "Westward Ho!" These two volumes are the journal of his
voyage. Records of natural history, sketches of tropical landscape, chapters
on education, views of society, all find their place. "We can only say
that Mr. Kingsley's account of a 'Christmas in the West Indies' is in
every way worthy to be classed among his happiest productions."—*
STANDARD.

THE ROMAN AND THE TEUTON. A Series of Lectures
delivered before the University of Cambridge. 8vo. 12s.

PLAYS AND PURITANS, and other Historical Essays. With
Portrait of Sir WALTER RALEIGH. Crown 8vo. 5s.

*In addition to the Essay mentioned in the title, this volume contains
other two—one on "Sir Walter Raleigh and his Time," and one on
Froude's "History of England."*

Kingsley (Henry, F.R.G.S.)—For other Works by same
Author, *see* BELLES LETTRES CATALOGUE.

TALES OF OLD TRAVEL. Re-narrated by HENRY KINGSLEY,
F.R.G.S. With *Eight Illustrations* by HUARD. Fourth Edition.
Crown 8vo. 6s.

*"We know no better book for those who want knowledge or seek to
refresh it. As for the 'sensational,' most novels are tame compared with
these narratives."—*ATHENÆUM.

Labouchere.—DIARY OF THE BESIEGED RESIDENT
IN PARIS. Reprinted from the *Daily News*, with several New
Letters and Preface. By HENRY LABOUCHERE. *Third Edition.*
Crown 8vo. 6s.

Laocoon.—Translated from the Text of Lessing, with Preface and
Notes by the Right Hon. SIR ROBERT J. PHILLIMORE, D.C.L.
With Photographs. 8vo. 12s.

Leonardo da Vinci and his Works.—Consisting of a
Life of Leonardo Da Vinci, by MRS. CHARLES W. HEATON,
Author of "Albrecht Dürer of Nürnberg," &c., an Essay on his
Scientific and Literary Works by CHARLES CHRISTOPHER
BLACK, M.A., and an account of his more important Paintings
and Drawings. Illustrated with Permanent Photographs. Royal
8vo. cloth, extra gilt. 31s. 6d.

"A beautiful volume, both without and within. Messrs. Macmillan

*are conspicuous among publishers for the choice binding and printing of
their books, and this is got up in their best style. ·. . . No English
publication that we know of has so thoroughly and attractively collected
together all that is known of Leonardo."—TIMES.*

Liechtenstein.—HOLLAND HOUSE. By Princess MARIE
LIECHTENSTEIN. With Five Steel Engravings by C. H. JEENS,
after Paintings by WATTS and other celebrated Artists, and
numerous Illustrations drawn by Professor P. H. DELAMOTTE, and
engraved on Wood by J. D. COOPER, W. PALMER, and JEWITT &
Co. Third and Cheaper Edition. Medium 8vo. cloth elegant.
16s.

> Also, an Edition containing, in addition to the above, about 40
> Illustrations by the Woodbury-type process, and India Proofs of
> the Steel Engravings. Two vols. medium 4to. half morocco
> elegant. 4l. 4s.
> *" When every strictly just exception shall have been taken, she may be
> conscientiously congratulated by the most scrupulous critic on the produc-
> tion of a useful, agreeable, beautifully-illustrated, and attractive book."*—
> TIMES. *"It would take up more room than we can spare to enumerate
> all the interesting suggestions and notes which are to be found in these
> volumes. . . . . The woodcuts are admirable, and some of the autographs
> are very interesting."*—PALL MALL GAZETTE.

Macarthur.—HISTORY OF SCOTLAND. By MARGARET
MACARTHUR. Being the Third Volume of the Historical Course
for Schools, Edited by EDWARD A. FREEMAN, D.C.L. 18mo. 2s.
*" It is an excellent summary, unimpeachable as to facts, and putting
them in the clearest and most impartial light attainable."*—GUARDIAN.
*" No previous History of Scotland of the same bulk is anything like so
trustworthy, or deserves to be so extensively used as a text-book."*—GLOBE.

Macmillan (Rev. Hugh).—For other Works by same Author,
see THEOLOGICAL and SCIENTIFIC CATALOGUES.

HOLIDAYS ON HIGH LANDS ; or, Rambles and Incidents in
search of Alpine Plants. Second Edition, revised and enlarged.
Globe 8vo. cloth. 6s.
*"Botanical knowledge is blended with a love of nature, a pious en-
thusiasm, and a rich felicity of diction not to be met with in any works
of kindred character, if we except those of Hugh Miller."*—TELEGRAPH.
"Mr. M.'s glowing pictures of Scandinavian scenery."—SATURDAY
REVIEW.

Mahaffy.—SOCIAL LIFE IN GREECE FROM HOMER TO
MENANDER. By the Rev. J. P. MAHAFFY, M.A., Fellow of
Trinity College, Dublin. Crown 8vo. 7s. 6d.
*" No omission greatly detracts from the merits of a book so fresh in
its thought and so independent in its criticism."*—ATHENÆUM.

Martineau.—BIOGRAPHICAL SKETCHES, 1852—1868. By HARRIET MARTINEAU. Third and Cheaper Edition, with New Preface. Crown 8vo. 6s.

"Miss Martineau's large literary powers and her fine intellectual training make these little sketches more instructive, and constitute them more genuinely works of art, than many more ambitious and diffuse biographies."—FORTNIGHTLY REVIEW.

Masson (David).—For other Works by same Author, *see* PHILO-SOPHICAL and BELLES LETTRES CATALOGUES.

LIFE OF JOHN MILTON. Narrated in connection with the Political, Ecclesiastical, and Literary History of his Time. By DAVID MASSON, M.A., LL.D., Professor of Rhetoric and English Literature in the University of Edinburgh. Vols. I. to III. with Portraits, £2 12s. Vol. II., 1638—1643. 8vo. 16s. Vol. III. 1643—1649. 8vo. 18s.

This work is not only a Biography, but also a continuous Political, Ecclesiastical, and Literary History of England through Milton's whole time.

CHATTERTON : A Story of the Year 1770. By DAVID MASSON, LL.D., Professor of Rhetoric and English Literature in the University of Edinburgh. Crown 8vo. 5s.

" One of this popular writer's best essays on the English poets."—STANDARD.

THE THREE DEVILS : Luther's, Goethe's, and Milton's ; and other Essays. Crown 8vo. 5s.

Maurice.—THE FRIENDSHIP OF BOOKS ; AND OTHER LECTURES. By the REV. F. D. MAURICE. Edited with Preface, by THOMAS HUGHES, M.P. Crown 8vo. 10s. 6d.

" The high, pure, sympathetic, and truly charitable nature of Mr. Maurice is delightfully visible throughout these lectures, which are excellently adapted to spread a love of literature amongst the people."—DAILY NEWS.

Mayor (J. E. B.)—WORKS edited by JOHN E. B. MAYOR, M.A., Kennedy Professor of Latin at Cambridge :—

CAMBRIDGE IN THE SEVENTEENTH CENTURY. Part II. Autobiography of Matthew Robinson. Fcap. 8vo. 5s. 6d.

LIFE OF BISHOP BEDELL. By his SON. Fcap. 8vo. 3s. 6d.

Mendelssohn.—LETTERS AND RECOLLECTIONS. By FERDINAND HILLER. Translated by M. E. VON GLEHN. With Portrait from a Drawing by KARL MÜLLER, never before published. Second Edition. Crown 8vo. 7s. 6d.

" This is a very interesting addition to our knowledge of the great German composer. It reveals him to us under a new light, as the warm-hearted comrade, the musician whose soul was in his work, and the home-loving, domestic man."—STANDARD.

Merewether.—BY SEA AND BY LAND. Being a Trip through Egypt, India, Ceylon, Australia, New Zealand, and America—all Round the World. By HENRY ALWORTH MEREWETHER, one of Her Majesty's Counsel. Crown 8vo. 8s. 6d.

"A most racy and entertaining account of a trip all round the world. It is a book which, without professing to deal in description, gives the reader a most vivid impression of the places, persons, and things it treats of."—GLASGOW DAILY NEWS.

Michael Angelo Buonarroti ; Sculptor, Painter, Architect. The Story of his Life and Labours. By C. C. BLACK, M.A. Illustrated by 20 Permanent Photographs. Royal 8vo. cloth elegant, 31s. 6d.

"The story of Michael Angelo's life remains interesting whatever be the manner of telling it, and supported as it is by this beautiful series of photographs, the volume must take rank among the most splendid of Christmas books, fitted to serve and to outlive the season."—PALL MALL GAZETTE. *"Deserves to take a high place among the works of art of the year."*—SATURDAY REVIEW.

Mitford (A. B.)—TALES OF OLD JAPAN. By A. B. MITFORD, Second Secretary to the British Legation in Japan. With upwards of 30 Illustrations, drawn and cut on Wood by Japanese Artists. New and Cheaper Edition. Crown 8vo. 6s.

"These very original volumes will always be interesting as memorials of a most exceptional society, while regarded simply as tales, they are sparkling, sensational, and dramatic, and the originality of their ideas and the quaintness of their language give them a most captivating piquancy. The illustrations are extremely interesting, and for the curious in such matters have a special and particular value."—PALL MALL GAZETTE.

Morison.—THE LIFE AND TIMES OF SAINT BERNARD, Abbot of Clairvaux. By JAMES COTTER MORISON, M.A. Cheaper Edition. Crown 8vo. 4s. 6d.

The PALL MALL GAZETTE *calls this* "*one of the best contributions in our literature towards a vivid, intelligent, and worthy knowledge of European interests and thoughts and feelings during the twelfth century. A delightful and instructive volume, and one of the best products of the modern historic spirit.*"

Murray.—THE BALLADS AND SONGS OF SCOTLAND, IN VIEW OF THEIR INFLUENCE ON THE CHARACTER OF THE PEOPLE. By J. CLARK MURRAY, LL.D., Professor of Mental and Moral Philosophy in McGill College, Montreal. Crown 8vo. 6s.

Napoleon.—THE HISTORY OF NAPOLEON I. By P. LANFREY. A Translation with the sanction of the Author. Vols. I. and II. 8vo. price 12s. each. [*Vol. III. in the Press.* *The* PALL MALL GAZETTE *says it is* "*one of the most striking* *pieces of historical composition of which France has to boast," and the* SATURDAY REVIEW *calls it " an excellent translation of a work on every ground deserving to be translated. It is unquestionably and immeasurably the best that has been produced. It is in fact the only work to which we can turn for an accurate and trustworthy narrative of that extraordinary career. . . . The book is the best and indeed the only trustworthy history of Napoleon which has been written."*

Owens College Essays and Addresses.—By PROFESSORS AND LECTURERS OF OWENS COLLEGE, MANCHESTER. Published in Commemoration of the Opening of the New College Buildings, October 7th, 1873. 8vo. 14*s.*

This volume contains papers by the Duke of Devonshire, K. G., F.R.S.; Professor Greenwood (Principal); Professor Roscoe, F.R.S. ; Professor Balfour Stewart, F.R.S. ; Professor Core ; W. Boyd Dawkins, F.R.S.; Professor Reynolds ; Professor Williamson, F.R.S. ; Professor Gamgee; Professor Wilkins ; Professor Theodores ; Hermann Breymann; Professor Bryce, D.C.L. ; Professor Jevons ; and Professor Ward.

Palgrave (Sir F.)—HISTORY OF NORMANDY AND OF ENGLAND. By Sir FRANCIS PALGRAVE, Deputy Keeper of Her Majesty's Public Records. Completing the History to the Death of William Rufus. Vols. II.—IV. 21*s.* each.

Palgrave (W. G.)—A NARRATIVE OF A YEAR'S JOURNEY THROUGH CENTRAL AND EASTERN ARABIA, 1862-3. By WILLIAM GIFFORD PALGRAVE, late of the Eighth Regiment Bombay N. I. Sixth Edition. With Maps, Plans, and Portrait of Author, engraved on steel by Jeens. Crown 8vo. 6*s.*

" He has not only written one of the best books on the Arabs and one of the best books on Arabia, but he has done so in a manner that must command the respect no less than the admiration of his fellow-countrymen."—FORTNIGHTLY REVIEW.

ESSAYS ON EASTERN QUESTIONS. By W. GIFFORD PALGRAVE. 8vo. 10*s.* 6*d.*

" These essays are full of anecdote and interest. The book is decidedly a valuable addition to the stock of literature on which men must base their opinion of the difficult social and political problems suggested by the designs of Russia, the capacity of Mahometans for sovereignty, and the good government and retention of India."—SATURDAY REVIEW.

ESSAYS ON ART. Extra fcap. 8vo. 6*s.*

Mulready—Dyce—Holman Hunt—Herbert—Poetry, Prose, and Sensationalism in Art—Sculpture in England—The Albert Cross, &c.

Pater.—STUDIES IN THE HISTORY OF THE RENAIS-
SANCE. By WALTER H. PATER, M.A., Fellow of Brasenose
College, Oxford. Crown 8vo. 7s. 6d.
*The PALL MALL GAZETTE says: "The book is very remarkable
among contemporary books, not only for the finish and care with
which its essays are severally written, but for the air of deliberate
and polished form upon the whole."*

Patteson.—LIFE AND LETTERS OF JOHN COLERIDGE
PATTESON, D.D., Missionary Bishop of the Melanesian Islands.
By CHARLOTTE M. YONGE, Author of "The Heir of Redclyffe."
With Portraits after RICHMOND and from Photograph, engraved
by JEENS. With Map. Fourth and Cheaper Edition. Two Vols.
crown 8vo. 12s.
*"Miss Yonge's work is in one respect a model biography. It is made
up almost entirely of Patteson's own letters. Aware that he had left his
home once and for all, his correspondence took the form of a diary, and
as we read on we come to know the man, and to love him almost as if we
had seen him."—*ATHENÆUM. *"Such a life, with its grand lessons of
unselfishness, is a blessing and an honour to the age in which it is lived;
the biography cannot be studied without pleasure and profit, and indeed
we should think little of the man who did not rise from the study of it
better and wiser. Neither the Church nor the nation which produces
such sons need ever despair of its future."—*SATURDAY REVIEW.

Prichard.—THE ADMINISTRATION OF INDIA. From
1859 to 1868. The First Ten Years of Administration under the
Crown. By ILTUDUS THOMAS PRICHARD, Barrister-at-Law.
Two Vols. Demy 8vo. With Map. 21s.
*"It is a work which every Englishman in India ought to add to his
library."—*STAR OF INDIA.

Raphael.—RAPHAEL OF URBINO AND HIS FATHER
GIOVANNI SANTI. By J. D. PASSAVANT, formerly Director
of the Museum at Frankfort. With Twenty Permanent Photographs. Royal 8vo. Handsomely bound. 31s. 6d.
*The SATURDAY REVIEW says of them, "We have seen not a few
elegant specimens of Mr. Woodbury's new process, but we have seen
none that equal these."*

Reynolds.—SIR JOSHUA REYNOLDS AS A PORTRAIT
PAINTER. AN ESSAY. By J. CHURTON COLLINS, B.A.
Balliol College, Oxford. Illustrated by a Series of Portraits of
distinguished Beauties of the Court of George III.; reproduced
in Autotype from Proof Impressions of the celebrated Engravings,
by VALENTINE GREEN, THOMAS WATSON, F. R. SMITH, E.
FISHER, and others. Folio half-morocco. £5 5s.
This volume contains twenty photographs, nearly all of which are full

length portraits. They have been carefully selected from a long list, and will be found to contain some of the artist's most finished and celebrated works. Where it is possible brief memoirs have been given. The autotypes, which have been made as perfect as possible, will do something to supply the want created by the excessive rarity of the original engravings, and enable the public to possess, at a moderate price, twenty faithful representations of the choicest works of our greatest national painter.

Robinson (H. Crabb).—THE DIARY, REMINISCENCES, AND CORRESPONDENCE, OF HENRY CRABB ROBIN-SON, Barrister-at-Law. Selected and Edited by THOMAS SADLER, Ph.D. With Portrait. Third and Cheaper Edition. Two Vols. Crown 8vo. 12s.

The DAILY NEWS *says: "The two books which are most likely to survive change of literary taste, and to charm while instructing generation after generation, are the 'Diary' of Pepys and Boswell's 'Life of Johnson.' The day will come when to these many will add the 'Diary of Henry Crabb Robinson.' Excellences like those which render the personal revelations of Pepys and the observations of Boswell such pleasant reading abound in this work."*

Rogers (James E. Thorold).—HISTORICAL GLEAN-INGS : A Series of Sketches. Montague, Walpole, Adam Smith, Cobbett. By Prof. ROGERS. Crown 8vo. 4s. 6d. Second Series. Wiklif, Laud, Wilkes, and Horne Tooke. Crown 8vo. 6s.

Seeley (Professor). — LECTURES AND ESSAYS. By J. R. SEELEY, M.A. Professor of Modern History in the University of Cambridge. 8vo. 10s. 6d.

CONTENTS :—*Roman Imperialism:* 1. *The Great Roman Revolution;* 2. *The Proximate Cause of the Fall of the Roman Empire;* 3. *The Later Empire.*—*Milton's Political Opinions — Milton's Poetry —Elementary Principles in Art—Liberal Education in Universities — English in Schools—The Church as a Teacher of Morality—The Teaching of Politics : an Inaugural Lecture delivered at Cambridge.*

Sime.—HISTORY OF GERMANY. By JAMES SIME, M.A. 18mo. 3s. Being Vol. V. of the Historical Course for Schools, Edited by EDWARD A. FREEMAN, D.C.L.

" This is a remarkably clear and impressive History of Germany. Its great events are wisely kept as central figures, and the smaller events are carefully kept not only subordinate and subservient, but most skilfully woven into the texture of the historical tapestry presented to the eye."— STANDARD.

Somers (Robert).—THE SOUTHERN STATES SINCE THE WAR. By ROBERT SOMERS. With Map. 8vo. 9s.

Strangford.—EGYPTIAN SHRINES AND SYRIAN SEPUL-CHRES, including a Visit to Palmyra. By EMILY A. BEAUFORT (Viscountess Strangford), Author of "The Eastern Shores of the Adriatic." New Edition. Crown 8vo. 7s. 6d.

Tacitus.—THE HISTORY OF TACITUS. Translated into English by A. J. CHURCH, M.A. and W. J. BRODRIBB, M.A. With a Map and Notes. New and Cheaper Edition, revised. Crown 8vo. 6s.

This work is characterised by the SPECTATOR *as a "scholarly and faithful translation."*

THE AGRICOLA AND GERMANIA. Translated into English by A. J. CHURCH, M.A. and W. J. BRODRIBB, M.A. With Maps and Notes. Extra fcap. 8vo. 2s. 6d.

The ATHENÆUM *says of this work that it is "a version at once readable and exact, which may be perused with pleasure by all, and consulted with advantage by the classical student."*

Thomas.—THE LIFE OF JOHN THOMAS, Surgeon of the "Earl of Oxford" East Indiaman, and First Baptist Missionary to Bengal. By C. B. LEWIS, Baptist Missionary. 8vo. 10s. 6d.

Thompson.—HISTORY OF ENGLAND. By EDITH THOMP-SON. Being Vol. II. of the Historical Course for Schools, Edited by EDWARD A. FREEMAN, D.C.L. Fourth Edition. 18mo. 2s. 6d.

"Freedom from prejudice, simplicity of style, and accuracy of statement, are the characteristics of this volume. It is a trustworthy text-book, and likely to be generally serviceable in schools."—PALL MALL GAZETTE. *"In its great accuracy and correctness of detail it stands far ahead of the general run of school manuals. Its arrangement, too, is clear, and its style simple and straightforward."*—SATURDAY REVIEW.

Todhunter.—THE CONFLICT OF STUDIES ; AND OTHER ESSAYS ON SUBJECTS CONNECTED WITH EDUCATION. By ISAAC TODHUNTER, M.A., F.R.S., late Fellow and Principal Mathematical Lecturer of St. John's College, Cambridge. 8vo. 10s. 6d.

CONTENTS :—*1. The Conflict of Studies. II. Competitive Examinations. III. Private Study of Mathematics. IV. Academical Reform. V. Elementary Geometry. VI. The Mathematical Tripos.*

Trench (Archbishop).—For other Works by the same Author, *see* THEOLOGICAL and BELLES LETTRES CATALOGUES, and pp. 27, 28, of this Catalogue.

GUSTAVUS ADOLPHUS IN GERMANY, and other Lectures on the Thirty Years' War. By R. CHENEVIX TRENCH, D.D., Archbishop of Dublin. Second Edition, revised and enlarged. Fcap. 8vo. 4s.

B

Trench, Archbishop—*continued.*

PLUTARCH, HIS LIFE, HIS LIVES, AND HIS MORALS. Five Lectures by RICHARD CHENEVIX TRENCH, D.D., Archbishop of Dublin. Second Edition, enlarged. Fcap. 8vo. 3s. 6d.

The ATHENÆUM *speaks of it as "A little volume in which the amusing and the instructive are judiciously combined."*

Trench (Mrs. R.)—REMAINS OF THE LATE MRS.

RICHARD TRENCH. Being Selections from her Journals, Letters, and other Papers. Edited by ARCHBISHOP TRENCH. New and Cheaper Issue, with Portrait. 8vo. 6s.

Wallace.—THE MALAY ARCHIPELAGO: the Land of the

Orang Utan and the Bird of Paradise. By ALFRED RUSSEL WALLACE. A Narrative of Travel with Studies of Man and Nature. With Maps and Illustrations. Fifth Edition. Crown 8vo. 7s. 6d.

Dr. Hooker, in his address to the British Association, spoke thus of the author:—" Of Mr. Wallace and his many contributions to philosophical biology it is not easy to speak without enthusiasm; for, putting aside their great merits, he, throughout his writings, with a modesty as rare as I believe it to be unconscious, forgets his own unquestioned claim to the honour of having originated, independently of Mr. Darwin, the theories which he so ably defends."

" The result is a vivid picture of tropical life, which may be read with unflagging interest, and a sufficient account of his scientific conclusions to stimulate our appetite without wearying us by detail. In short, we may safely say that we have never read a more agreeable book of its kind."— SATURDAY REVIEW.

Waller.—SIX WEEKS IN THE SADDLE: A PAINTER'S

JOURNAL IN ICELAND. By S. E. WALLER. With Illustrations by the Author. Crown 8vo. 6s.

" An exceedingly pleasant and naturally written little book. . . . Mr. Waller has a clever pencil, and the text is well illustrated with his own sketches."— TIMES. *" A very lively and readable book."—* ATHENÆUM. *" A bright little book, admirably illustrated."—* SPECTATOR.

Ward (Professor).—THE HOUSE OF AUSTRIA IN THE

THIRTY YEARS' WAR. Two Lectures, with Notes and Illustrations. By ADOLPHUS W. WARD, M.A., Professor of History in Owens College, Manchester. Extra fcap. 8vo. 2s. 6d.

" We have never read," says the SATURDAY REVIEW, *" any lectures which bear more thoroughly the impress of one who has a true and vigorous grasp of the subject in hand."*

Ward (J.)—EXPERIENCES OF A DIPLOMATIST. Being

recollections of Germany founded on Diaries kept during the years 1840—1870. By JOHN WARD, C.B., late H.M. Minister-Resident to the Hanse Towns. 8vo. 10s. 6d.

Warren.—AN ESSAY ON GREEK FEDERAL COINAGE. By the Hon. J. LEICESTER WARREN, M.A. 8vo. 2s. 6d.

Wedgwood.—JOHN WESLEY AND THE EVANGELICAL REACTION of the Eighteenth Century. By JULIA WEDGWOOD. Crown 8vo. 8s. 6d.

"In style and intellectual power, in breadth of view and clearness of insight, Miss Wedgwood's book far surpasses all rivals."—ATHENÆUM.

Wilson.—A MEMOIR OF GEORGE WILSON, M.D., F.R.S.E., Regius Professor of Technology in the University of Edinburgh. By his SISTER. New Edition. Crown 8vo. 6s.

"An exquisite and touching portrait of a rare and beautiful spirit."— GUARDIAN.

Wilson (Daniel, LL.D.)—Works by DANIEL WILSON, LL.D., Professor of History and English Literature in University College, Toronto :—

PREHISTORIC ANNALS OF SCOTLAND. New Edition, with numerous Illustrations. Two Vols. demy 8vo. 36s.

"One of the most interesting, learned, and elegant works we have seen for a long time."—WESTMINSTER REVIEW.

PREHISTORIC MAN. New Edition, revised and partly re-written, with numerous Illustrations. One vol. 8vo. 21s.

CHATTERTON: A Biographical Study. By DANIEL WILSON, LL.D., Professor of History and English Literature in University College, Toronto. Crown 8vo. 6s. 6d.

Wyatt (Sir M. Digby).—FINE ART: a Sketch of its History, Theory, Practice, and application to Industry. A Course of Lectures delivered before the University of Cambridge. By Sir M. DIGBY WYATT, M.A. Slade Professor of Fine Art. 8vo. 10s. 6d.

"An excellent handbook for the student of art."—GRAPHIC. *"The book abounds in valuable matter, and will therefore be read with pleasure and profit by lovers of art."*—DAILY NEWS.

Yonge (Charlotte M.)—Works by CHARLOTTE M. YONGE, Author of "The Heir of Redclyffe," &c. &c. :—

A PARALLEL HISTORY OF FRANCE AND ENGLAND : consisting of Outlines and Dates. Oblong 4to. 3s. 6d.

CAMEOS FROM ENGLISH HISTORY. From Rollo to Edward II. Extra fcap. 8vo. Second Edition, enlarged. 5s.

A SECOND SERIES, THE WARS IN FRANCE. Extra fcap. 8vo. 5s. Second Edition.

"Instead of dry details," says the NONCONFORMIST, *"we have living pictures, faithful, vivid, and striking."*

B 2

Young (Julian Charles, M.A.)—A MEMOIR OF CHARLES MAYNE YOUNG, Tragedian, with Extracts from his Son's Journal. By JULIAN CHARLES YOUNG, M.A. Rector of Ilmington. ·With Portraits and Sketches. *New and Cheaper Edition.* Crown 8vo. 7s. 6d.

"*In this budget of anecdotes, fables, and gossip, old and new, relative to Scott, Moore, Chalmers, Coleridge, Wordsworth, Croker, Mathews, the third and fourth Georges, Bowles, Beckford, Lockhart, Wellington, Peel, Louis Napoleon, D'Orsay, Dickens, Thackeray, Louis Blanc, Gibson, Constable, and Stanfield, etc. etc., the reader must be hard indeed to please who cannot find entertainment.*"—PALL MALL GAZETTE.

POLITICS, POLITICAL AND SOCIAL ECONOMY, LAW, AND KINDRED SUBJECTS.

Baxter.—NATIONAL INCOME : The United Kingdom. By R. DUDLEY BAXTER, M.A. 8vo. 3s. 6d.

Bernard.—FOUR LECTURES ON SUBJECTS CONNECTED WITH DIPLOMACY. By MONTAGUE BERNARD, M.A., Chichele Professor of International Law and Diplomacy, Oxford. 8vo. 9s.

"*Singularly interesting lectures, so able, clear, and attractive.*"—SPECTATOR.

Bright (John, M.P.)—SPEECHES ON QUESTIONS OF PUBLIC POLICY. By the Right Hon. JOHN BRIGHT, M.P. Edited by Professor THOROLD ROGERS. Author's Popular Edition. Globe 8vo. 3s. 6d.

"*Mr. Bright's speeches will always deserve to be studied, as an apprenticeship to popular and parliamentary oratory; they will form materials for the history of our time, and many brilliant passages, perhaps some entire speeches, will really become a part of the living literature of England.*"—DAILY NEWS.

LIBRARY EDITION. Two Vols. 8vo. With Portrait. 25s.

Cairnes.—Works by J. E. CAIRNES, M.A., Emeritus Professor of Political Economy in University College, London.

ESSAYS IN POLITICAL ECONOMY, THEORETICAL and APPLIED. By J. E. CAIRNES, M.A., Professor of Political Economy in University College, London. 8vo. 10s. 6d.

"*The production of one of the ablest of living economists.*"—ATHENÆUM.

Cairnes—*continued.*

POLITICAL ESSAYS. 8vo. 10s. 6d.

The SATURDAY REVIEW *says, " We recently expressed our high admiration of the former volume; and the present one is no less remarkable for the qualities of clear statement, sound logic, and candid treatment of opponents which were conspicuous in its predecessor. . . . We may safely say that none of Mr. Mill's many disciples is a worthier representative of the best qualities of their master than Professor Cairnes."*

SOME LEADING PRINCIPLES OF POLITICAL ECONOMY NEWLY EXPOUNDED. 8vo. 14s.

CONTENTS :—*Part I. Value. Part II. Labour and Capital. Part III. International Trade.*

" A work which is perhaps the most valuable contribution to the science made since the publication, a quarter of a century since, of Mr. Mill's ' Principles of Political Economy.' "—DAILY NEWS.

Christie.—THE BALLOT AND CORRUPTION AND EXPENDITURE AT ELECTIONS, a Collection of Essays and Addresses of different dates. By W. D. CHRISTIE, C.B., formerly Her Majesty's Minister to the Argentine Confederation and to Brazil; Author of "Life of the First Earl of Shaftesbury." Crown 8vo. 4s. 6d.

Clarke.—EARLY ROMAN LAW. THE REGAL PERIOD. By E. C. CLARKE, M.A., of Lincoln's Inn, Barrister-at-Law, Lecturer in Law and Regius Professor of Civil Law at Cambridge.

" Mr. Clarke has brought together a great mass of valuable matter in an accessible form."—SATURDAY REVIEW.

Corfield (Professor W. H.)—A DIGEST OF FACTS RELATING TO THE TREATMENT AND UTILIZATION OF SEWAGE. By W. H. CORFIELD, M.A., M.B., Professor of Hygiene and Public Health at University College, London. 8vo. 10s. 6d. Second Edition, corrected and enlarged.

" Mr. Corfield's work is entitled to rank as a standard authority, no less than a convenient handbook, in all matters relating to sewage." —ATHENÆUM.

Fawcett.—Works by HENRY FAWCETT, M.A., M.P., Fellow of Trinity Hall, and Professor of Political Economy in the University of Cambridge :—

THE ECONOMIC POSITION OF THE BRITISH LABOURER. Extra fcap. 8vo. 5s.

MANUAL OF POLITICAL ECONOMY. Fourth Edition, with New Chapters on the Nationalization of the Land and Local Taxation. Crown 8vo. 12s.

The DAILY NEWS *says: "It forms one of the best introductions to the*

Fawcett (H.)—*continued.*

principles of the science, and to its practical applications in the problems of modern, and especially of English, government and society."

PAUPERISM : ITS CAUSES AND REMEDIES. Crown 8vo. 5s. 6d.

The ATHENÆUM *calls the work "a repertory of interesting and well-digested information."*

SPEECHES ON SOME CURRENT POLITICAL QUES-TIONS. 8vo. 10s. 6d.

" *They will help to educate, not perhaps, parties, but the educators of parties."—*DAILY NEWS.

ESSAYS ON POLITICAL AND SOCIAL SUBJECTS. By PROFESSOR FAWCETT, M.P., and MILLICENT GARRETT FAWCETT. 8vo. 10s. 6d.

" *They will all repay the perusal of the thinking reader."—*DAILY NEWS.

Fawcett (Mrs.)—Works by MILLICENT GARRETT FAWCETT.

POLITICAL ECONOMY FOR BEGINNERS. WITH QUES-TIONS. New Edition. 18mo. 2s. 6d.

The DAILY NEWS *calls it "clear, compact, and comprehensive;" and the* SPECTATOR *says,* "*Mrs. Fawcett's treatise is perfectly suited to its purpose."*

TALES IN POLITICAL ECONOMY. Crown 8vo. 3s.

" *The idea is a good one, and it is quite wonderful what a mass of economic teaching the author manages to compress into a small space... The true doctrines of International Trade, Currency, and the ratio between Production and Population, are set before us and illustrated in a masterly manner."—*ATHENÆUM.

Freeman (E. A.), M.A., D.C.L.—COMPARATIVE POLITICS. Lectures at the Royal Institution, to which is added " The Unity of History," being the Rede Lecture delivered at Cambridge in 1872. 8vo. 14s.

"*We find in Mr. Freeman's new volume the same sound, careful, comprehensive qualities which have long ago raised him to so high a place amongst historical writers. For historical discipline, then, as well as historical information, Mr. Freeman's book is full of value."—*PALL MALL GAZETTE.

Godkin (James).—THE LAND WAR IN IRELAND. A History for the Times. By JAMES GODKIN, Author of "Ireland and her Churches," late Irish Correspondent of the *Times.* 8vo. 12s.

"*There is probably no other account so compendious and so complete."—*FORTNIGHTLY REVIEW.

Goschen.—REPORTS AND SPEECHES ON LOCAL TAXATION. By GEORGE J. GOSCHEN, M.P. Royal 8vo. 5s.
"*The volume contains a vast mass of information of the highest value.*"
—ATHENÆUM.

Guide to the Unprotected, in Every Day Matters Relating to Property and Income. By a BANKER'S DAUGHTER. Fourth Edition, Revised. Extra fcap. 8vo. 3s. 6d.
"*Many an unprotected female will bless the head which planned and the hand which compiled this admirable little manual. . . . This book was very much wanted, and it could not have been better done.*"—MORNING STAR.

Hill.—CHILDREN OF THE STATE. THE TRAINING OF JUVENILE PAUPERS. By FLORENCE HILL. Extra fcap. 8vo. cloth. 5s.

Historicus.—LETTERS ON SOME QUESTIONS OF INTERNATIONAL LAW. Reprinted from the *Times*, with considerable Additions. 8vo. 7s. 6d. Also, ADDITIONAL LETTERS. 8vo. 2s. 6d.

Jevons.—Works by W. STANLEY JEVONS, M.A., Professor of Logic and Political Economy in Owens College, Manchester. (For other Works by the same Author, *see* EDUCATIONAL and PHILOSOPHICAL CATALOGUES.)

THE COAL QUESTION : An Inquiry Concerning the Progress of the Nation, and the Probable Exhaustion of our Coal Mines. Second Edition, revised. 8vo. 10s. 6d.
"*The question of our supply of coal,*" says the PALL MALL GAZETTE, "*becomes a question obviously of life or death. . . . The whole case is stated with admirable clearness and cogency. . . . We may regard his statements as unanswered and practically established.*"

THE THEORY OF POLITICAL ECONOMY. 8vo. 9s.
"*Professor Jevons has done invaluable service by courageously claiming political economy to be strictly a branch of Applied Mathematics.*"
—WESTMINSTER REVIEW.

Macdonell.—THE LAND QUESTION, WITH SPECIAL REFERENCE TO ENGLAND AND SCOTLAND. By JOHN MACDONELL, Barrister-at-Law. 8vo. 10s. 6d.
"*His book ought to be on the table of every land reformer, and will be found to contain many interesting facts. Mr. Macdonell may be congratulated on having made a most valuable contribution to the study of a question that cannot be examined from too many points.*"—EXAMINER.

Martin.—THE STATESMAN'S YEAR-BOOK: A Statistical and Historical Annual of the States of the Civilized World. Handbook for Politicians and Merchants for the year 1875. By FREDERICK MARTIN. Twelfth Annual Publication. Revised after Official Returns. Crown 8vo. 10s. 6d.

The Statesman's Year-Book is the only work in the English language which furnishes a clear and concise account of the actual condition of all the States of Europe, the civilized countries of America, Asia, and Africa, and the British Colonies and Dependencies in all parts of the world. The new issue of the work has been revised and corrected, on the basis of official reports received direct from the heads of the leading Governments of the world, in reply to letters sent to them by the Editor. Through the valuable assistance thus given, it has been possible to collect an amount of information, political, statistical, and commercial, of the latest date, and of unimpeachable trustworthiness, such as no publication of the same kind has ever been able to furnish. "As indispensable as Bradshaw."— TIMES.

Phillimore.—PRIVATE LAW AMONG THE ROMANS, from the Pandects. By JOHN GEORGE PHILLIMORE, Q.C. 8vo. 16s.

Rogers.—COBDEN AND POLITICAL OPINION. By J. E. THOROLD ROGERS. 8vo. 10s. 6d.

" Will be found most useful by politicians of every school, as it forms a sort of handbook to Cobden's teaching."—ATHENÆUM.

Smith.—Works by Professor GOLDWIN SMITH :—

A LETTER TO A WHIG MEMBER OF THE SOUTHERN INDEPENDENCE ASSOCIATION. Extra fcap. 8vo. 2s.

THREE ENGLISH STATESMEN : PYM, CROMWELL, PITT. A Course of Lectures on the Political History of England. Extra fcap. 8vo. New and Cheaper Edition. 5s.

Social Duties Considered with Reference to the ORGANIZATION OF EFFORT IN WORKS OF BE-NEVOLENCE AND PUBLIC UTILITY. By a MAN OF BUSINESS. (WILLIAM RATHBONE.) Fcap. 8vo. 4s. 6d.

Stephen (C. E.)—THE SERVICE OF THE POOR ; Being an Inquiry into the Reasons for and against the Establish-ment of Religious Sisterhoods for Charitable Purposes. By CAROLINE EMILIA STEPHEN. Crown 8vo. 6s. 6d.

"The ablest advocate of a better line of work in this direction than we have ever seen."—EXAMINER.

Thornton.—Works by W. T. THORNTON, C.B.:—

ON LABOUR : Its Wrongful Claims and Rightful Dues; Its Actual Present State and Possible Future. Second Edition, revised. 8vo. 14s.

A PLEA FOR PEASANT PROPRIETORS : With the Outlines of a Plan for their Establishment in Ireland. New Edition, revised. Crown 8vo. 7s. 6d.

WORKS CONNECTED WITH THE SCIENCE OR THE HISTORY OF LANGUAGE.

Abbott.—A SHAKESPERIAN GRAMMAR : An Attempt to illustrate some of the Differences between Elizabethan and Modern English. By the Rev. E. A. ABBOTT, M.A., Head Master of the City of London School. For the Use of Schools. New and Enlarged Edition. Extra fcap. 8vo. 6s.

"*Valuable not only as an aid to the critical study of Shakespeare, but as tending to familiarize the reader with Elizabethan English in general.*"—ATHENÆUM.

Besant.—STUDIES IN EARLY FRENCH POETRY. By WALTER BESANT, M.A. Crown 8vo. 8s. 6d.

Breymann.—A FRENCH GRAMMAR BASED ON PHILOLOGICAL PRINCIPLES. By HERMANN BREYMANN, Ph.D., Lecturer on French Language and Literature at Owens College, Manchester. Extra fcap. 8vo. 4s. 6d.

"*We dismiss the work with every feeling of satisfaction. It cannot fail to be taken into use by all schools which endeavour to make the study of French a means towards the higher culture.*"—EDUCATIONAL TIMES.

Hadley.—ESSAYS PHILOLOGICAL AND CRITICAL. Selected from the Papers of JAMES HADLEY, LL.D., Professor of Greek in Yale College, &c. 8vo. 16s.

"*Rarely have we read a book which gives us so high a conception of the writer's whole nature ; the verdicts are clear and well-balanced, and there is not a line of unfair, or even unkindly criticism.*"—ATHENÆUM.

Hales.—LONGER ENGLISH POEMS. With Notes, Philological and Explanatory, and an Introduction on the Teaching of English. Chiefly for use in Schools. Edited by J. W. HALES, M.A., late Fellow and Assistant Tutor of Christ's College, Cambridge ; Lecturer in English Literature and Classical Composition at King's College School, London; &c. &c. Third Edition. Extra fcap. 8vo. 4s. 6d.

Hare.—FRAGMENTS OF TWO ESSAYS IN ENGLISH PHILOLOGY. By the late JULIUS CHARLES HARE, M.A., Archdeacon of Lewes. 8vo. 3s. 6d.

Helfenstein (James).—A COMPARATIVE GRAMMAR OF THE TEUTONIC LANGUAGES : Being at the same time a Historical Grammar of the English Language, and comprising Gothic, Anglo-Saxon, Early English, Modern English, Icelandic (Old Norse), Danish, Swedish, Old High German, Middle High German, Modern German, Old Saxon, Old Frisian, and Dutch. By JAMES HELFENSTEIN, Ph.D. 8vo. 18s.

Morris.—Works by the Rev. RICHARD MORRIS, LL.D., Member of the Council of the Philol. Soc., Lecturer on English Language and Literature in King's College School, Editor of " Specimens of Early English," etc., etc.

HISTORICAL OUTLINES OF ENGLISH ACCIDENCE, comprising Chapters on the History and Development of the Language, and on Word-formation. Fourth Edition. Fcap. 8vo. 6s.

ELEMENTARY LESSONS IN HISTORICAL ENGLISH GRAMMAR, containing Accidence and Word-formation. 18mo. 2s. 6d.

Oliphant.—THE SOURCES OF STANDARD ENGLISH. By T. L. KINGTON OLIPHANT, of Balliol College, Oxford. Extra fcap. 8vo. 6s.

"*Mr. Oliphant's book is, to our mind, one of the ablest and most scholarly contributions to our standard English we have seen for many years.*"—SCHOOL BOARD CHRONICLE. "*The book comes nearer to a history of the English language than anything we have seen since such a history could be written, without confusion and contradictions.*"—SATURDAY REVIEW.

Peile (John, M.A.)—AN INTRODUCTION TO GREEK AND LATIN ETYMOLOGY. By JOHN PEILE, M.A., Fellow and Assistant Tutor of Christ's College, Cambridge, formerly Teacher of Sanskrit in the University of Cambridge. New and revised Edition. Crown 8vo. 10s. 6d.

"*The book may be accepted as a very valuable contribution to the science of language.*"—SATURDAY REVIEW.

Philology.—THE JOURNAL OF SACRED AND CLASSICAL PHILOLOGY. Four Vols. 8vo. 12s. 6d.

THE JOURNAL OF PHILOLOGY. New Series. Edited by W. G. CLARK, M.A., JOHN E. B. MAYOR, M.A., and W. ALDIS WRIGHT, M.A. Nos. I., II., III., and IV. 8vo. 4s. 6d. each. (Half-yearly.)

Roby (H. J.)—A GRAMMAR OF THE LATIN LANGUAGE, FROM PLAUTUS TO SUETONIUS. By HENRY JOHN ROBY, M.A., late Fellow of St. John's College, Cambridge. In Two Parts. Part I. containing :—Book I. Sounds. Book II. Inflexions. Book III. Word Formation. Appendices. Second Edition. Crown 8vo. 8s. 6d. Part II.—Syntax, Prepositions, &c. Crown 8vo. 10s. 6d.

"The book is marked by the clear and practical insight of a master in his art. It is a book which would do honour to any country."—ATHENÆUM. *"Brings before the student in a methodical form the best results of modern philology bearing on the Latin language."*—SCOTSMAN.

Taylor.—Works by the Rev. ISAAC TAYLOR, M.A.:—

ETRUSCAN RESEARCHES. With Woodcuts. 8vo. 14s.

The TIMES *says :—" The learning and industry displayed in this volume deserve the most cordial recognition. The ultimate verdict of science we shall not attempt to anticipate ; but we can safely say this, that it is a learned book which the unlearned can enjoy, and that in the descriptions of the tomb-builders, as well as in the marvellous coincidences and unexpected analogies brought together by the author, readers of every grade may take delight as well as philosophers and scholars."*

WORDS AND PLACES ; or, Etymological Illustrations of History, Ethnology, and Geography. By the Rev. ISAAC TAYLOR. Third Edition, revised and compressed. With Maps. Globe 8vo. 6s.

In this edition the work has been recast with the intention of fitting it for the use of students and general readers, rather than, as before, to appeal to the judgment of philologers.

Trench.—Works by R. CHENEVIX TRENCH, D.D., Archbishop of Dublin. (For other Works by the same Author, *see* THEOLOGICAL CATALOGUE.)

Archbishop Trench has done much to spread an interest in the history of our English tongue, and the ATHENÆUM *says, "his sober judgment and sound sense are barriers against the misleading influence of arbitrary hypotheses."*

SYNONYMS OF THE NEW TESTAMENT. New Edition, enlarged. 8vo. cloth. 12s.

"He is," the ATHENÆUM *says, "a guide in this department of knowledge to whom his readers may entrust themselves with confidence."*

ON THE STUDY OF WORDS. Lectures Addressed (originally) to the Pupils at the Diocesan Training School, Winchester. Fifteenth Edition, enlarged. Fcap. 8vo. 4s. 6d.

ENGLISH PAST AND PRESENT. Eighth Edition, revised and improved. Fcap. 8vo. 4s. 6d.

Trench (R. C.)—*continued.*

A SELECT GLOSSARY OF ENGLISH WORDS USED
FORMERLY IN SENSES DIFFERENT FROM THEIR
PRESENT. Fourth Edition, Enlarged. Fcap. 8vo. 4*s.*

ON SOME DEFICIENCIES IN OUR ENGLISH DICTION-
ARIES : Being the substance of Two Papers read before the
Philological Society. Second Edition, revised and enlarged.
8vo. 3*s.*

Whitney.—A COMPENDIOUS GERMAN GRAMMAR. By
W. D. WHITNEY, Professor of Sanskrit and Instructor in Modern
Languages in Yale College. Crown 8vo. 6*s.*
"*After careful examination we are inclined to pronounce it the best
grammar of modern language we have ever seen.*"—SCOTSMAN.

Wood.—Works by H. T. W. WOOD, B.A., Clare College,
Cambridge :—

THE RECIPROCAL INFLUENCE OF ENGLISH AND
FRENCH LITERATURE IN THE EIGHTEENTH
CENTURY. Crown 8vo. 2*s.* 6*d.*

CHANGES IN THE ENGLISH LANGUAGE BETWEEN
THE PUBLICATION OF WICLIF'S BIBLE AND THAT
OF THE AUTHORIZED VERSION ; A.D. 1400 to A.D. 1600.
Crown 8vo. 2*s.* 6*d.*

Yonge.—HISTORY OF CHRISTIAN NAMES. By CHAR-
LOTTE M. YONGE, Author of "The Heir of Redclyffe." Two
Vols. Crown 8vo. 1*l.* 1*s.*

R. CLAY, SONS, AND TAYLOR, PRINTERS, LONDON.

GOLDSMITH'S MISCELLANEOUS WORKS.

With Biographical Introduction by Professor MASSON.

"Cheap, elegant, and complete."—*Nonconformist.*

SPENSER'S COMPLETE WORKS.

Edited, with Glossary, by R. MORRIS, and Memoir, by J. W. HALES.

"Worthy—and higher praise it needs not—of the beautiful ' Globe Series.'"—*Daily News.*

POPE'S POETICAL WORKS.

Edited, with Notes and Introductory Memoir, by Professor WARD.

"The book is handsome and handy."—*Athenæum.*

DRYDEN'S POETICAL WORKS.

Edited, with a Revised Text and Notes, by W. D. CHRISTIE, M.A., Trinity College, Cambridge.

"It is hardly possible that a better or more handy edition of this poet could be produced."—*Athenæum.*

COWPER'S POETICAL WORKS.

Edited, with Notes and Biographical Introduction, by W. BENHAM, M.A., Professor of Modern History in Queen's College, London.

"An edition of permanent value. Altogether a very excellent book."—*Saturday Review.*

VIRGIL'S WORKS.

Rendered into English Prose. With Introductions, Notes, Analysis, and Index, by J. LONSDALE, M.A., and S. LEE, M.A.

"A more complete edition of Virgil in English it is scarcely possible to conceive than the scholarly work before us."—*Globe.*

HORACE.

Rendered into English Prose. With Reviewing Analysis, Introduction, and Notes, by J. LONSDALE, M.A., and S. LEE, M.A.

"This charming version is the closest and most faithful of all renderings of Horace into English."—*Record.*

MACMILLAN AND CO. LONDON.

MACMILLAN'S GOLDEN TREASURY SERIES.

Uniformly printed in 18mo., with Vignette Titles by Sir Noel Paton, T. Woolner, W. Holman Hunt, J. E. Millais, Arthur Hughes, &c. Engraved on Steel by Jeens. Bound in extra cloth, 4s. 6d. each volume. Also kept in morocco and calf bindings.

THE GOLDEN TREASURY OF THE BEST SONGS AND LYRICAL POEMS IN THE ENGLISH LANGUAGE. Selected and arranged, with Notes, by Francis Turner Palgrave.

THE CHILDREN'S GARLAND FROM THE BEST POETS. Selected and arranged by Coventry Patmore.

THE BOOK OF PRAISE. From the Best English Hymn Writers. Selected and arranged by Lord Selborne. A new and enlarged Edition.

THE FAIRY BOOK; the Best Popular Fairy Stories. Selected and rendered anew by the Author of "John Halifax, Gentleman."

THE BALLAD BOOK. A Selection of the Choicest British Ballads. Edited by William Allingham.

THE JEST BOOK. The Choicest Anecdotes and Sayings. Selected and arranged by Mark Lemon.

BACON'S ESSAYS AND COLOURS OF GOOD AND EVIL. With Notes and Glossarial Index. By W. Aldis Wright, M.A.

THE PILGRIM'S PROGRESS from this World to that which is to come. By John Bunyan.

THE SUNDAY BOOK OF POETRY FOR THE YOUNG. Selected and arranged by C. F. Alexander.

A BOOK OF GOLDEN DEEDS of All Times and All Countries. Gathered and narrated anew. By the Author of "The Heir of Redclyffe."

THE POETICAL WORKS OF ROBERT BURNS. Edited, with Biographical Memoir, Notes, and Glossary, by Alexander Smith. Two Vols.

MACMILLAN AND CO., LONDON.

GOLDEN TREASURY SERIES (*Continued*).

THE ADVENTURES OF ROBINSON CRUSOE. Edited from the Original Edition by J. W. CLARK, M.A., Fellow of Trinity College, Cambridge.

THE REPUBLIC OF PLATO. Translated into English, with Notes by J. Ll. DAVIES, M.A. and D. J. VAUGHAN, M.A.

THE SONG BOOK. Words and Tunes from the Best Poets and Musicians. Selected and arranged by JOHN HULLAH, Professor of Vocal Music in King's College, London.

LA LYRE FRANÇAISE. Selected and arranged, with Notes, by GUSTAVE MASSON, French Master in Harrow School.

TOM BROWN'S SCHOOL DAYS. By AN OLD BOY.

A BOOK OF WORTHIES. Gathered from the Old Histories and written anew by the Author of "The Heir of Redclyffe."

A BOOK OF GOLDEN THOUGHTS. By HENRY ATTWELL, Knight of the Order of the Oak Crown.

GUESSES AT TRUTH. By Two BROTHERS. New Edition.

THE CAVALIER AND HIS LADY. Selections from the Works of the First Duke and Duchess of Newcastle. With an Introductory Essay by EDWARD JENKINS, Author of "Ginx's Baby," &c. 18mo. 4s. 6d.

THEOLOGIA GERMANICA. — Translated from the German, by SUSANNA WINKWORTH. With a Preface by the REV. CHARLES KINGSLEY, and a Letter to the Translator by the CHEVALIER BUNSEN, D.D.

SCOTTISH SONG: A SELECTION OF THE CHOICEST LYRICS OF SCOTLAND. Compiled and arranged with brief notes by MARY CARLYLE AITKEN.

MILTON'S POETICAL WORKS. With Introductions, Notes, and Memoir by Professor MASSON. With Two Portraits engraved by JEENS. Two Vols.

MACMILLAN AND CO., LONDON.